Rumors AND A Rake

By Jane Maguire

Rumors and a Rake

Copyright © 2022 Jane Maguire

Cover design by Holly Perret
Edited by Nevvie Gane

ISBN: 978-17778926-3-0

www.janemaguireauthor.com

The Inconveniently Wed Series
By Jane Maguire

Book 1: **Secrets and a Scandal**
Book 2: **Rumors and a Rake**

To anyone who has ever felt the fear and done it anyway.

Rumors and a Rake

Chapter 1

September 1819

Lady Catherine Adderley had arrived in hell, in the form of a house party.

"We are here at last!" cried her traveling companion, Lavinia Bathurst, pressing her face against the carriage window as the stately exterior of Oakwood Hall came into view. "Isn't it wonderful?"

The house, with its tidy red brick and expansive mullioned windows, was indeed impressive, although Catherine wouldn't have been mistaken in remarking that it wasn't nearly so grand as the Bathursts' country seat in Devonshire, or her own family's estate of Highfield Park in Kent. However, she knew this wasn't what Lavinia meant. Rather, the appeal lay, for Lavinia anyway, in the fact that this was the first house party to which they'd been invited since making their debuts. For Catherine, the opportunity brought considerably less excitement.

"Must you really gawk like that?" Lady Bathurst snapped at her daughter from her seat on the opposite side of the carriage, sparing Catherine the need to reply. "One would think you were some sort of oblivious farm girl and not a well-bred lady. I'm sure I need not remind you that a number of eligible gentlemen have accepted Lady Wellesley's invitation to come here for the week. You will be far from the only desperate young miss who failed to secure a match this Season and is now vying for their attention. How you expect to shine brighter than the rest while displaying the basest of manners, I surely do not know."

"I apologize, Mama," Lavinia said with a sigh, peeling her face from the glass and settling her hands primly in her lap. Yet the rebuke failed to dim the delight in her lively blue eyes.

"Make yourselves ready," instructed Lady Bathurst, reaching up to smooth her elegant, silvery blonde coiffure. The carriage rolled to a halt at the top of the drive, and a footman approached to help them alight. She started to rise but, on second thought, turned back to look Catherine squarely in the eye. "Oh, and Catherine?" She arched a flaw-lessly shaped brow. "It may behoove you *not* to look as though you've just immersed your arm in a pail of leeches."

With that, the carriage door flew open, and Lady Bath-urst accepted the waiting footman's hand, leaving Catherine sitting in shocked silence. She paused only a second before scrambling to her feet, her expression now perfectly neutral, or so she hoped. She thought she had grown adept at con-cealing her emotions, at appearing serene even when faced with events that made her want to flee in terror. Apparently, she had given herself too much credit.

A flush began creeping over her cheeks, and she glanced around for a distraction, desperate to make the un-settling realization go away so she could maintain her composure. She counted the number of buttons on the footman's jacket. The number of shrubs in front of the house. The number of steps she climbed to lead her to the front door, that would open and bring her to fresh misery …

"Welcome, my dears. How glad I am that you have arrived."

Lady Wellesley's greeting as the butler admitted them into the wood-paneled entrance hall was so jovial that it made Catherine's trepidation seem foolish. Unfortunately, that knowledge did nothing to quell it. She stood there stiffly, holding herself tall despite her overwhelming urge to shrink away, as Lady Wellesley exchanged pleasantries with Lady Bathurst and Lavinia.

Fortunately, Lady Wellesley appeared to notice nothing amiss in her demeanor as she turned to her and gave her hand an affectionate squeeze. "And dear Catherine. How well you look. Perfectly lovely, just like your poor mother."

Catherine bowed her head, flashing her teeth in what she hoped passed for a smile. "Thank you. I'm very pleased to be here."

"Charming!" Lady Wellesley continued to gaze at her, giving her an approving nod. "Now, allow me to show you to your rooms. You may wish to rest for a spell before dinner, or if you choose, you may join the ladies who have already arrived in the drawing room. Lord Wellesley has taken the gentleman to the library, but I daresay they'll be in to mingle by and by."

Indeed, murmurs of conversation and laughter wafted down the corridor, causing Catherine's heart to start beating a little faster. With Lady Bathurst and Lady Wellesley now facing away from her as they started up the stairs, she gave her head an impatient shake. All would be well if she could only make herself stop worrying.

As a fresh distraction, she looked down and concentrated on Lady Wellesley's silky skirts gliding over each step. In a way, it was difficult *not* to look at the woman, who had a small stature but a drawing presence. She had encountered Lady Wellesley several times throughout the Season and had always found her good humored and affable. She could almost feel at ease with her, but for the fact the woman was a notorious gossip, holding an elaborate house party every year so she could then report all the salacious doings that happened right under her nose. It did little to affect Catherine, who was far too quiet, her behavior much too subdued, to make herself the subject of rumor. Nonetheless, being thrust into such an environment was somewhat unsettling.

"Here we are," announced Lady Wellesley, pulling Catherine from her anxious thoughts. They had stopped before a heavy oak door which Lady Wellesley cast open before gesturing into the room. "Althea, Lavinia, this is your chamber for the week. And Catherine, I have you just next door. I hope everything will be to your liking."

Catherine began moving down the corridor toward the next doorway, anticipating the reprieve. "Thank you. I'm certain it will be lovely."

Lady Wellesley nodded approvingly at her once more. "Well, if you require anything, you need only ring for it. As

I said, you are welcome to join the ladies in the drawing room if you desire. Otherwise, I shall see you at dinner."

Catherine placed her hand on the door handle, eagerly awaiting her solitary chamber. But no sooner had Lady Wellesley turned back in the direction of the stairs than Lavinia nearly flew over to her. "Let's make ourselves ready quickly so we can go to the drawing room at once!"

"Now wait a moment," Lady Bathurst said, still standing poised by her own doorway. "I advise you to take this period before dinner to rest. After all, you will both want to look your finest when we go down to join the gentlemen."

"Indeed," put in Catherine, "a repose would be just the thing." Not that she felt tired, but whatever it took to prolong her quiet time.

"But Mama," Lavinia said, appearing not to have heard her friend, "how are we supposed to interact with gentlemen if we remain in our rooms? They may choose to join the ladies in the drawing room before dinner, and if so, the other girls will put their claims on them first."

Slight lines appeared on Lady Bathurst's forehead as she mulled it over. "Very well. I suppose we'll change our dresses and go down. Catherine?"

"I'm rather fatigued after the journey and think I need to rest first," she lied without missing a beat. "Perhaps I could join you later."

"As you wish." Lavinia bounced back toward her door, her mind clearly on other things. "Do not take too long!"

At last, Catherine could press on the brass handle beneath her hand and let herself into the room, which welcomed her with its woodland tapestries adorning the walls and a fire burning in the grate. She went straight to the curtained bed, threw herself backward onto the counterpane, and kicked off her traveling boots. Now that she was alone, she allowed herself to let out a slow, shaky breath. Her claim of tiredness had mostly been an untruth. Yet mentally …

Why, oh why, couldn't she be more like Lavinia? Lavinia gleaned joy from every social event she attended. The more, the better. She had no trouble meeting new acquaintances and thinking of charming things to say to potential suitors. Now that her older sister, Anne, had been married off, she would be apt to redouble her efforts, and it likely wouldn't be long before she succeeded. If anything, her fault lay in being *too* gregarious.

On the other hand, Catherine's body tensed and filled with apprehension at the very thought of immersing herself in a crowd. Perhaps it was the result of spending too much time alone in the country. Growing up as a motherless child, she had no one but an older brother who spent years away on the Continent and a father who had better things to do than devote attention to a mere daughter. Whatever the reason, being surrounded by strangers made her heart race. Having gentlemen attempt to charm her left her either fumbling or silent. Whenever possible, she escaped the bustle of a congested ballroom or drawing room by finding a quiet terrace or back room where no one would notice her.

Much like she was doing right now. Except ... didn't that defeat the purpose of coming here in the first place? And indeed, no one had forced her to come here; she'd done so of her own accord, and with a motive.

She had already let her anxiety overrule her once this year when she departed London early, leaving the Season behind. Without a second thought, she'd accompanied her brother and sister-in-law to the country as they awaited the birth of their first child. She hadn't regretted her decision in the least. With Edward and Eliza there, the echoey house was no longer lonely, and once her darling niece, Sophia, had arrived, everything felt warm and complete. She had a baby to dote on and a brother and sister-in-law who welcomed her and loved her just as she loved them.

But as she'd watched Edward and Eliza in their joy, marveling over the little being they had created and showering each other with affection, something within her stirred. What would it be like if she had something like that of her own? A husband to care about, children to love ... Every time she noticed Eliza trace her finger over the curves of Sophia's face as the baby slept, or she caught Edward pause to pull Eliza into a quick embrace even during busy moments throughout the day, she thought there must be nothing nicer in the world. However, one thing remained certain. If she kept herself shut away at their country estate, cut off from society, she would never find out for sure.

She pushed herself up to a sitting position, filled with new resolve. This party provided an excellent second chance for anyone who hadn't succeeded on the marriage mart during the Season, just as Lady Bathurst had said. And if she could force herself to participate in social events rather than hide from them, if she could find a way to engage in flirtation rather than get flustered, then surely at least some of the gentlemen would prove themselves agreeable. In fact, there was one in particular...

"Good afternoon, my lady. May I assist you in removing your traveling clothes?"

Any lingering doubts vanished with the entrance of Betsy, her lady's maid. Betsy's arrival had been so well-timed, it had to be a sign she was meant to carry through with her plan.

"Yes, thank you," she said, stepping onto the embroidered carpet and holding herself tall. "Let's try to make haste, for I would like to join the other guests in the drawing room."

If the out-of-character request surprised Betsy, she gave no indication of it. In fact, the lady's maid got her mistress ready quickly enough that by the time Catherine descended the stairs, she'd had so little opportunity to dwell on the matter that her hands only shook slightly. She stopped outside the crowded drawing room, peeping around the corner to observe the guests within. It would be better if she simply walked in without overthinking it, but she couldn't bring herself to do so without first knowing who she would encounter there.

However, Lavinia gave her no such opportunity. "Catherine!" she called, locking eyes with her from across the room. She'd been speaking with Lady Rose Smythe, a mutual acquaintance who had completed her second Season without a proposal, much to the lady's disappointment. Lavinia uttered a hasty farewell and rushed to the doorway to grab Catherine's arm, dragging her to an unoccupied corner.

"I'm glad you came down so quickly," Lavinia said, her eyes bright with exhilaration. "Rose just told me the most thrilling tidbit of information."

"I thought spreading gossip was Lady Wellesley's domain," Catherine remarked wryly. Despite herself, her ears began to perk up.

"Oh, everyone will be discussing this. A most unexpected pair of guests have decided to join the party. Can you guess their identity?" Fortunately, Lavinia paused only a moment before whispering, "The Marchioness of Langley is coming, accompanied by none other than her only surviving son. Viscount Kendrick."

Lavinia announced the name with a flourish, while a deep pit formed in Catherine's stomach. During the carriage ride, Lady Bathurst had discussed the party's guest list in great detail. Those names had most definitely not been on it.

"The marchioness has not appeared in public all Season, even though her mourning period for her elder son ended some months ago," Lavinia continued, barely able to get the words out fast enough. "But apparently, she and Lady Wellesley are old friends. No one ever thought Lord Kendrick would accompany her to something as mundane as a house party, not with the way he cavorts about town. But word is, now that he's heir to the marquessate, and with his father quite unwell, he thinks to settle down and choose a bride. Can you imagine? The man is simply delicious. You *have* made his acquaintance, haven't you?"

Catherine's head began to spin from all the chatter, and she wished beyond anything she had stayed upstairs and saved her resolve for another day. Or better yet, an event other than this house party.

"I met him once," she said, her tone clipped, "and I fail to see why his presence would garner such excitement. He's the worst kind of rake, known for having a different mistress in his bed each night. Even if he did marry, I cannot imagine him as the type to settle down, and I daresay his disreputable behavior would continue just as it does now. A respectable lady would do well to stay far away from him."

Now she was the one gossiping, but when it came to this particular gentleman, the words were more than warranted.

Lavinia drew her eyebrows together, her announcement clearly not having the desired effect. "Really,

Catherine, you are always so severe. Besides, how could you know such a thing?"

Catherine couldn't stop the flush from creeping across her cheeks. What should she say? She *knew*. She would sooner expire on the spot than admit how, but she knew.

She had come to this party with so many good intentions. She would make herself visible. She would participate in conversations. She would make a concerted effort to flirt and charm. If things didn't work out with the gentleman who had first caught her attention, she would give others she had previously avoided a chance. She would try her best to exhibit the confidence befitting of the daughter, and now sister, of an earl.

But she could do none of those things in the presence of Lord Kendrick.

Her eyes began darting around when they met with the most wonderful distraction at the other side of the room. She curved her lips into a small smile, slightly inclining her head.

Lavinia, impatient at receiving no reply, turned her gaze in the direction of Catherine's. Upon taking notice of the source of the distraction, she let out an unladylike sniff. "You cannot be serious."

They both peered at the same man, Sir Arthur Croft, who sat alone in an armchair and had just happened to glance up from his newspaper. Yet clearly, the impressions they gained from the sight couldn't have been more different.

Though Lavinia rarely did things with the intention of being unkind, a surge of annoyance trickled through Catherine at the subtle insult to both her and the gentleman. "What, pray, is wrong with Sir Arthur?"

"For one thing, he's a mere baronet." Lavinia wrinkled her nose. "And for another thing, he's just so ... so ... uninspiring."

Catherine suppressed a sigh. Perhaps Lavinia saw only a man with a narrow chin and straw-colored hair showing signs of receding despite his youth. Perhaps she saw a man who was slow to laugh and always had his nose in a book or paper. But Lavinia didn't understand. Due to her conviviality, she could never appreciate a man who didn't overwhelm her with boisterous chatter of horse races or fox hunts. She could never see value in a man who was content to merely sit beside her and read in companionable silence. She would turn up her nose at a man who approached her with quiet courtesies instead of declarations that made him sound like a lovesick poet.

Perhaps these characteristics *did* make a man uninspiring. But they also made him safe.

"Sir Arthur is perfectly agreeable," she said under her breath, "and he is coming this way, so you had best mind your manners."

"You may have him." Lavinia had already turned her attention elsewhere in the room. "I just noticed Elizabeth Carey. I must go ask if she's heard the news about Lord Kendrick."

Lavinia rushed away to gossip with another of their acquaintances, leaving Catherine standing alone waiting for Sir Arthur's unhurried footsteps to reach her. She kept the slight smile plastered across her face, trying to appear welcoming. Sir Arthur had always found her pleasant enough before and had seemed content with their conversations despite their sparsity. As he was a reserved person himself, perhaps he needed her to take the next step and drop little hints of her interest.

She was ready. She could do this. Besides, she now had an extra motive.

Focusing her efforts on Sir Arthur would help her block out memories of certain wayward viscounts.

Chapter 2

A brilliant light bore through Philip Hadleigh's eyelids, piercing him like thousands of tiny knives.

"My lord, it's time to awaken."

A hammer pounded at his head, each rapid blow on the verge of crushing his skull.

"Come, my lord, it is imperative that you get out of bed immediately."

Thankfully, the incessant hammering abated, leaving him at peace until a gush of tepid water splashed across his face, pouring into his mouth and nose.

"Lord Kendrick, I really must insist!"

Philip sat bolt upright, spluttering, as he pried open his bleary eyes. Morning sunlight streamed through the window where the curtains had been cast open, causing another deep stab in his head that forced him to turn away. That proved no better, for leaning down near the shadowed side of the bed, only inches away from him, was the perturbed face of his valet, Robertson.

Seeing his master's eyes finally open, Robertson straightened himself up, placing his hands firmly on his hips. "Lord Kendrick, are you listening at all?"

Philip blinked, trying to absorb all that transpired. Had Robertson been shaking him? And had he really dared to douse him in the morning's wash water?

Philip collapsed back against his pillow, screwing his eyes shut. "A moment," he croaked, his mouth feeling like it was stuffed with wool.

Every part of him ached, from the roots of his hair to his toenails. He tried to force his muddled brain into action so he could determine what, exactly, had gotten him in such a state.

He had been perfectly fine yesterday. After paying several necessary calls in the afternoon, he had gone to eat dinner at White's, where a few friends joined him. What could be more innocuous than that?

But then … they hadn't remained at White's, had they? No, all of them, probably seven or eight in total, had crowded into a carriage and gone somewhere … the theater. The performance had already ended, but the actresses remained backstage, including the charming Lucia Ferri, a most eager young woman with a delightful pair of—

No, he couldn't allow himself to get distracted when the night's events remained a mystery. He coaxed his brain to work a little harder until another image appeared, of a second crowded carriage ride that included the chatter of ladies, including Lucia, bouncing atop his lap until they reached … Lord Sherwood's townhouse.

Yes, that was it. No wonder. Evenings at Sherwood's tended to result in some sort of debauchery or another. Wisps of memories danced around his throbbing head. Glasses of whiskey … absinthe … a betting book … a greased pig running through the library …

A *pig*? Surely that hadn't *really* happened.

Philip groaned and gingerly stretched out his limbs, but instead of gliding over the sheets, his foot connected with soft flesh. He turned his head and drew an eye open, only to be met with the sight of lush ebony hair spilling across the pillow next to him. Somehow, he had found his way home, and it would seem Lucia had accompanied him. Interesting.

"My lord, your mother would like to see you at once."

Robertson's voice reached him, although it floated in his pool of thoughts as though not quite real. "Mmm," he mumbled, reaching out to mindlessly stroke one of Lucia's silky curls. "Yes. Send a message that I'll call before dinner."

He closed his eyes again, wishing he could return to a dreamlike state. He just needed to rest a while longer. Then, perhaps this god-awful aching would abate, and he and Lucia could—

"Lord Kendrick, the marchioness is already here!"

For the second time, he scrambled to sit and to make himself form a coherent sentence, although all he could muster was, "What?"

Robertson peered down at him, his drooping face making him look rather like a dejected bloodhound. "As I've been trying to tell you, my lord, this is quite urgent."

Philip uttered a string of oaths and reached clumsily for the silver tray glinting on his bedside table until Robertson, ever the proficient valet, retrieved the cup of black coffee from it and thrust it into his hands.

"Here, my lord, drink this at once. I'll then set to work at making you presentable. Or at least passable," he muttered, heading to the wardrobe to fetch a clean suit of clothes.

Philip groaned again. Damn, blast, and bloody hell, what was his mother doing here? She never visited him at his bachelor's lodgings. In fact, the marchioness never went anywhere at all. Her retreat from the world had started four years ago, after John's death, but the subsequent loss of her beloved Charles had caused her to pull away entirely, keeping herself confined to her house, devoid of visitors. Why she and his father had bothered journeying to London for the Season when her grief and his ill health prevented them from mingling in society, he hadn't the faintest clue. And as for why they stayed in London with the Season now at an end, that also remained a mystery.

He stole a wistful glance at Lucia, still peacefully sleeping despite the commotion, although any amorous desires had vanished at the announcement his mother waited in the next room.

Robertson cocked an eyebrow, his mouth pinched in a line of pure distaste. "Please, my lord, never mind that now. I'll see that the—ahem—lady departs without drawing notice. You must focus on getting dressed so you can cease keeping the marchioness waiting."

Philip gulped down the rest of his coffee and cast the cup back onto the tray. It served him right for continuing to employ the valet his father had hired to accompany him to

Oxford some years ago. He should have engaged his own man, someone more inclined to sense when visitors were unwelcome. Nonetheless, he gave in to Robertson's ministrations, and within ten minutes, he had gained his nod of approval, albeit a reluctant one.

His mother awaited him on the settee in the sparsely furnished sitting room, seated as regally as ever. Yet he couldn't help but notice the changes she had undergone over the past months. Her dark hair, the same glossy brunette all three of her sons had inherited, was now streaked heavily with gray, and deep lines creased her pale face.

Her eyes, though, held a faint light amongst the sadness that lingered there, and she looked him up and down, assessing him as though he were a foreign object.

At last, she inclined her head, apparently granting him her seal of approval. "Good day, Philip. I trust you are well."

It was a testament to Robertson's skills that she hadn't turned up her nose and strode out in repulsion. Philip shuffled toward her, suddenly unsure of what to do with himself. "Very well," he said, despite how his stomach roiled. "I hope this day finds you in good health also."

"Yes." She murmured the word, and her face took on a faraway expression before she startled herself out of her distractedness and gestured to the spot beside her. "Please sit. I have something I must discuss with you."

As the settee provided the only seat in the room, aside from an overstuffed armchair in the opposite corner, he lowered himself next to his mother, careful not to sit on her stiff lilac skirts. He was ensconced in a cloud of her perfume, the same lily of the valley scent she had worn for as long as he could remember. The same scent that had hit him many years ago as she sat at his bedside while he struggled to breathe, thinking it might be the last thing he ever inhaled. It was funny how despite all the monumental changes that had taken place since then, some small things remained the same.

He squeezed his hands into fists and abruptly released them, annoyed by his sudden burst of sentimentality. It was no doubt due to the aftereffects of the absinthe, a drink which he made a mental note never to imbibe again. He looked at his mother, keeping his face neutral. "Go on."

The marchioness cleared her throat. "I have decided to attend Lady Wellesley's house party in Essex."

"I see." Philip could think of no comment to make besides that. After all, Lady Wellesley's annual house party, an event notorious for attracting the Season's rejected debutantes who aimed to catch the attention of gentlemen still on the prowl, was not the sort of house party that appealed to him. He supposed he should feel glad that his mother felt ready to reintegrate with society, but why did such an announcement warrant her coming to his lodgings and rousing him from bed at whatever hellish hour it was?

"I would like you to accompany me."

He stared at her blankly, the pounding in his head increasing in intensity. Had he possibly misheard her? But no, he couldn't have, for she regarded him with widened eyes, clearly awaiting a response.

"I'm afraid I cannot. Other commitments ..." he muttered thickly, his intellectual abilities still not restored enough to invent a more proficient excuse.

His mother's eyes narrowed, and the crease between her brows deepened. "What other commitments, pray tell? Gaming? Whoring? Making wagers at Gentleman Jackson's? You may not have shown your face at Langley House since the beginning of the Season, but do not think that means I know nothing of your conduct."

Philip's mind drifted to the time back in February when he *had* visited Langley House, his parents' London residence. His mother had lain in the darkened drawing room with her tearstained face pressed against the sofa, a damaged, hollow shell of her former self. He had thought she was lost, that there was no coming back from such a state. Apparently, he hadn't given her enough credit.

"Philip, I think it best we speak with honesty." For just a second, that void, broken look from the previous months flashed across his mother's face, although she quickly composed herself and crossed her hands across her lap in a neat stack. "You have now received the courtesy title, and you stand to inherit the marquessate. It is not what any of us envisioned, but alas, situations cannot always be of our choosing. There is no one else."

The marchioness spoke the last phrase with great emphasis, and his stomach churned so violently that he had to be on the verge of casting up his accounts. He swallowed, forcing the bile in his throat back down. His mother was wasting her breath, for as much as he tried to ignore the truths of which she reminded him, he could never quite shake that unwanted knowledge from his head.

"You are aware that your father is unwell." The words were part statement, part question, although they needed no reply. Of course he was aware. All of society knew that the Marquess of Langley's health had been in steady decline over the past couple of years. "I daresay he will not live much longer."

If she heard Philip's sharp intake of breath, she didn't let on. In fact, she kept her voice and face expressionless, as if discussing something as trivial as the weather. Such a declaration would have likely reduced another woman to tears, but he supposed one didn't experience grief like the marchioness had and live to overcome it without becoming somewhat hardened.

"And so, the time for all this"—she swept her hand around the room, from the bare wooden floor to the unlit fireplace, to the closed bedroom door, and then to Philip himself—"has come to an end. Your antics made little difference when you were a third son, but now your father's legacy is at stake. Do not let him depart the world thinking the marquessate will end up in the hands of some distant relation. Not when circumstances should have been so different. The simple truth is, you must marry, and soon."

Her speech hit him like a right hook to the jaw. Why did she keep rehashing facts of which he was already all too aware? He had no business being a viscount or a marquess. He was the last person on earth who should linger around innocent young ladies with the intention of marriage. He was totally wrong for the tasks at hand, a dissipated, unwanted third son called upon only because, through a hard blow from fate, he was the only one who remained.

Yet how could he say no? He would fail miserably at the whole business; of that, he had no doubt. But after all his parents had lost, if he could accompany his mother to this inane house party or go along with whatever other schemes she concocted to at least fill his father's final weeks with the illusion that he had a respectable son and heir …

He stifled a sigh. "Would leaving on the morrow suffice?"

His mother blinked, her mouth slightly agape. Clearly, she had expected him to object. She watched him for a moment, perhaps noticing his greenish tinge, but then shook her head. "I'm afraid not, for the party is starting today, so we will already be late as it is. We had best set out at once so we can arrive tomorrow and only miss one day of the affair."

"Splendid." He stumbled to his feet, trying not to gag as he imagined hours ahead in a bouncing carriage. "A moment, if you please. I must ask Robertson to prepare."

He would also ask Robertson for some headache powder and another very strong cup of coffee.

"Of course." The marchioness flashed him something that nearly looked like a smile. "I'm certain it will not take him long. My own trunks have already been prepared and are waiting in the carriage, so as soon as he's through, we can be on our way."

Philip took a moment to peer at his mother, trying to solve the puzzle she had become. However, he quickly gave up and started toward his bedroom, unable to tackle such a feat at present. All he knew was how grossly he had underestimated her.

But for that matter, he had underestimated himself as well. Everyone knew he was a scoundrel, focused solely on his own pleasure. He had never been of much use to his parents, and in turn, he had taken little interest in them. He didn't want to make a show of performing charitable acts for others, not when he had so much living to do for himself. And live he did, placing no deed, and no woman, off limits.

Yet it would seem that underneath all his layers of depravity, small scraps of a heart remained.

Perhaps. Or perhaps it was simply an effect of the absinthe.

Chapter 3

"There you go, my lady." Betsy leaned in to refasten the final pin in Catherine's elegant chignon. "Will you return downstairs now?"

"Yes." She gazed into the mirror before her, its surface reflecting back her shiny golden curls and dark, solemn eyes. "Thank you, that will be all for now. I'll go down in a moment."

Betsy's departing curtsey appeared in the mirror, and as soon as she vanished, Catherine reached up to pinch her cheeks, trying to add some color to them.

Now that dinner was through, many of the younger guests planned to assemble in the library for an evening of parlor games. As part of her newfound resolve, she had agreed to join in, although she couldn't handle the event without having a short reprieve first.

At least the whole affair had grown a little easier. She and Sir Arthur had engaged in a successful conversation the previous day on the subject of their favorite books. They had spoken again today during Lady Wellesley's picnic by the lake, where he had told her about Calverton Manor, his estate in Oxfordshire. Unfortunately, they hadn't been seated next to one another at dinner, but although parlor games didn't seem much to his taste either, he had assured her he would see her in the library. Which was why she needed to liven herself up and conceal how she'd spent most of the previous night tossing and turning.

It appeared now that her added discomfiture may have been unfounded. For while Lavinia had spent much of the picnic gazing into the distance, hoping to spot Lord Kendrick strolling across the lawn toward them, there had been no sign of the viscount's arrival. Likewise, while many of the ladies had cast glances at the doorway as they waited in the drawing room to be called in for dinner, certain that Lady Langley and Lord Kendrick would enter at any minute, they both remained absent. Catherine still heard whisperings of the pair, but as a second dinner had come and gone with no sign of them, it seemed more and more likely that their addition to the party was only a rumor. Or so she hoped.

That didn't change the fact she had dreamed of him.

It was the same old episode she had dreamed about so often right after it occurred. That evening back in February, in London, at the Countess of Whitmore's musicale …

She, Edward, and Eliza had accepted Lady Whitmore's invitation for "an evening of musical delights," thinking it would be a welcome change from an overcrowded soiree or ball. The event had indeed been uncrowded, a definite point in its favor. Yet the hired soprano sang so shrilly, and Lady Whitmore's daughter then spent so much time gliding her bow across an out-of-tune violin, that Catherine still found herself in need of a retreat. After murmuring an excuse to Eliza, who appeared on the edge of bolting herself, she had slipped from her gilded chair near the back of the room and into the corridor. She tiptoed along the dim, vacant space, putting distance between herself and the music, before stopping in front of a closed door near the back of the house. As no trace of light peaked out from underneath the door, she nudged it open, allowing her eyes to adjust to the darkness. She could just make out soaring rows of shelves lining the walls, dotted with the shadows of books. It would seem she had entered the library, the perfect place to sit alone for a moment.

Except that a sudden rustle of skirts made her freeze in place. Low murmurs floated through the air, followed by a woman's high-pitched giggle. She was definitely not alone in the room.

She took a silent step backward, wanting to escape whatever scene she had intruded upon without detection. The murmurs grew louder, turning into noises that sounded more like moans, and she backed up again, nearly close enough to the doorway to make a hasty retreat.

And she would have, had the dark blanket of clouds not shifted, allowing moonlight to stream through the expansive windows. She caught sight of him then, sprawled out in an armchair near the window, his head tilted back, his eyes closed. They had met each other only once, at Lady Cranford's ball, as she recalled, but she would recognize that unruly dark hair and chiseled jawline anywhere. They belonged to Viscount Kendrick, the notorious scoundrel and rake. She hadn't known he was present this evening.

Furthermore, he had company. A woman sat atop his lap, her skirts hiked up and her legs dangling to each side of him. Although she faced away from Catherine, the prominent feather emerging from her coiffure marked her as Lady Blakely, a widow at least ten years the viscount's senior. Catherine *had* noticed Lady Blakely earlier, sitting several rows in front of her, but hadn't realized the woman had also slipped away.

With Lady Blakely and Lord Kendrick absorbed in one another, she had every opportunity to flee this unwanted situation, but some unnameable force kept her glued to the spot. Lord Kendrick's eyes flew open, and she tensed her whole body, certain he had noticed her. However, he merely leaned forward to press his mouth to Lady Blakely's throat, working his way downward as he began tugging at her bodice. Lady Blakely wriggled against his lap, pushing her body closer to his, and his free hand went to her bare thigh, sliding upward until she let out an animal-like squeal.

Catherine was an innocent. An ignorant girl of eighteen who had passed far too many hours alone in the country. That didn't mean she was oblivious to what transpired right in front of her. Her heart pounded forcefully enough to make her whole body feel like it shook, with the core of the sensation settling itself at the spot between her legs.

Finally, she regained her ability to move, to tiptoe back another few steps until she could burst through the library door and bolt down the corridor.

That's where the dream always ended, the point where she awoke with a racing heart and heated skin. The unwelcome memory had stayed away from her dreams for weeks now. Until last night, when it had returned more vividly than ever, leaving her awake staring at the ceiling for hours, afraid of what might await her if she went back to sleep.

She had no need to keep pinching her cheeks, for they had turned a ghastly shade of red all of their own accord. She glared at herself, willing her face to cool.

Why was she such a ninny? A true lady would have put the events of that night out of her head at once. Besides, Lord Kendrick wasn't coming here after all, and she had no reason to be reminded of his untoward behavior. On the contrary, Sir Arthur awaited her downstairs, a true gentleman eager to strengthen their acquaintanceship. Nothing mattered beyond that.

Seeing her cheeks had lightened to a more pleasing pink, she pushed herself up from the vanity stool and rushed out of the room before her thoughts could get the better of her again.

For once, she hurried to join the crowd, not letting the buzz of chatter or peals of boisterous laughter disconcert her in the least. If she had to humiliate herself at charades or kiss the candlestick, then so be it, as long as she eventually achieved her desired outcome.

She stepped into the crowded library without a moment's hesitation, on the lookout for Sir Arthur. However, the person who skipped up to her was Lavinia, holding a gentleman's unbound cravat.

"You have arrived right on time." Lavinia's face glowed with excitement, her voice so high that it sounded rather like she had overindulged in wine at dinner. "We're about to start a game of blindman's bluff, and I'm to be the one blindfolded. Lord Carington has generously donated his cravat for the purpose."

That evoked chuckles throughout the room, and Lord Carington, with his shirt hanging loose around the neck, flashed Lavinia a lewd smile. Catherine quickly turned her face to the floor.

"Well, let's begin." Lavinia pulled the cravat over her eyes, securing it in a tight knot behind her head. "Lord Carington, perhaps you'll spin me?"

"With pleasure." The young, ruddy-haired earl showed his teeth in another suggestive grin and reached to take hold of Lavinia's waist.

Catherine took the opportunity to gaze about the room. Had she somehow missed Sir Arthur? Throughout the sea of faces, his remained noticeably absent, though perhaps he had needed a short reprieve as well and would soon be in.

"I'm coming for yoooou!" Lavinia's singsong voice rang directly in her ear. Drat. Why had Lord Carington turned Lavinia in her direction? And why did she keep letting herself get distracted?

She moved to take a large step away, far from Lavinia's reach, when her foot caught in the curved leg of an armchair. She jerked herself upright to keep from falling, just as Lavinia's hands connected with her shoulders. Oh dear, oh blast, oh *hell*, why hadn't she been more careful?

"Ooh, I've caught someone," exclaimed Lavinia with a giggle. She brought her hands up to Catherine's coiffure, letting them rest there only a moment before reaching down to the gauzy puffs of her sleeves.

"Catherine?" Lavinia tugged down the blindfold, meeting her face with a frown. "Why, that was too easy. You were right next to me to begin with. Why didn't you move?"

"I tripped," she muttered, feeling numerous sets of eyes upon her and wishing she could sink into the carpet.

Lavinia's pique quickly faded. "No matter, I suppose. It is now your turn to be blindfolded."

With a flourish, she handed Catherine the cravat, and as the subject of scrutiny, Catherine saw no option but to take it. Perhaps it would be best if she feigned a headache or an ankle injury … But no, she couldn't let herself back away now, not when she had come this far. If Lavinia enjoyed this game, she would find a way to enjoy it as well.

"Thank you," she said, pulling the knotted cravat across her eyes. At least in the darkness, she didn't have to watch others peering at her. "Lavinia, will you spin me?" She posed the question quickly, before Lord Carington could get any ideas.

"But of course." Giggling again, Lavinia twirled her in three dizzying circles before abruptly releasing her hands. "Do not stumble this time!"

But Catherine couldn't help but stumble a little as she tried to regain her balance. She tentatively inched forward, waving her arms out in front of her. It shouldn't be too difficult to recapture Lavinia, given how foolishly she was acting. But despite her giddiness, Lavinia remained silent and evasive.

No matter. She merely had to catch and identify *someone*, so the game's focus could shift away from her. She kept advancing with small steps, although whether she still moved toward the doorway, the direction in which she had initially faced, or Lavinia had spun her another way altogether, she couldn't say.

It made little difference, though, because her hand connected with a thick woolen coat. Not Lavinia, then. A gentleman. Could Sir Arthur have possibly entered the library at the opportune moment, walking right into her searching arms?

She raised her hands, letting them travel upward until they made contact with hair. However, whereas Sir Arthur's hair was straight and wispy, the locks beneath her fingers tumbled across their owner's forehead in thick waves. Her skin prickled at the horrifying thought that she had Lord Carington within her grasp. But no, it couldn't be him, for Lord Carington carried the scent of a filled brandy decanter. This man smelled like the outdoors, of fresh evening air and newly fallen leaves.

She tried to recall all the other gentlemen present, but her thoughts swirled about her head in a jumble, and no matches came to mind. All she could do was continue to trace her fingers downward, running the tips over the straight bridge of his nose and the sharp angles of his cheekbones. His skin had just a trace of a beard, the stubble of a man who hadn't had the opportunity to shave that day, and his jaw ended in a perfectly defined line.

Her stomach abruptly became heavy, as if she had swallowed a rock. Her heartbeat quickened, coming in urgent little thumps, alerting her addled brain that something was wrong. But the face that flashed in her mind wasn't here. It couldn't be ...

She halted in her tracks, her hands stuck to his face as if they were glued there despite the clamminess in her palms. He made a low sound in his throat. A sound of discomfort? Or worse, was he laughing at her? His skin began burning her fingertips, and she snatched them away, suddenly desperate to regain her sight. She clawed at the blindfold, ripping it from her eyes and letting the unwanted scrap of cotton fall to the floor.

And there he was. Right in front of her stood a figure with dark hair that hung roguishly over his forehead, pale gray eyes with just a hint of green at the centers, and a face so neatly angled that it looked like a sculptor had taken great care in carving it.

Lord Kendrick.

The room had gone silent except for her own heartbeat, which pounded through her ears. Breathing had become increasingly difficult, and her chest rose and fell heavily each time she forced air through her lungs.

She had promised herself that she would stop letting fear hold her back. That she would endure any discomforts necessary if they led her to her goal. However, some things were beyond bearing.

She pivoted away from him and ran.

Chapter 4

"Kendrick! It's not often I've seen you up and about at this hour. Come join me."

As Philip entered the breakfast room with the morning's early glimmers of light, the first thing that greeted him was the overly loud voice of his old acquaintance from school, Lord Carington. Carington motioned to the empty seat beside him at the long mahogany table, which already bustled with men preparing for the morning's partridge shooting.

Philip nodded his greeting. "I'll be there in a moment."

He sauntered over to the sideboard at the opposite end of the room, which was laden with every type of bread, meat, eggs, and fruit one could possibly desire. Somehow, though, none of it appealed to him. He didn't know why, especially after last night, when he'd abstained from having even a single snifter of brandy. Perhaps the aftereffects of the evening at Sherwood's would be slow to dissipate.

After taking a reluctant spoonful of coddled eggs and a thick slice of buttered toast, he made his way back to the seat beside Carington. "Fine morning," he muttered, for lack of anything better to say.

"Yes, but never mind the small talk." Carington gazed at him, his ruddy hair, pointed teeth, and sharp chin making him look rather like a fox. "You're not renowned for being an avid shooter, and I've sure as hell never seen you linger around groups of ladies looking to get leg-shackled. So what in blazes are you doing here?"

"I could ask you the same question," Philip snapped, already tense from Carington's thunderous tone. After all, Carington wasn't known as a paragon of proper behavior either.

The man merely chuckled. "After several undesirable outcomes at the card table, I find my coffers stretched rather thin. I'm seeking a wife who can help remedy that problem."

"Well, I wish you every success with your endeavor," Philip remarked dryly, turning his attention to his piece of toast. He popped it in his mouth, where it immediately turned to sawdust.

"And you?" Carington continued to stare at him, un-willing to let the matter go.

Philip bit back a curse. Memories flooded him again: his mother sobbing in her darkened drawing room, his fa-ther fading a little more each day, thinking all was lost. However, he would have sooner had Carington fetch his hunting rifle and shoot him on the spot than discuss any of these matters with the man.

He reached for his teacup and took a mouthful of the piping liquid, washing down the crumbs that stuck in his throat. "The same old activities grow dull after a time," he said, shrugging his shoulders. "I thought I might try seeking a new source of divertissement."

"Ah." Carington grinned. "Well, you were in the library for a time last night. Did any of those 'divertissements' catch your eye?"

Philip took another long swallow from his teacup, wishing he could be through with this conversation. With any luck, Carington would recognize his hesitancy as a sign to shut up.

"Sadly, there wasn't an unhappy young wife or a worldly widow in sight," Carington boomed, not bothered by Philip's pause in the least. "Although I suppose that would rather defeat the purpose. Fortunately, there were a number of other pleasing possibilities. That Bathurst chit is an eager young thing. They always are, you know, once their siblings wed and they remain unattached."

"Mmm." Philip tried to feign a modicum of interest, but in truth, he'd taken little notice of the lady in question.

"Of course, the most exquisite of them all is Lady Catherine, and she should have a generous dowry now that her brother has married well. It's too bad she's such a little mouse, although she certainly had her hands all over you last night."

"It's too bad indeed," cut in Philip, unable to tolerate Carington's ensuing sniggering. "I imagine she would bring as much warmth to my bed as a chunk of arctic ice. I prefer my women a little less … frosty."

He regretted his declaration the second he made it. Really, he'd just wanted Carington to get that name out of his mouth, and saying such a thing seemed a good way to put the discomforting sensation within him to rest. Instead, it had made the feeling so much worse.

He was no stranger to a woman's touch. Skilled, welcoming, eager touches, given by slender fingers, thick fingers, bare fingers, fingers adorned by wedding rings ...

An innocent, awkward touch should have done nothing for him. Yet there was something about Lady Catherine's silk-gloved fingers tentatively tracing over the angles of his face—at least, before she had trembled and ran—that had stirred something unnameable and uncomfortable inside him. It was too absurd to even think of.

Carington remained unfazed. "If you say so. If she's not to your liking, how about—"

"If you'll excuse me." Philip shoved out his chair and jumped to his feet, unable to tolerate another minute in Carington's presence. "I find I'm not inclined to join the shooting after all."

Carington peered up at him with knit brows. "Is something the matter?"

"Not at all. Just a bit of fatigue." Philip tried to appear nonchalant. "I suppose that's what comes of spending the night engaged in other pursuits besides sleeping."

Carington's eyes widened before he broke into a smirk. "You don't say. And who, exactly, was the fortunate lady?"

"Really, Carington. A gentleman doesn't kiss and tell."

With that, Philip strolled out of the room as if he hadn't a care in the world, not bothering to give Carington a second glance.

In truth, he had passed a restful, and solitary, night. His stomach no longer churned, his head no longer pounded, and his limbs no longer ached. Why, then, did he feel so out of sorts?

***

Catherine ran through the corridors of Oakwood Hall, hardly knowing where she was going. To her bedroom? Outdoors? It didn't signify, as long as she put ample distance between herself and the breakfast room.

If she had learned anything throughout the Season, it was that not speaking allowed one to listen. And when listening, one could hear some very interesting things.

She was no stranger to the whisperings about her. She overheard them often when shielding herself behind a potted palm in a ballroom, in a darkened alcove, or on a hidden garden bench.

What a funny creature, that Catherine Adderley. One would almost think she lacks the ability to speak.

Lady Catherine has her mother's looks; it's a shame she lacks charm to go with them.

Or worst of all, *No wonder she behaves so peculiarly. Everyone knows she's not truly an earl's daughter.*

Still, none of those things had cut her the same way as what she had just overheard. *I imagine she would bring as much warmth to my bed as a chunk of arctic ice.*

Her face flamed, and her chin trembled as she strode across the floorboards. Damn him. His presence ruined everything.

As Sir Arthur had spoken yesterday of his intention to join the shooting, she had decided to go to the breakfast room early in hopes of seeing him before he departed. And she would have, had that awful Lord Carington, with his resounding voice, not been seated at the end of the table closest to the doorway, conversing with the even more terrible Lord Kendrick.

I prefer my women a little less ... frosty.

Sir Arthur had sat at the other end of the breakfast room, unengaged in conversation. He probably still did and would be perfectly able to talk with her, but it no longer mattered. She just needed to get away, forget her resolve for the time being, and simply be alone.

However, her haste made her clumsy, and she found herself crashing into another figure in the middle of the corridor.

"Oh!" The figure, an older woman dressed in a simple mauve gown, gave a cry of surprise.

"I'm terribly sorry." Somehow, her cheeks became even hotter, and she turned her eyes to the floor, awaiting the woman's reproach.

The woman, though, merely paused a moment before saying in a soft voice, "Lady Catherine. How like your mother you look."

Catherine dared to meet her gaze, but the woman's thin, lined face, adorned by a coiffure of brown hair mixed with gray, looked unfamiliar. She certainly hadn't noticed her at the picnic or at dinner. Indeed, they had never met before, but as they continued to peer at one another, an unsettling flicker of recognition popped into her mind.

"Allow me to introduce myself," the woman said, although there was no longer any need. Catherine knew exactly to whom she spoke. "I was a friend of your mother's. Marian Hadleigh, the Marchioness of Langley."

So confirmed what Catherine had already deduced. Of course she would crash into Lady Langley, of all people. She had already experienced the ultimate humiliation on account of Lord Kendrick. She may as well humiliate herself in front of his mother as well.

"Lady Catherine Adderley," she murmured, sinking into a curtsey with all the grace she could muster. "A pleasure to make your acquaintance."

The pleasantries aside, she could now return to her objective of fleeing, but something about the way the marchioness looked at her held her in place. The woman had stormy gray eyes, similar to her son's. But they were so filled with a subtle melancholy, she thought they must be the saddest eyes she'd ever seen.

Perhaps that's what having such a scoundrel for a son did to a mother.

She regretted her ungenerous assessment at once. It was common knowledge that the Marquess and

Marchioness of Langley had been parents to three sons until the second had been killed in the Battle of Waterloo, and the eldest had succumbed to illness not long after. *That* had to be the source of the worst sorrow imaginable.

"Marian. Catherine. Good morning."

The even voice that called out from the other end of the corridor caused her to break her gaze with Lady Langley. Coming toward them was Lady Bathurst, further complicating her plan to retreat somewhere alone.

"Good morning, Althea." The marchioness greeted Lady Bathurst in a way that suggested a friendship between them. "I just had the pleasure of making Lady Catherine's acquaintance."

Catherine eyed Lady Langley carefully, searching for any hints of displeasure at the manner in which their meeting had occurred. Fortunately, the marchioness kept her face bland, seemingly willing to keep Catherine's clumsiness a secret.

"Lovely," Lady Bathurst said. "Is she not the image of her mother?"

Catherine bit back a hum of annoyance at the repeated comparison and attempted to smile beneath Lady Bathurst's scrutinizing look.

"You've awoken rather early," Lady Bathurst remarked, fortunately turning the topic of conversation to something other than the late Georgina Adderley. "Lavinia is still abed. Have you breakfasted already?"

"Yes." It was a lie, but she would never manage to eat while her stomach still fluttered as it did.

"And do you intend to join the ladies' excursion to the village?"

"No." She should have let Lady Langley speak first, but now that their meeting's power to distract her began to fade, her desire to flee became all the more profound. "No, I have a small headache and think it best I lie down before it has the opportunity to intensify."

She must not have spoken the untruth with enough conviction, for Lady Bathurst regarded her with a frown. Thankfully, though, she decided not to press the matter further. "As you wish. Be sure to request some headache powder if you have need of it."

"Thank you, I will. Good day, Lady Bathurst. Lady Langley."

Catherine barely took the time to nod her farewell before picking up her skirts and resuming her hasty journey down the corridor, feeling the two older ladies' eyes bore into her back as she went. Now that she had parted ways with them, perhaps they, too, would discuss what an odd creature she was over cups of tea in the breakfast room. It made no difference, though, if she didn't have to hear it.

Having gotten herself upstairs and near the ladies' wing, she continued with the purpose of shutting herself in her bedroom. Fortunately, the corridor remained empty for the final stretch to her doorway, and she stumbled inside, regretting her decision to leave the room in the first place.

The brocade counterpane had already been smoothed over, the pillows stacked neatly in place, but she flung herself upon them, burrowing into the softness. Perhaps she would be wisest to continue feigning a headache and stay here for the remainder of the week.

She closed her eyes, wishing for sleep to come and erase her memories, at least for a time. However, rustling noises and the low murmurs of Lavinia and her maid began drifting over from next door, every footstep and giggle pounding into her head. She breathed out a long sigh. She wasn't tired anyway.

She reached for the novel on her bedside table, pulling out the bookmark where it rested against chapter three. If she couldn't sleep, the next best thing would be to get caught up in the pages of a book, the story of a desperate damsel and the valiant gentleman who managed to treat her with an ounce of chivalry.

She must have passed quite a long time with her novel, for the house grew silent around her, and the stack of pages left to be read became thin. But as for what the words on any of the previous pages said, she hadn't a clue.

She threw the book down on the bed, giving another sigh that came out as a short huff of breath. It would have been vastly more satisfying to hurl the book across the room and scream so loudly that even the servants below stairs would hear. Her father had been proficient at shouting until he got his way; perhaps, she would discover she had inherited his ability if she tried it. But of course, she would never do such a thing. Instead, she jumped from the bed and rummaged through the wardrobe for a shawl. Her room was certainly safe, but it would also drive her mad if she had to pass another hour there alone with her thoughts. Besides, with the ladies in the village and the men out hunting, the rest of the house would be safe as well, and she desperately needed a change of scenery.

Oakwood Hall had lovely grounds, and with the sun streaming invitingly through the windows, outdoors seemed the best choice for an excursion. This time, she took unhurried steps as she made her way through the corridors and back downstairs, although no unexpected passersby came about with whom she could have a collision. She made her way to the deserted drawing room and through the doors that led to the terrace, the burst of crisp air helping to clear her head. She surveyed the landscape before her, from the neatly trimmed topiaries to the collection of rosebushes, which now hung heavy with rosehips, but none of these locations seemed quite private enough. Instead, she strolled farther away from the house, toward the more rustic terrain beyond, where expansive clusters of oak trees displayed their first hints of gold.

The trees would help block her from the view of anyone who happened to peer through the windows of Oakwood Hall, and that knowledge allowed her to move more freely. She sprinted down the slight incline as if she could outrun her troubled thoughts, not stopping until she reached the clearing in the trees that revealed a hidden pond.

The surface shimmered beneath the rays of morning sunshine, as smooth as a sheet of glass.

She gazed into the water as if it were a mirror, taking stock of her murky reflection. While she had never known her mother, repeated viewings of the portrait in the gallery back at Highfield Park allowed her to see what others recognized: the same golden hair, the same slender face with the delicate nose and rosebud lips. She supposed she should feel lucky to be thought as beautiful as the former countess, but the notion followed her around like a curse. For when people came to know her, it only emphasized how terribly she lacked her mother's allure, how inept she was, how reserved, how frigid …

She would bring as much warmth to my bed as a chunk of arctic ice.

Catherine kicked her foot across the pond's surface, her reflection vanishing as the water splashed up around her. Even outdoors on a picturesque day, she couldn't escape her misery. She thrust her foot through the water once more, wishing she was the type who could scream her troubles away, but then another idea took hold. The water temperature was surprisingly pleasant, and the air uncommonly warm for a morning in late September.

She gazed all around her, but the only other movement came from the slight rustle of the trees. That being the case, she cast off her sodden slipper and then the dry one, followed by her silky stockings. She glanced around again to be sure the area remained deserted and began unfastening the row of tiny buttons at the back of her dress. The garment slackened against her frame, and she pushed it to the ground before setting to work on her petticoat and stays. Those items also discarded, she stood at the pond's edge in only her shift, holding herself tall and squaring her shoulders.

She closed her eyes and filled her lungs with the fragrant autumn air. And then, she jumped.

Water rushed over her, much colder now that she was entirely submerged in it. Yet it was perfect. Her limbs tingled in the briskness, beginning to thrash toward the surface, but she forced herself to stay under and glide through the crystal water.

This is what she needed to wash the memories away. Here, she could think back to an earlier time: of being a young girl with a cheerful nurse who taught her to swim in the lake at Highfield Park. They had swum as much as possible in the summer, back when her days had been quiet and uncomplicated. Remembering them left her weightless, unhindered, free.

Until something grabbed her. Something tight snaked around her waist, dragging her with it. She was no longer a child; she knew lake monsters weren't real, yet some creature had her in its clutches, and she couldn't force her eyes open to face it. Instead, she kicked and flailed, her mouth opening in a silent scream that filled her lungs with water as they plowed through the depths. It seemed like it hauled her down, straight to the bottom, where she would never take a breath again.

She struggled harder, thrashing her limbs wildly, until somehow, they began drifting upward, and suddenly, a blast of air hit her face. She inhaled it in ravenous gulps, coughing out pond water as she went.

"Catherine."

She was breathing again. She was alive. And with that vital fact established, it now occurred to her that the creature still held her in its grasp. Furthermore, it had spluttered out her name. Her heart, which had seemed to be on the verge of quieting, now resumed its intensive thumps. She hadn't reached safety after all.

Very slowly, she cracked an eye open, prepared to face her captor.

Chapter 5

Philip had never been a strong swimmer. It was the type of activity that his brothers had participated in as he observed from his bed by the window for much of his youth. However, as he had stood shaded behind a tree trunk and watched Lady Catherine Adderley plunge into the chilly depths of the pond, only to fail to reemerge, his lack of skills didn't cross his mind. He thought only of reaching her and hauling her up before the water consumed her altogether.

But the creature in his arms was no delicate flower who hung limply as he pulled her to shore. She struck and thrashed at him, her eyes screwed shut, as she coughed up mouthfuls of water.

"Catherine." He choked out her name, his throat burning after having swallowed pond water as well. He needed to speak to her, though, to help break her out of her panic, so she would realize help had come and she was safe.

At last, her eyelids flickered open, her dark eyes regarding him intently. Until a second later, when she kicked him squarely in the shin.

"Ugh, hell," he groaned, instinctively releasing his grip on her as pain shot through his leg.

She floated beside him, looking to be on the verge of striking him again. "What do you think you're doing?"

His waiting damsel no longer appeared to need rescue. She had righted herself and begun treading water, bobbing above the surface with ease. However, she had become far from docile. On the contrary, the way she had practically spit the question, combined with her steely glower, suggested she was livid.

"What do you mean?" He had long considered himself proficient in speaking with casual charm, but the irate woman before him was such an enigma that he couldn't keep the note of perplexity from his voice. "I was attempting to save you from drowning. But by all means, no need to thank me."

Her bare arms slid across the water in even strokes while her expression still looked murderous. "Why would I thank you when I wasn't drowning?"

"Weren't you?" He propelled himself backward toward the shore, clearly no longer needed in the middle of the pond. Unlike Lady Catherine's effortless floating, his movements were clumsy. He let out a pent-up breath when his hands connected with the grassy bank and he could haul himself out of the water. He shook himself off, although everything from his woolen coat to his top boots remained saturated. "Then what, may I ask, were you doing submerged in the middle of the pond?"

She turned her eyes away from him, instead opting to stare at the movement of her legs beneath the water. "I was … swimming."

"Why, of course. Swimming." He nodded emphatically. "As one often does in the midst of autumn."

It was fortunate he had already removed himself from the pond, for she looked like she wished to drown him. She had to be out of her head, jumping into a pond and lingering beneath the surface like that. Yet she seemed no worse the wear for it. The briskness didn't bother her in the least, and she was clearly a proficient swimmer. Had he possibly ... overreacted?

His neck grew hot, and the sensation threatened to creep into his face. He squeezed his hair, letting the chilly drips run over him. How had Lady Catherine, the woman afraid of her own shadow, managed to ruffle him? If this kept up, he would need to jump back into the pond for another dose of the bracing water.

"Did Lady Wellesley not provide you with more compelling entertainment?" Somehow, he maintained his usual nonchalant tone. "I thought I heard tell of a ladies' shopping trip or some such delightful excursion."

"I found myself disinclined to attend." She still refused to meet his gaze and started pushing herself backward to put more distance between herself and the shore. But suddenly, her head whipped up, and she fixed her inquisitive brown eyes upon him. "And what are you doing here? I surveyed the area very carefully to ensure I was alone. Besides, Lord Wellesley took the gentlemen off partridge shooting at the *opposite end* of the estate."

Philip bent over and began tugging at his boots so he had reason to avoid her piercing stare. What could he even say in response? That he had hoped that by trudging around the estate alone, he could forget all the people around him and his reason for being there? That he had thought to escape the foreboding voice in his head that kept suggesting he would never be carefree again?

He stood barefoot on the grass, turning his boots upside down so the water could trickle out of them. Then, he lifted his head, cocking an eyebrow. "I found myself disinclined to attend."

Catherine had proven herself a proficient swimmer, but her body showed a hint of shivering for the first time since she'd entered the water. It made sense that she'd succumb to the briskness sooner or later.

"It being autumn and all, perhaps you should bring your current excursion to an end," he said, keeping an eye on her quivering chin.

Once more, she turned her face down. "I cannot."

"And why is that, precisely?"

She kept her voice low, almost out of his earshot. "I'm dressed in only my shift."

He swallowed back a laugh. Did she really think he was unaware of that fact? For one thing, her discarded garments lay in a pile near his feet. And for another, the sight that had greeted him as he came through the trees had been none other than Lady Catherine Adderley dropping her powder blue dress to the ground, followed by her petticoat and stays. He had known he was an intruder at once, but with Lady Catherine before him, all long limbs and soft curves barely concealed by the filmy fabric of her shift, he'd found it impossible to look away.

But now, it would seem he'd have to.

"I'll divert my eyes," he said, going against every principle he normally obeyed. Better that than have her freeze to death in the pond.

She bit her lip, still not moving. She would no doubt prefer that he departed the scene altogether, but he couldn't shake the suspicion that she would plunge into the water once more if left alone.

"Go on, love," he urged, speaking with a gentleness he hadn't known he possessed. He turned so that his back was to the pond, and even though she could no longer see his face, he pressed his eyelids closed.

At first, no sounds emerged from behind him, but eventually, he could detect the gentle lap of water as she swam toward him and the squelch as she pulled herself upward and her feet hit the grassy shoreline.

Then, more silence, except for her quickened breathing right behind him until she cleared her throat. "I require my shawl."

His eyes flew open, meeting with the length of patterned silk that lay in front of his feet. Wordlessly, he bent to retrieve the article and turned just enough to pass it back to her. He did it quickly, thinking it unwise to further agitate her given how uneasy she seemed, but that didn't stop him from catching the briefest glimpse of her.

The sight of her in her shift before she jumped into the water had been enough to stop him in his tracks. But now that the wet garment clung to her, leaving no curve to the imagination, displaying the shadows of two peaked nipples and a darkened patch between her legs, it was torture to look away. He could gaze upon such a sight for hours, studying every angle and curve, taking in her smooth perfection. Even better, how would it feel to run his fingers over her face, just as she had done to him? He wouldn't stop there, of course; he would glide them downward, exploring every inch of her, for even a woman like Lady Catherine couldn't be totally immune to pleasure.

He had to stop thinking that way or jumping back in the pond would become an absolute necessity. However, it was momentously difficult to fight off every urge he would normally concede to without a second thought.

Lady Catherine rustled around behind him. Judging by the sound of fabric rubbing against skin, she must be trying to use her shawl as a towel. Not that the flimsy scrap would do much good.

"Lord Kendrick."

She called his name so clearly that he instinctively turned to face her. However, she now had the shawl draped about her so that much of her body was concealed.

She motioned to the ground. "You are still standing between me and the remainder of my clothing."

You're not the first lady to find herself in such a predicament. The remark started to form on his tongue, yet he swallowed it back, aware it would be exactly the wrong thing to say to her. Instead, he stepped to the side, allowing her free access to the rest of her garments. Apparently, he *could* act like a gentleman when he so chose.

However, Lady Catherine didn't move. She eyed him once more with her striking gaze and took a deep breath. "Lord Kendrick, we seem to have had a misunderstanding today. Nonetheless, I cannot come to any conclusion but that you tried to offer me your assistance, and for that, I owe you my thanks. However, I think it best for us to part ways now and forget this incident ever occurred."

He peered at her in return, watching as water droplets fell from the ends of the golden waves that framed her face and onto her toes. She was correct about there being no further need for his presence here. Now that she had exited the pond and felt autumn's crispness accentuated against her damp skin, it seemed unlikely she would return to the water. If she had any sense, she would quickly return to the house and curl up by the fire.

Still, he didn't want to leave. Not with her here alone, unsettled, unclothed … Doing so would feel rather like defeat.

But there was nothing else left.

"As you wish," he said, inclining his head with impeccable politeness. "Good day, Lady Catherine."

And he strode back toward the trees.

***

After checking to make sure Lord Kendrick did, in fact, continue walking in the opposite direction, Catherine snatched up her stays, lacing them about herself in a loose and untidy knot. She threw her petticoat over her head, pulled on her stockings, stepped into her dress—

"Drat." Her chilled fingers clawed at the row of buttons in the back, desperately trying to force them into their loops, but it was futile. The buttons were so tiny, and until the numbness in her fingertips subsided, she would never manage to fasten them all.

Lord Kendrick paused in his jaunt, turning back to face her. "Is something the matter?"

Double drat. The man must have ears like a pointer. She pinched the gaping fabric together at her back. "No, not at all."

He leaned against the expansive oak trunk next to him. "If you're having difficulty with your dress, I can assist you."

"No." She could barely spit out the word fast enough. "No, that will be quite unnecessary."

"You're correct, of course." He ran a hand through his dripping locks as if he hadn't a care in the world. "It would be much better for you to return to the house with your dress hanging open. With any luck, your timing will coincide with the men returning from the shooting."

She had made up her mind early that morning that she hated him, and the day's subsequent events had turned her loathing into a feeling too powerful to name. It was impossible to put enough space between them. She would gladly board a ship to the other side of the earth and make a permanent departure from England if it meant never seeing him again, and still, the distance wouldn't be sufficient.

But at the moment, there seemed no other option but to accept his assistance. She gave the buttons a final tug, but they slipped out of her fingers unfastened, and she ripped her hands away from the dress with a cry. She was set to experience additional mortification in some form or another. As he had been the cause of her humiliation up to this point, it was just as well to continue the trend.

"Come here, then, if you are so inclined to be helpful." She issued her order as sternly as an army commander. But apparently, he didn't find her too off-putting, for he strolled toward her with a hint of a smile.

She glared at him in return, thinking, for the thousandth time, of how every choice she'd made at this house party seemed to be the wrong one. But maybe, once she got her dress fastened and headed on her way, she could find a way to do better moving forward. The first step would be avoiding Lord Kendrick's presence at all costs.

Her skin had grown cold in the autumn air, but when his hands connected with the back of her dress, her body turned to fire. His fingertips seared her, each touch sending flames licking up her back as he made his way through the row of buttons. Since her emergence from the water, her limbs had been trembling, but she abruptly tensed all her muscles, willing herself not to move, not even to breathe. He was tall enough to stand above her by several inches, and she could sense his face near the top of her head, his nose inhaling the scent of her hair. She wanted to turn around and slap him, to wipe away that trace of smugness and send him reeling away from her. Except ... perhaps that wasn't what she truly desired after all.

It made little difference what she wanted, for his fingertips left her nearly as quickly as they had come, leaving her buttons fastened in a neat row. Frequent practice had likely made him adept at such a task.

"I sincerely thank you," she said, as warmly as a blast of pond water in the middle of winter. She turned to face him but took several steps back, not wanting to be within his reach. "I'm certain I require no additional assistance, so you may as well head on your way now."

"Are you not returning to the house?"

"I am," she affirmed, "but you have raised a valid point. There could now be others lurking about, so we had best not be seen together. People could jump to all sorts of erroneous conclusions. It would be more prudent for you to return to the house ahead of me. I'll follow a short time later."

"You go first, and I'll follow later." His gaze traveled up and down her body. "You're clearly freezing."

His scrutiny, his proximity, suddenly became too much. No man deserved to have eyes that gray and penetrating, to have cheekbones that high, to have a smile that indolent and suggestive all at the same time. No one should be that effortlessly self-assured, that carefree, that able to act as though everything existed for his pleasure and everything was easy.

It would be simplest to agree with him and flee the scene at once, just as she so often felt the temptation to do. That way, they could be done with each other, and she could try, once again, to put him out of her mind. But something had come over her, some tangled sensation within, that gave her a spurt of boldness and refused to let her back down.

"Oh, not to worry. After all, some women are frostier than others." She watched him carefully, seeking any trace of a reaction. "And when a woman is as frigid as a chunk of arctic ice, I suppose she can manage a little cold."

As the meaning of her words set in, his eyes widened while his complexion turned slightly gray. And Lord Kendrick, the man with the flirtatious grin and a clever remark always on the tip of his tongue, stood open-mouthed with nothing to say.

After a day of failures, she finally had one small victory. With that accomplished, she spun on her heels and stormed away, leaving him standing alone by the pond.

Chapter 6

With great difficulty, Catherine forced herself downstairs for dinner that evening. She had grown comfortable sitting by the fireplace in her room, trying to regain warmth in her fingers and toes. The environment was far superior to the bustling yet underheated dining room. Furthermore, when Lady Bathurst came to her room after returning from the village and inquired after her health, it would have been so easy to say her headache had worsened and she would need to continue resting.

However, that newly generated part of her, the side that refused to shrink from a challenge, still hadn't disappeared. And so, she had rung for Betsy, asking her to fetch the new lace-adorned evening gown with the lowcut bodice and take extra care with her hairstyle.

She arrived downstairs just as the guests began proceeding from the drawing room to the dining room, and she scurried along in the lowly lit corridor, trying to join the back of the line without attracting notice.

Unfortunately, Lady Wellesley, strolling with her arm atop Lord Carington's, caught sight of her at once.

"Catherine, come join us," she called in a singsong voice, extending her free arm.

Catherine pinched her lips together and gritted her teeth before showing them in the most genuine smile she could muster. She traipsed over to them, inclining her head in greeting. "Good evening. Please forgive my lateness."

"Think nothing of it." Lady Wellesley reached for her arm, leading her down the corridor. "I'm pleased to see you have recovered from your megrim."

"I'm much better, thank you." Murmurs of conversation echoed behind them, and she fought the urge to look back and see if she could spot Sir Arthur in the procession. Or any other certain gentleman.

"Lord Kendrick?"

As if somehow reading her thoughts, Lady Wellesley called the very name she *didn't* want to hear as soon as they set foot in the vast, oak-paneled dining room. It turned out he stood only several couples behind them, arm in arm with Lady Rose, looking as polished as ever in his black dinner attire and tidily knotted cravat.

"I think we should change our arrangement this evening. Lord Kendrick, kindly switch places with Lord Carington. I should like you to be my dinner companion."

"I shall consider myself the luckiest of men," he said, strolling over to her and gazing at her as if she were the only woman in the room.

Lady Wellesley had him accompany her to her seat at the head of the table, her creased cheeks turning slightly pink. But before sitting, she turned back to Catherine. "Come along, my dear. You may take the seat next to Lord Kendrick."

Catherine's small pang of satisfaction at Lord Carington's setting down paled in comparison to her dread at now dealing with an even worse man. As she lowered herself onto the stiff brocade seat of her dining chair, her stomach began to churn. Why had Lady Wellesley taken a sudden interest in Lord Kendrick? And more importantly, why had her attention extended to Catherine? Could she possibly know something of what had transpired that morning? It was impossible, of course; Lady Wellesley and her companions had been far away in the village. Still, the thought made Catherine's insides twist so fiercely that the bowl of vegetable soup a footman placed in front of her nearly made her gag.

Lord Kendrick turned to her, as nonchalant as ever. "Did you pass a pleasant day, Lady Catherine?"

Lady Wellesley had started a conversation with the neighbor to her left, the middle-aged Lord Milton, yet her head remained slightly turned in their direction. Likewise, the Marchioness of Langley, seated across the table and a good half dozen places away from them, looked to be concentrating on her soup, but her eyes were fixed subtly upon her son. Despite appearances to the contrary, they were being watched. Making it crucial that Catherine not fumble.

She pressed a tiny spoonful of soup between her lips, forcing it down with a heavy swallow. Then, she turned to Lord Kendrick, refusing to let her voice tremble. "Yes, thank you, although sadly, a headache prevented me from attending the shopping excursion in the village."

"A true disappointment, to be sure." He managed the words without a trace of irony. "Did your health allow you to seek out another diversion instead?"

She fought an overwhelming urge to kick him beneath the table. What did he mean by alluding to the morning's events? Did he not realize they were on dangerous territory? But if he noticed the scrutiny they were under, he didn't let it show. Indeed, his face remained as serene as ever. Which meant she would need to find a way to keep herself composed as well.

"As a matter of fact, it did. It was such a lovely day that I managed a stroll. Oakwood Hall has the most pristine grounds." She threw in the compliment, thinking it couldn't hurt in keeping her high in Lady Wellesley's favor.

"I agree." Lord Kendrick's affirmation caused Lady Wellesley's mouth to curve into a smile, even though, by all appearances, she still spoke with Lord Milton. "The gardens are picturesque, and if you continue toward the oak wood, there's a charming little pond. Did you venture that way?"

The man had no shame whatsoever. Not that she'd been unaware of that fact before now. If she could only slam her foot into his shin again.

"I did. Charming, as you say." She slipped in another small mouthful of soup, struggling to keep the spoon steady in her hand. She needed to turn the conversation away from herself at once, and if he insisted on playing this game, she would join him. "And you, Lord Kendrick? Did you enjoy the shooting this morning?"

"I regret that malaise kept me from joining in. I, too, passed a solitary morning."

His ability to lie so smoothly was impressive. It would have annoyed her had it not been working to her benefit.

"I hope you found yourself recovered enough to attend the billiards tournament after luncheon," she said, remembering the rowdy shouts that had floated up from Lord Wellesley's study to her bedroom throughout the afternoon.

"Unfortunately, I did not. At this gathering of delightful guests, I spent the day by myself, if you can imagine."

She couldn't imagine, for if he hadn't attended the billiards tournament, it was likely because he had opted to pass the hours before dinner in another lady's bedroom. Yet something about his words made them sound not just filled with superficial charm but sincere.

He leaned slightly closer to her, lowering his voice to a murmur that only she could hear. "You see, Lady Catherine, it is sometimes possible to spend *too* much time in the company of others. For when doing so, one must engage in all manner of conversations. That can sometimes lead to saying things one might come to regret."

Was that supposed to be some form of apology? She peered at him while trying to prevent her mouth from gaping. The man bewildered her to no end. He churned up that unnameable feeling in her again, the one that felt rather like loathing but entirely different at the same time.

"Indeed, Lord Kendrick," she said, keeping her voice low. "I recognize the value of both silence and restraint."

Now that they whispered, Lady Wellesley no longer pretended to engage in conversation with Lord Milton.

Instead, she stared at them unabashedly, looking like the wheels in her head turned with vigor. Likewise, the marchioness still glanced their way with alertness.

They had returned to unsteady ground just as quickly as they had left it. A situation that Catherine needed to remedy without delay. She straightened herself up, turning to Lady Wellesley with a gentle smile. "The soup is delicious. Do you think your cook might share the recipe so I can bring it to our own cook at Highfield Park?"

For the rest of the meal, she let Lady Wellesley lead the conversation and took extra care not to be seen in confidence with Lord Kendrick again. After all, they had nothing left to say to one another. All that mattered now were the after-dinner activities when she could speak to Sir Arthur, who was seated so far down the table from her that a candelabrum nearly blocked him from view.

When Lady Wellesley announced it was time for the ladies to retreat to the drawing room, Catherine practically shot from her seat. Despite her lack of continued direct conversation with Lord Kendrick, the fact that he merely sat and laughed and *breathed* beside her had been too much to ignore.

Getting up and walking away from the table, where the air somehow turned lighter the farther she went, was so refreshing that she didn't even feel the need to retire to her bedroom for a spell. No, this evening, she would go straight to the drawing room and wait for the gentlemen, namely Sir Arthur, to join them.

Lord Carington gazed up at the ladies as they fluttered toward the doorway, his eyes gleaming. "Shall we have another evening of games in the library?"

"Yes, let's." Lavinia, always eager for new entertainment, spoke up at once. "Perhaps a game of hide and seek?"

The way he grinned at Lavinia made Catherine's skin prickle. "That sounds just the thing, assuming all other company is agreeable."

Murmurs of assent from the younger guests hummed around the room while Catherine suppressed a groan. Hide and seek was a convenient game when one wished to slip away and be alone, and even better when one wished to engage in scandalous behavior with another. However, when it came to encouraging a simple conversation, hide and seek was terrible.

Perhaps, though, all was not lost. If she could speak with Sir Arthur before the game started, maybe they could forgo playing and return to the drawing room with the older guests to continue their conversation.

With that in mind, she went to the drawing room and waited patiently, settling herself in an armchair with a cup of tea to warm her fingers. Fortunately, she didn't have to wait long before several gentlemen peeked their heads through the doorway to ask if the ladies were ready to commence the game.

She strolled down the corridor with a surprising lightness in her step, nodding along with Lavinia's enthusiastic chatter. However, when they reached the library, of all the gentlemen assembled, including one she pretended not to see, there was no sign of Sir Arthur.

"Who shall be the seeker?" Lavinia asked as Catherine scanned the room, just in case Sir Arthur stood by a book-shelf or sat in an armchair concealed from view. But no, it would seem he was once again late in joining the revelry, if he planned to come at all.

"I believe I'd be up to the task."

The keen voice came from none other than Lord Carington, not surprising her in the least. Having him as the seeker would give her all the more incentive to find a clever hiding spot. Or better yet, slip upstairs and not return until later.

"Very well, Lord Carington." Lavinia's pale eyelashes fluttered. "Close your eyes, then, and begin counting. Shall we agree to keep our hiding spots to this level of the house only?"

"Indeed. One, two …"

Lord Carington's swift start to the counting caused shrieks from some of the ladies, followed by the hasty dis-persal of all the room's occupants. Catherine bolted along with them, determined not to have a repeat of her failure at blindman's bluff. However, once out in the corridor, she glanced from side to side, unmoving. Should she wait here in the hopes Sir Arthur would come along? Find a hiding spot now and search for him later? Whisper a hurried excuse to Lavinia and return upstairs and wait to try speaking with Sir Arthur until tomorrow?

"Forty-four, forty-five ..."

Drat, Lord Carington seemed to be hurrying his counting. She hastened down the lowly lit corridor toward the
stairs, thinking she may go up, when Lord Carington's voice
rang out again.

"Here I come!"

The man had clearly cheated by counting so rapidly, yet
there was little use in dwelling on that at present. She slipped
through the nearest doorway and into a darkened room,
softly pulling the door shut behind her. The remains of the
fire in the grate illuminated the space just enough to define
it as Lord Wellesley's study. A large desk with a solid, heavy
front stood in the middle of the room. Perhaps she could
push back the chair behind it and crawl underneath.

She turned back to the doorway, debating her options,
when a woman's high-pitched squeal, followed by peals of
laughter and Lord Carington's low murmur, sounded from
the corridor.

That decided it. She sprang for the desk, ducking
around the chair so she could push herself into the space
beneath the desktop. And came face to face with Lord
Kendrick.

Of course she did. By now, she should have expected
this type of indignity.

"I'm terribly sorry," she said in the faintest of whispers,
her heart thudding. "I didn't realize this space was already
occupied." Her cheeks flamed, although at least it was too
dark for him to notice.

"Wait," he whispered as she started to retreat. "You may as well join me."

"I'll do no such thing …" she began to say, but Lord Carington's footsteps in the corridor became louder, along with a delirious giggle that could only belong to Lavinia.

Lord Carington's voice rang out as clear as a church bell. "Now, let's see who I can get my hands on next."

Her body tensed, and her eyes darted toward the door one more time. Then, before she could give it another second's thought, she scooted under the desk into the cramped space beside Lord Kendrick.

***

Philip sat with his body curled into a tight ball, while next to him, Lady Catherine did the same. It didn't stop them from overlapping or her heat from pressing into him.

The door opened with a slight creak, and in plodded Carington, his footsteps heavy against the stone floor.

"Whom will I find in here, I wonder?" he drawled. His words were accompanied by a feminine titter that sounded like Lavinia Bathurst's.

Beside Philip, Lady Catherine remained as still as a statue, her chest barely moving even as she breathed. The only thing that gave her away was her rapid heartbeat, which vibrated against his arm.

Carington's footsteps neared the desk, and for the first time, Philip considered what the implications might be were they discovered here together. Carington would have no end of suggestive comments, none of which would please Lady Catherine.

However, despite their hiding place not being overly clever, Carington unknowingly stumbled past them with Miss Bathurst clinging to his arm. He went straight to the window, partially covered by a set of fringed curtains, at the back of the room.

"Aha!" he shouted, casting back the heavy fabric, only to reveal a bare window. That promptly sent Miss Bathurst into a fit of giggles.

In the dark, Philip rolled his eyes. The man had to be foxed, and the lady along with him.

Philip spun his head to the side as the faintest rustling sound came next to him. Lady Catherine had clamped her hand to her mouth. Had the inanity of the situation become too much for her? He peered at her, trying to communicate silently that this would all come to an end soon if she could only stay hidden a few moments longer.

But Lady Catherine didn't appear distressed. Rather, her eyes crinkled slightly at the corners, and she made a barely perceptible sound from the back of her throat. Why, if he wasn't mistaken, she was trying not to laugh. It was the first time he had noticed her express genuine amusement, and the sight tugged at his chest in a very odd way.

"No one's here," muttered Carington, his tone full of bewilderment. "Ah, well, let's try the breakfast room. Come along, Vinny."

He grabbed Lavinia's waist, adding his chuckle to her high-pitched snicker. They staggered back toward the desk, close enough that Miss Bathurst's feet nearly got tangled with the chair. However, at this point, they only had eyes for each other, and Carington leaned down to whisper something imperceptible in the lady's ear. In another moment, they were out of the room, slamming the door behind them.

Lady Catherine shifted her hand away from her mouth, revealing that she bit down tightly on her lip. She abruptly released her teeth, gazing at the doorway with wide eyes. "How utterly ridiculous."

And with that, Lady Catherine actually giggled. Not a high, grating sound like Miss Bathurst had made, but a quiet, clear little laugh that sent a jolt of longing straight to his groin.

With the threat of discovery now passed, he expected her to pull away at once, unable to escape his proximity fast enough. But she didn't. She remained exactly where she was, pressed against him.

He had known his share of women, and Lady Catherine was by far the most perplexing of them.

Didn't she abhor him? While she had gone through dinner with every outward appearance of politeness, he wasn't blind to the aversion in her eyes. Which perhaps he deserved, but really … he was a renowned scoundrel. What did she expect?

Besides, hadn't she realized the benefit in them discussing their morning openly at the dinner table? Lady Wellesley had regarded them so intently, had given off such a sense of all-knowingness, that it didn't hurt to say something to throw her off the truth.

Furthermore, after the way Lady Catherine had unnerved him at the pond, why shouldn't she experience some disconcertment in return?

But now, the detestation and the discomposure were both gone. Her eyes took on a dreamlike appearance in the darkness, and she tilted her head so that their faces nearly touched. She was a woman like any other, warm and pliant against him. A very foolish woman who didn't realize that she lingered in a fox's den.

Her inhibition, her solemness, and her sheer innocence had caused him to attempt to set aside the worst of his rakish ways around her. Still, he wasn't a bloody saint.

And so, he kissed her. Her lips were so close that he needed only to move in a few inches to reach them. They were even better than he imagined: as smooth as rose petals and as plump as a ripened plum. He pressed his mouth against them gently, half expecting her to dart away with the unfamiliar sensation. But Lady Catherine didn't move. She stayed with her mouth against his, perfectly still, until he felt her apply just the slightest amount of pressure to his lips as she allowed her own to part.

Shocks of longing lurched within him as he absorbed her heated exhale. He dared to trace his tongue around the opening of her mouth, coaxing her lips farther apart, and he placed his palm atop the golden tendrils at her nape, guiding her closer to him.

He thought for sure she would gasp in horror or give him another kick in the shin. But no, she still didn't shy away. Her fingers stretched to skim the edge of his face, and slowly, her tongue reached out to connect with his. He ran over it in languid circles, drinking in her sweet, intoxicating taste.

Her caresses, tentative and inexperienced, were exactly what he wanted. They drove him wild.

The heat of her mouth captivated him, and her pearly skin begged to be touched. He brought his hand forward, running it across the smoothness of her throat and then lower, right to where the edge of her lacy bodice sat temptingly low against the swell of her breasts.

It was really a wonder she didn't shove him away, but no, she stayed locked in the kiss as her fingers began sifting through his hair. This was bliss and torture all at the same time. If only he could tug away her bodice so her breasts were fully exposed to him, so he could taste the rosy buds as he brought his hand lower and lower until he reached the spot that would make her moan with pleasure—

There it was. In a matter of seconds, her hand had left his hair to deliver a swift slap across his face, leaving him recoiling with a stinging cheek. Some part of him had known this was coming.

She pinched her lips together, gazing at him with huge, astonished eyes. And then, without a word, Lady Catherine clambered away from the desk and darted across the room.

"Catherine," he began to call, but her name died on his lips. She was already gone. Apparently, even the threat of discovery by Carington was preferable to spending another minute in his clutches.

He scrambled out from under the desk, suddenly feeling ridiculous for cowering there like an errant child hoping to escape punishment. He stood alone in the darkened room, smoothing his rumpled clothing, waiting for the blood to stop pounding so intensely through his veins.

He was Philip Hadleigh, the infamous rogue. Nothing troubled him. In fact, the more difficult external circumstances became, the more he took it as a reason to live with abandon.

However, in this situation, it seemed Lady Catherine had the right of it. For he could think of nothing he'd like to do right now more than flee.

Chapter 7

Philip sank deep into the tub of steaming bathwater, letting the warmth soak through his limbs. The sun from earlier in the week had been replaced by a dreary mist, but that hadn't stopped him from persuading a group of gentlemen to proceed with the day's planned fishing excursion. For he knew better, after what had transpired two days ago, than to allow himself another idle morning. So what if the lot of them had returned damp, muddy, and miserable, with empty baskets besides? It merely gave them all an added incentive to bathe prior to the ball scheduled for that evening.

He dunked his head under the water, giving it a shake before popping back up. Perhaps Lady Catherine had good reason for her swimming excursion, for in that brief moment, he could understand the solace that came from being submerged in water. But he couldn't think about that now. Really, he shouldn't think of her at all. Even though he'd never seen a more tempting sight than Catherine Adderley floating in the pond with her eyes blazing at him. Even though she'd stood mere inches away from him in a wet shift that begged him to remove it.

Whether she had avoided him or he had avoided her, he couldn't exactly say, but whatever the case, they never had cause to speak since their evening in the study. Even Lady Wellesley wasn't so indiscreet as to force them together at dinner a second time, and Lady Catherine had forgone additional parlor games in favor of passing the time reading or embroidering. That was, when she hadn't been engaged in conversation with Sir Arthur Croft, hanging on to his every word. A mistake if ever there was one, but what difference did it make to him?

If he knew what was good for him, he would have found another young lady upon whom to turn his attention. There was no shortage of them in attendance, and he wasn't oblivious to the way they often directed their coy smiles or fluttering eyelashes at him. But even though that was the reason for him being here, he just couldn't muster up the enthusiasm. He supposed he could consider it yet another way in which he'd proven his uselessness and disappointed his parents. Surprisingly, though, the marchioness didn't appear distressed over his lack of a potential bride. Rather, during the brief moments they encountered one another throughout the day, she looked almost … pleased.

That being the case, he had little cause to feel troubled, and anyway, what was the point in wasting time on so useless an emotion? Besides, everything would improve with tonight's ball. Scores of neighbors and friends would add to the present company. New women, eager and experienced, would welcome his advances and gladly slip away into a hidden corner of the garden or sneak into the library with him, locking the door behind them. That was all he needed to set him to rights.

He allowed his hand to glide through the water, suddenly aware that he had developed an aching cockstand. This was what came of pretending he was anything other than a rake and leaving London, and the zealous woman in his bed, too abruptly.

He took himself in hand, stroking over the throbbing flesh as he conjured up Lucia's image. Dark hair, generous curves, a ready and welcoming grin … He tried to hear her laughter, to imagine her hands caressing him instead of his own.

But the figure in his mind shifted so that her body elongated, her dark eyes became solemn, and her hair turned the most brilliant shade of gold. She stood before him in a soaked shift, the clinging fabric revealing so much yet not enough, as her fingers made featherlight motions across his jawline.

Damn it, this wasn't supposed to happen. Not with Lady Catherine, who was reserved and naive and *frosty*. The thought should have been enough to unnerve him, but instead, his arousal burned more deeply than ever, and his hand continued pumping as though not even his own. The Catherine of his imagination nuzzled against him, allowing him to feel the heat from every perfect curve, silently begging him to touch her. Maybe just this *one time*, he could permit himself this fantasy and then get her out of his system for good.

Catherine's tentative fingers reached for his swollen flesh, tracing over the rigid tip as she stared at him, unwavering, with just a hint of a smile. That was all it took for him to spend into the bathwater as his body shook with violent spasms of pleasure. His climax seemed to go on and on, and when the last shudders faded away, he dropped his weight backward so he rested against the edge of the tub. His body had slackened, and his heart rate began to slow. Strangely, he didn't feel satisfied in the least.

***

The ballroom buzzed with activity, from the lively playing of the orchestra to the couples spinning about the dancefloor to the people who stood to the side and created a steady hum of conversation. The giant crystal chandelier showered them all with glittering light, putting the whole scene on display. It was the type of situation from which Catherine was apt to run away, only for the fact she had promised herself to no longer be so fainthearted. Still, she took a step closer to the wall as if to camouflage herself against the papered surface.

"Lady Catherine."

No sooner had she settled herself than a quiet voice called her name, and she turned to see the nondescript figure of Sir Arthur, slightly red-faced from the heat of the ballroom.

She managed a smile she didn't truly feel. "Good evening, Sir Arthur. I'm very pleased to see you."

Her words should have been sincere. The man she had set her sights on due to their mutual quietness had reciprocated her interest and now had the confidence to approach her. They had spoken numerous times throughout the week, with Sir Arthur even going so far as to ask if she thought his extensive library at Calverton Manor might please her.

Given her marriage aspirations, she could presumably take that as a promising sign. For some reason, though, his presence before her now created nothing but a dull emptiness inside.

"I'm finding myself growing a touch overheated." Sir Arthur gave his cravat a tug. "Would you like to take a stroll?"

Really, what would be better than leaving this overcrowded room and furthering her relationship with Sir Arthur in a quieter setting? Yet that feeling of dullness wouldn't leave her, and she found herself wanting to stay where she was, cacophony and all.

"Lady Catherine?" Sir Arthur peered at her expectantly, awaiting her response.

"That would be very nice, thank you," she squeaked awkwardly, accepting his proffered arm so he could lead her toward the terrace. As they walked, she silently berated herself for her trepidation. By being alone with Sir Arthur, she was getting exactly what she wanted, and with the house party nearing its end, there was no time left to lose. Why should she change her mind about her purpose now? She and Sir Arthur would suit. They could live a peaceful, comfortable life together. She had never required more than that, and there was no reason she should.

The terrace offered them a welcome breath of fresh air, but the space remained crowded with guests. Sir Arthur gazed at the multitude of couples with a frown. "Perhaps we could walk into the garden a ways to find somewhere more tranquil."

Catherine glanced back at the terrace doors. Lady Bathurst had given her a discreet nod on their way out, but surely that only signified consent for a stroll on the terrace and not an unchaperoned meeting in the garden. However, would anyone truly find fault in her taking a brief walk with Sir Arthur Croft? Unlike *some* gentlemen, he had no sort of salacious reputation. On the contrary, he was viewed as the picture of reserved decorum, and she along with him. Any doubts she felt were only because of her anxiety trying to take over again, and she wouldn't allow that to happen.

"As you wish." She gave him another half-hearted attempt at a smile. If she could just force herself to keep doing so, real happiness would eventually come from the facade.

Fortunately, the terrace had become such a hive of activity that no one seemed to remark them descending the stone steps. Sir Arthur led her toward the collection of topiaries, their perfect angles and curves just shadows against the night sky. They strolled alongside a line of towering pyramid-shaped trees, Sir Arthur coming to a halt when they reached a bench behind the last one in the row.

"Would you care to sit?"

His question made her realize she had neglected to engage him in conversation as they walked. At least he didn't appear to have found her silence off-putting, from what she could see of his expression in the darkness, anyway.

"Yes, thank you."

In truth, she would have preferred strolling back in the direction from which they'd come, but she didn't let that prevent her from taking a seat upon the marble surface and smoothing out the satin and gauze of her skirts.

Sir Arthur hesitated a moment before lowering himself beside her. They had shared the same sofa and settee before, but none quite so narrow as this bench. Here, their legs practically touched, although given how the topiaries obstructed them from the view of those on the terrace, she supposed it made little difference.

He turned to her with a smile of his own. "That's better, don't you think? I sometimes find the noise of these events rather overwhelming."

"Yes, I agree." And she did. Of course she agreed, but she couldn't get herself to fully settle on this bench either, even though only the faintest strains of music reached them, and there wasn't another person in sight.

"I must confess, though, I'm rather disappointed that this house party will soon come to an end."

"Indeed," she said with automatic politeness. "Lord and Lady Wellesley have been generous hosts who have offered us no end of entertainments."

"To be sure," Sir Arthur answered quickly but then paused and gazed down at his lap. His milky skin still contained a reddish tinge. "But that hasn't been my primary source of joy here and the reason I so regret leaving."

Despite how he had rushed his words and still refrained from looking at her, she had made out what he said quite plainly. Her heart gave a little flutter at the implied meaning and at what she suspected might come next, but the sensation felt more like nausea than excitement.

Sir Arthur took a deep breath and turned his eyes upon her. "Lady Catherine, I hope you realize that my greatest pleasure this week has been spending time in your company."

"How kind of you." She lowered her gaze demurely, now struggling with maintaining eye contact herself. Yet he had just said exactly what she had wanted to hear, the words that should have filled her with elation.

"I hope we can continue our friendship," he said, leaning in close enough that his coffee-scented breath tickled her face. "And that perhaps you have interest in making it something more."

I would like that very much, she should have said, but her throat had grown tight, and her tongue didn't want to move. Sir Arthur was introverted himself; surely, he wouldn't mind if she took a silent moment to compose her thoughts. But suddenly, one of his clammy fingers reached for her chin, tilting it upward so their gazes locked and their faces nearly touched.

Before she could make a sound, his lips were upon hers. If she'd harbored any doubts regarding the profundity of his feelings, the kiss swiftly dispelled them. She should have been bursting with anticipation and joy and leaning in to him with subtle eagerness. Instead, she sat stiffly, the push of his mouth doing nothing to erase her feeling of dullness.

Viewing Sir Arthur from this angle made him appear blurry and almost fishlike. And for the first time, she could see him as Lavinia did: a man who evoked little inspiration.

It wasn't supposed to be this way. And it wouldn't have been if not for—no, she shouldn't allow herself to even think of that other man's name. But how could she help it when, once again, he had ruined everything? That night beneath the desk, a single touch from his lips had captivated her, causing her to cast away all restraint and propriety. His fingers against her skin had set every nerve ending ablaze, and the taste of his mouth had left her in a frenzy, starving for more. Her momentary flash of sanity that night had been the only thing that kept her from total ruination in a rake's clutches. She could never take that risk again.

She tried closing her eyes, making herself concentrate on the feel of Sir Arthur's caresses as she awaited the sparks they would ignite within her. But nothing happened. The unrefined movements of his lips were too much, and his mouth was just so … wet.

She withdrew slightly, resisting the urge to wipe her mouth. "Sir Arthur …" She trailed off, the look on his face giving her pause. His cheeks had become more flushed than ever, and his eyes glittered in a way that made them look almost wild.

"You are so lovely, Lady Catherine," he murmured close to her ear. Then, he pulled her back against him for another embrace, crushing his lips against hers.

She wrenched her head away, no longer concerned about manners. Her stomach churned, but not with the pleasurable flutters she'd been waiting for. The feeling was pure dread. "Sir Arthur, I hardly think this is appropriate."

He gave a quick chortle, a sound so cutting she was suddenly glad he didn't laugh often. He reached for her, placing his clammy hands firmly on either side of her face. "I appreciate your attempts at modesty, but there is no need. You have made no secret of your interest, and I return it wholeheartedly."

He pulled her to him again, his humid lips overtaking hers as he continued to grip her face. She tried jerking her neck, but his hands tightened against her, giving her no escape. Perhaps she could kick at his shin. It had worked with Lord Kendrick. Or better yet, bring a knee to his groin.

But as much as she wanted to get away, she couldn't muster the necessary strength to try harder. After all, Sir Arthur was showering her with affection, just as she'd desired. Wasn't that the whole point of her coming here? Hadn't she encouraged his attention?

Every inch of her body became heavy, and her shoulders slumped. Yet again, she had muddled things in the worst way possible. Her eyes stung at the thought, and bile burned her throat as she endured the repeated plundering of Sir Arthur's tongue.

But this was exactly what she had wished for.

"Get the hell away from her."

The voice cut through the night air like a saber, causing Sir Arthur to drop his hands and gawk at its source.

Catherine remained frozen in place, staring at Sir Arthur's wrinkled cravat and crimson face. She had no need of darting around to see who had approached them. She would know that voice anywhere. It was the one that, try as she might, she couldn't stop from floating through her dreams.

Once again, the rake who ruined everything had come to her rescue.

Chapter 8

In strolling alone outside instead of parading about the ballroom, Philip had broken two of his recently made vows. The first, simply to no longer stroll alone outside. And the second, to avoid Lady Catherine at all costs.

But in making this second vow, he'd neglected to consider Lady Catherine's penchant for getting herself into binds. The fact that he'd misjudged the situation and made an ass of himself the last time he'd come to her aid meant little to him now. For in front of him, he saw a stiff, unwilling woman being ravaged by Sir Arthur Croft. If that was merely how the two of them looked when engaged in a passionate embrace, he would deal with the consequences of his misperception later. But the thought of standing idle while she legitimately required help was more than he could stomach.

Lady Catherine didn't turn to face him, but the way Sir Arthur stared at him, almost like a puppy who had just been scolded, alerted him that his instincts were correct. And as the meaning of that sank in, his blood began racing, and he stomped across the grass toward them without another second's thought.

"Get up," he snapped at Sir Arthur, his nails involuntarily digging into his palms as he noticed the way the man's thigh pushed against Lady Catherine's.

To Sir Arthur's immense benefit, he obeyed the command without protest and staggered to his feet. A good thing, because Philip had no more time to waste on him right now, not when Lady Catherine had begun noticeably trembling.

He slid into the seat Sir Arthur had just vacated so he could stop staring at her back and peer into her face. "Are you all right, love?"

She nodded, but her complexion was ashen, and her slender arms kept shaking. She was most definitely not all right. With that realization, Philip leaped to his feet again, flinging a swift punch into Sir Arthur's jaw. The pathetic milksop stumbled backward with a moan, tumbling into the grass below him.

Philip glared down at him, using every ounce of restraint he had to keep from delivering another blow. "What the blasted, bloody hell were you doing?"

Sir Arthur struggled into a sitting position, keeping one hand clutched to his jaw. "Really, Lord Kendrick, I could ask the same of you. I would have thought that you, of all people, wouldn't be troubled by my private encounter with my betrothed."

"Your *what*?" Philip snarled. Each breath he took felt like fire.

Lady Catherine jumped up from the bench, striding over to him so she, too, could look down at the hapless Sir Arthur. "Your *what*?"

"Please do not fret, Lady Catherine." Sir Arthur's mouth curled into a small smile. "I have every intention of doing right by you and offering you marriage."

Philip balled his hands into tight fists, which quivered as he continued glowering at Sir Arthur's smug face. "Is this a goddamn joke?"

Lady Catherine stepped forward, placing herself between Sir Arthur and additional harm. However, if looks could kill, she would have made the man expire on the spot.

"Thank you for the offer," she said, her voice like steel, "but I wholeheartedly decline."

"You decline?" Sir Arthur echoed her words thickly, his expression uncomprehending. "But what other choice do you have?"

Philip's chest felt on the verge of exploding with rage. "What do you mean, what other choice ..." But the words he had begun shouting faded as he turned around in response to Sir Arthur's subtle head nudge.

The grass upon which Sir Arthur had tumbled was out in the open, unconcealed by the sprawling topiaries. At least they were far from the house. Not far enough, though, to escape detection from those on the terrace. Philip could just make out a cluster of tiny figures standing against the railing. All peering in their direction.

"Bollocks," he muttered under his breath. He should have had the sense to shove Sir Arthur into the trees instead of away from them.

Sir Arthur kept gazing at his so-called betrothed, seemingly unfazed by Philip's wrath. "Never mind this unpleasantness, Lady Catherine. People will forget this unfortunate scene once we announce the happy news of our engagement. Your reputation will remain unscathed."

"Bollocks indeed," she cried with a ferocity Philip didn't know she possessed. She spun on her heels, flinging herself back upon the obscured stone bench. And with that, the fury drained from her face, and she dropped her head into her hands.

"I'll be ruined," she whispered to herself, her limbs once more starting to tremble. "My whole family will be ruined. I'll have to marry him."

Philip glanced back and forth, torn between his desire to comfort Lady Catherine and kill Arthur Croft.

Perhaps he should have said something to her about Sir Arthur before. Not that he had ever been certain of anything. Not that he even knew Sir Arthur well, for they didn't often run in the same circles, and he was several years the man's junior. Still, rumors circulated around the gentlemen's clubs that Sir Arthur, for all his reservedness and decorum, had a difficult time keeping female servants in his employ. Whatever one could make of that. Right now, Philip suspected that the implications of nefariousness weren't far off the mark.

He raised his foot, ready to deliver a kick to Sir Arthur's gut, when a spark of an idea took hold and stopped him in his tracks.

It was a ridiculous idea. Probably the most inane he had ever come up with, and he had carried out numerous foolhardy ideas over the years. But the more he thought of it, the more it made sense. They were in an impossible situation, which couldn't end the way anyone truly desired. It could, however, end in a way that saved Lady Catherine from ruin and helped him with his own quandary. A mutually beneficial arrangement, despite the multitude of problems it would create.

He abandoned his attack on Sir Arthur and hurried back to the bench to sit beside Lady Catherine. Very gently, he pressed on her gloved hand just until her eyes locked with his.

"Marry me instead."

***

Not for the first time that evening, the downward spiral of events caused Catherine to question whether she had entered some hellish dream. For she thought she'd heard Lord Kendrick propose marriage to her, and under no circumstances on earth could that have legitimately happened.

Except the real Lord Kendrick sat beside her on the bench, so close she could detect his body heat, with his stormy gaze fixed upon her. His words echoed through her mind so clearly that they had to have been real. *Marry me instead.*

"What an absurd proposition!" Sir Arthur's voice broke through the heavy silence before she had the chance to express a coherent thought. His brows scrunched together in bemusement. "Of course she cannot marry you. Everyone knows you are not the marrying type. An association with you would tarnish her reputation far worse than anything you accuse me of doing. Lady Catherine and I will wed, just as intended."

Lord Kendrick bolted from his seat and lunged at Sir Arthur. "Like hell—"

"Stop!" Her shriek pierced the air, causing both men to turn to her with wide eyes. It would seem she had a little of her father, the former earl, in her after all. No doubt the commotion she made traveled back to the terrace, but if she was to be ruined anyway, what difference did it make?

"Stop," she repeated in a voice much quieter but just as severe. "Sir Arthur?"

"Yes?" He looked at her hopefully, although he remained on the ground and grasped at the other side of his face. Lord Kendrick must have managed to strike him again.

"I have nothing more to discuss with you if you would kindly refrain from making additional comments. I can assure you, they are quite unwanted. Lord Kendrick, if you would please sit with me a moment."

She had no idea where that speech had come from, for she had certainly never ordered anyone about in such a manner, especially not two men at once. The aftereffects of her despondency, terror, and fury, combined with the knowledge that her life as she knew it was over, had created a force within her unlike anything she'd ever known. Her companions must have noticed the change, for Sir Arthur closed his mouth, and Lord Kendrick rushed back to seat himself on the bench, although he refrained from touching her.

"Why would you say such a thing?" She kept her voice low, hoping the words would escape Sir Arthur's detection. "It would be impossible, without question."

"It would not," Lord Kendrick murmured back at her. "Unless there is some reason you are not free to legally wed? Because I assure you, I'm quite able."

"Of course I'm legally able," she hissed. "It's only that …"

She trailed off, suddenly feeling like she had overstepped her newfound power. She could list dozens of reasons why they shouldn't marry. They wouldn't suit. He was a rake. He wasn't the type to settle down with one woman, especially a woman like her. However, she was loath to repeat the same slights Sir Arthur had already thrown at him. And so, she said nothing.

"I know it seems absurd." His unwavering gaze drew her in, making it look like he was confiding in her as a trusted friend. "In case you are unaware of my situation and find yourself questioning my motives, let me be honest with you. If reports of my father's health are accurate, I stand to inherit his marquessate sooner rather than later. I'm expected to marry and carry on the line. Not what anyone anticipated, of course …"

Lord Kendrick's body tensed, and for the second time since she'd made his acquaintance, he faltered with his words. It was the most awkward, unromantic thing a man could say while proposing marriage. But it was the truth and not just a careless phrase uttered with the intention to allure and persuade. It alerted her to the possibility that beneath all those layers of charm, perhaps something deeper rested. After all, within the last several years, he had lost both of his brothers, and it sounded like he stood to lose his father as well. Could it be that he felt some depth of sorrow on that account? That perhaps he wasn't entirely carefree after all?

"You could become a marchioness." He had regained his composure and now dangled the marquessate in front of her like he offered her a prize.

She shook her head. "That is of no consequence to me. I just want … I want a family of my own."

She immediately regretted allowing herself to be vulnerable. But as he had been honest with her, she supposed it was just as well that she laid her truth out before him.

"And you shall have one if that is your desire. Clifton Manor, the family seat, is a fine place for children to grow up. Of course, there are other properties if that one is not to your liking. So many that after the business of children is through, we need never even see each other if you do not wish it."

She stared at him, trying to decipher the meaning of his words. If they wed, would he consider his family obligation fulfilled and cast her aside, no longer wanting to see her? He was a rogue, after all, going from woman to woman. How could she alone be enough? Her mind flashed back to the evening in the Whitmores' library when he had sat with Lady

Blakely upon his lap, kissing her, caressing her … The familiar burn spread across her belly, accompanied by a stab in her chest that felt suspiciously like jealousy.

"There are many things that remain to be seen." He spoke almost as if he had read her thoughts, and for the first time since he'd sat beside her, she looked down, willing herself not to blush. "But if you're agreeable, we can try to make a go of it. I know this situation is not of your choosing, but sometimes, fate can be unkind. I merely want you to know that marriage to"—he paused, taking a moment to scowl in Sir Arthur's direction—"that cretin is not your only option."

She, too, peered at Sir Arthur, who still sat on the ground nursing his injured jaw. His face had swelled, and the hair high on his forehead stuck up like ruffled feathers. The way she'd spent the week envisioning marriage to him now made her stomach heave. He had seemed so quiet, respectable, safe. How could she have known that his gentle manners were only an illusion? And worse, what if beneath the surface existed additional dark truths too terrible for her to imagine?

She quickly turned back to Lord Kendrick, who sat before her without a hair out of place. The only thing that gave away his agitation was his eyes, which flickered mercurially like storm clouds. Once again, his collectedness both enthralled and enraged her. How could he utter life-altering propositions and not appear anxious in the least? How come he had to be there at every turn, tempting her, making her desire things she had no business wanting? How could she expect happiness if she willingly ensnared herself in a scoundrel's clutches?

But an old expression kept tumbling through her head: *Better the devil you know than the devil you don't.*

She raised her voice so she could be certain Sir Arthur heard her. "Thank you, Lord Kendrick. I would like to accept your proposal."

Sir Arthur spluttered for only an instant before a vicious glare from Lord Kendrick caused him to fall silent.

With that, Lord Kendrick jumped to his feet, extending his hand to help her up as well. "Splendid. I suggest we return to the house and relay the happy news. Best not let talk on the terrace continue to escalate. Croft, if you value your wellbeing, you will remain here, out of sight, for the next quarter hour or so."

Catherine took his proffered hand. Her betrothed's hand. Despite everything, the skin beneath her glove started tingling.

They began their stroll toward the terrace, her mind swirling with hundreds of thoughts and emotions, none of which fully made sense. Fortunately, Sir Arthur had the decency to remain still and silent as they walked away. She didn't have it in her to endure additional commentary from him, telling her what a reckless decision she'd made. Her insides knotted tightly, and her heart beat more rapidly with each step they took closer to the house.

It didn't take long for the tiny figures on the terrace to become people with discernible features. People who waited for them, eager to latch on to an approaching scandal.

At one end of the cluster stood Lavinia, her eyes enthusiastic and bright, with her hand resting atop the arm of the slyly smiling Lord Carington. Lady Bathurst held herself rigidly beside them, her expression a mixture of disbelief and fury. At the other side of the terrace, Lady Langley stood with her hand grasping the railing, her face an expressionless mask that gave nothing away. From the brief time she had spent in the marchioness's company, Catherine suspected she wasn't the type of woman prone to outward displays of emotion. Still, Catherine could make no mistake that the marchioness watched them with interest. And then, at the top of the steps in the center of them all, was Lady Wellesley, looking as though a magnificent gift had just been delivered to her door. Or rather, her terrace.

Philip wasted no time in flashing Lady Wellesley one of his easy smiles. The smile that had likely led to many a woman's ruin. "Just the lady I hoped to see."

He led Catherine up the steps, stopping directly before Lady Wellesley, whose gold-embroidered skirts made her a glittering beacon beneath the glow of the lanterns adorning the terrace. Catherine gave a tight smile of her own and strengthened her grip on Lord Kendrick's arm, as if doing so would help her absorb some of his nonchalance. These ladies viewed her as the image of her mother. If there was ever a time for her to take on her mother's renowned charm and poise, now would be it.

"Lady Wellesley, I hope you will allow me to make an announcement." Everyone had turned to face them, but Lord Kendrick focused only on Viscountess Wellesley as if he held an intimate conversation with an old friend. "I had planned to announce this upon returning to the ballroom, but I find I cannot wait a moment longer to share the joyful news. And I think it only fitting that you hear it first, as I have your exceptional house party to thank for bringing me this happiness."

His words were pure flattery, bordering on ridiculous. Yet he had somehow known they were exactly the right thing to say to Lady Wellesley. The woman stepped toward them with an enthusiastic nod. "By all means, tell us."

Catherine imagined the way Lady Wellesley's mind must be racing, planning the letters she would write and the friends she would visit, with this piece of news always at the tip of her pen or tongue.

A hush had fallen over the terrace, a stillness that left all attention concentrated on them. Lord Kendrick leaned toward her almost imperceptibly, giving her a gentle reminder of his supporting presence. "I have asked for Lady Catherine's hand in marriage, and she has accepted."

The silence lasted a split second longer until the group erupted in chatter and activity. Sounds and movement swirled around her, and she became aware that Lord

Kendrick no longer stood within her grasp and that Lavinia now clasped her hands instead.

"Congratulations on your engagement, dearest Catherine." Lavinia leaned in to kiss her cheek and then brought her face close to Catherine's ear, lowering her voice to a whisper. "Later, you must tell me *everything.*"

Catherine tried to share in her friend's excitement. If such a thing were to happen to Lavinia, she would consider it impeccably good fortune. But as for how Catherine felt, now that the news had become official, well ... She had no more time to ponder that, for Lady Bathurst appeared beside them, her expression unchanged.

Catherine braced herself for a quiet berating, which would likely continue with greater intensity once they reached the privacy of her bedroom. Lady Bathurst wouldn't take kindly to being made to look like an irresponsible chaperone. Not that Catherine had done anything she'd expressly been forbidden to do, but nonetheless, she knew that was a poor excuse. She had behaved foolishly when she should have known better and gotten herself into a tangle because of it.

However, Lady Bathurst merely nodded to her, all traces of anger wiped from her face, leaving only a hint of confusion. "Congratulations, Catherine. I hope that in accompanying us here, you achieved the result you were looking for."

"I ..." She tried to come up with a courteous response, but words failed her. Whether Lady Bathurst intended her comment to be civil or as a subtle jibe, she had no clue. Her head still spun, and the events playing out before her didn't seem entirely real.

"My warmest felicitations, dear Catherine."

Before she could spend another moment sorting through her thoughts, Lady Wellesley called out to her and came to clasp her hands, pulling her forward. She had Lord Kendrick next to her, and beside him stood his mother, still the picture of stoicism.

"How happy I am for you both. And to think that poor Georgina's daughter became engaged under my roof. Just delightful! She was a friend to us all, you know." With this, she glanced at Lady Bathurst and Lady Langley, who murmured their assent.

"Oh, but there's Lord Wellesley just stepping onto the terrace. Come, Lord Kendrick, so you can tell him the news."

Lady Wellesley took hold of Lord Kendrick's arm before Catherine could make a sound, and just as quickly as they had appeared, they were gone. She watched them hurry away, taking this brief reprieve from conversation to let out a shaky exhale. She supposed she should be glad for Lord Kendrick's charm. Perhaps that, combined with Lady Wellesley's old friendship with Georgina Adderley, would entice the viscountess to forget about Sir Arthur Croft writhing in the garden when she recounted the tale of the engagement. Catherine could only hope that gossip about a notorious rogue making a marriage proposal would prove salacious enough without added details of another man's involvement.

Catherine turned her head forward again, suddenly aware that Lady Langley still stood in front of her. She should have offered a greeting or polite comment, but she couldn't force words out of her throat. Instead, she and the marchioness peered at each other, just as they had that morning in the corridor, the lady's gaze silently assessing her. Was Lady Langley shocked by the turn of events? Horrified? Pleased? Her stately posture and neutral expression betrayed none of these sentiments. Indeed, the only detectable trace of emotion came from the persistent look of sadness in her eyes. Oddly, that hint of melancholy made Catherine's heart do a little lurch, and she was hit by an unexpected desire to offer comfort to this woman she didn't even know.

Finally, the marchioness inclined her head. "Lord Langley and I will be pleased to welcome you to our family."

"Thank you," Catherine said, "I—"

However, Lady Langley had already turned away. She brought a gloved hand to her face, taking a quick swipe at her eyes before returning it to her side and resuming her regal stance. Perhaps she truly did hate the thought of having Catherine for a daughter-in-law. But then, with her face to the ground, she whispered words so softly that they had to be intended for her own benefit alone. Yet Catherine managed to just make them out.

"She'll do. She'll do very nicely indeed."

Chapter 9

Lavinia grinned at Catherine throughout the entire journey from Essex back to Kent. She wasn't even upset about her mother's insistence that they leave the house party a day early so that Catherine's marriage arrangements could be finalized before a scandal began to take hold. The thrill of having a notorious rake propose to her friend, especially a friend who had sworn against the rake in question, was enough to compensate.

As for Catherine, she watched her home of Highfield Park draw nearer with a mixture of relief and apprehension. The sprawling house with its gleaming white stone and lush grounds had been her refuge from the world for years. How good it would feel to flop upon her familiar bed, cuddle little Sophia in her arms, or take a quiet stroll through the gardens with Edward and Eliza. She would do all those things, and soon. But it wouldn't change the fact that her life had been forever altered and that before long, this would no longer be her home.

At her insistence, they had refrained from sending a message telling of their early arrival. She couldn't stand the thought of not explaining the situation herself and being bombarded with questions the second she walked through the door. As a result, no one appeared when their carriage came to a halt in front of the house, except for a groom who must have spotted them from the stables and come running.

It made no difference. She took the moment of quiet when she stepped to the ground to inhale the familiar autumn air and absorb the rays of early evening sunshine. She was home, at least for now.

"Why, Lady Catherine!"

Just as they began climbing the stone steps, the front door flew open to reveal the stooped figure of Higgins, the family's butler for far longer than she'd been alive. "And Lady Bathurst, and Miss Bathurst. We didn't expect you back until the morrow."

"I couldn't bear to stay away another moment." Catherine greeted him with a smile as her footsteps hit the black and white marble of the entrance hall, the sound echoing up to the soaring ceiling. Best pretend everything was as it should be, at least for a short while longer.

"Have the guest rooms been prepared yet?" she asked, keeping her tone light. "Lady Bathurst and Miss Bathurst will stay for the night before continuing their journey to Devonshire, as planned."

"I believe the housemaids finished the task a short time ago, my lady. All that remains is to light the fires."

"Thank you." She turned back to face Lavinia and Lady Bathurst. "Would you like me to show you to your rooms? Or, if you prefer, we could have tea in the drawing room."

Or at least she could try to sit through tea in the drawing room. She wasn't sure how she would manage such a feat with the unspoken news of her engagement weighing heavy on her.

"We will go to our rooms," Lady Bathurst said. "After our day of travel, a repose is in order before dinner."

"Of course." She began leading them toward the stairs, although she couldn't leave without asking the butler one more question. "Higgins, are Lord and Lady Ashton about?"

"Lady Ashton has not yet come in from outdoors, and I believe Lord Ashton is in his study. Shall I fetch them, my lady?"

"No," she rushed to answer. "No, not right now. That is, you can wait to announce our arrival until we've had the opportunity to refresh ourselves."

At Higgins's bow, she ascended the stairs with Lavinia and Lady Bathurst at her heels, unsure of what she preferred. On the one hand, the longer she kept her news hidden, the more it would eat at her from inside. But on the other, uttering it aloud in her home, her one safe space, would make it all so … real.

Fortunately, Lady Bathurst was content to shut herself in her bedroom at once, and even Lavinia seemed willing to rest without complaint. However, Catherine had gone to bed the night before after disclosing only the bare minimum. If this was the last opportunity they would have to speak in confidence, she couldn't let Lavinia go without first saying something.

"Lavinia?" she called softly, just as her friend began closing her bedroom door.

"Yes?" Despite Lavinia's mellowness after six days of constant excitement, her blue eyes still shone eagerly, and she stilled her hand against the door handle.

"You were right about Sir Arthur."

"Of course I was." Lavinia grimaced. "Loathsome little toad."

Catherine let out a giggle in spite of herself, although her laughter quickly became a frown. "Do you think everyone knows? About what happened with Sir Arthur?"

"To an extent, I imagine. But never mind that." Lavinia stepped back into the corridor and clasped Catherine's hands. "If anything, it will only make Sir Arthur appear more repulsive. What the ton truly cares about is your engagement to Lord Kendrick. He rescued you, and after you were so determined he was nothing but a reprobate. How perfectly romantic."

"Indeed." She spit the word as sharply as shards of ice.

Lavinia pulled back her hands and crossed her arms over her chest. "Catherine, you were dead wrong about Sir Arthur. Do you think it possible you misjudged Lord Kendrick as well?"

Her mind flashed back to his tension during the marriage proposal. Its existence suggested that while unhappiness didn't cloud his eyes the same way as his mother's, emotions lingered that he didn't readily disclose. That not everything was easy for him after all, and that perhaps he did have a care, and maybe he even cared for others …

"I hardly know." She sighed heavily, her chest becoming tight. "In any case, I apologize again that the whole affair necessitated our early departure from Oakwood Hall. I hope you are not too vexed with me."

There, that seemed a sufficient change of subject. They could stand at Lavinia's doorway all night discussing Lord Kendrick, and she still didn't see herself finding a way to make sense of him. It was wiser to drop the matter altogether.

"Not at all." Lavinia grinned, displaying her nearly constant good humor. "I was having a splendid time, but I have a feeling that many more pleasurable entertainments await me. Lord Carington said he enjoyed the event so much that he may host a party of his own before the Season begins anew. His estate is in Somerset, not so very far from me."

Catherine tried not to cringe. Lady Bathurst would be foolish indeed to allow Lavinia to attend such an event. People could say all they wanted about Lord Kendrick not being the marrying type, but from what she'd seen over the past week, the same was true of Lord Carington. Perhaps she'd never come across Lord Carington and another woman in a compromising position, but nonetheless, he appeared to be a rake through and through, and any secret bits of heart he might possess had to be *very* well hidden.

But then again, who was she to judge? She had muddled her own situation so profusely that she had no business doling out advice or assessing the character of others.

She merely encircled Lavinia in a quick embrace. "Thank you for your patience and understanding. Whatever happens, I wish you every happiness."

"And I you," Lavinia said, appearing surprised yet pleased by the sudden burst of affection. "We'll write to each other often. I want no detail omitted. But for the time being, would you mind if I rested for a spell? After all those late nights at Oakwood Hall and perhaps a touch too much wine, I'm rather fatigued."

Catherine returned Lavinia's sheepish smile. "Of course. Shall we see each other at dinner, then? If you don't feel too tired, that is."

"Yes, at dinner." Lavinia moved to close her door again. "Will you rest a while as well?"

"Perhaps," Catherine said, already beginning her journey down the corridor. By now, the fire in her bedroom would be lit, and she could retreat into the space's comforting warmth. But as tempting as that sounded, she instead made her way back down the stairs, willing her feet to keep going until she slipped into the study.

Edward looked up from the stacks of papers covering his polished walnut desk to notice her at once.

"Catherine!" He pushed a stray lock of hair, golden like hers, away from his face, and his blue eyes brightened. "Higgins just informed me of your arrival. We didn't anticipate your return until tomorrow. I hope you found the house party agreeable."

"Yes," she said quietly. It was a lie that didn't begin to scratch the surface of all she had to tell him, but it seemed easier than bursting out with the whole story while she still lingered in the doorway.

Despite their thirteen-year age difference and all the time they'd spent apart, Edward knew her too well, for his brow creased with concern. "Something is amiss. Come in and tell me."

She scurried over to the chair in front of his desk, letting herself sink into the slippery leather. "Is Eliza about?"

He glanced toward the window that overlooked the gardens with a hint of a smile. "As dusk has not quite fallen, I imagine she's still outdoors. But she should return soon, or we can fetch her, of course, if you need to speak with her immediately."

"No, there's no need to trouble her," Catherine answered quickly. However, there was no longer any point to her pretending nothing had transpired at the house party and all was normal. If she didn't get her secret off her chest at once, she felt she might explode. She made herself meet Edward's evaluating stare. "I can relay the news to her later. For now, I thought I might speak with you instead."

Edward's brisk nod was all the prompting it took for her story to come pouring out. She recounted the whole sordid tale of Sir Arthur and the rake who had unexpectedly intervened, barely pausing for breath, as Edward regarded her with a face as still as a statue.

"After Lord Kendrick sees his mother back to London, he'll come to formally request your permission for my hand," she said as her story drew to an end. "It is, of course, a mere formality, for I'm sure you see the necessity of the marriage."

She finally allowed herself to lean back and take a deep breath, aware of how her lungs ached and her heart pounded. Edward, on the other hand, stayed seated with his elbow atop the desk and his chin resting in his palm, his expression stony.

Despite her penchant for quiet, she found the current silence maddening. "Please say something," she begged, her soft words echoing across the room as if she had shouted them.

He shifted slightly to press his fingers into his temples. "A moment, Catherine. I'm trying to solve a predicament. I'm unsure where I should venture first: to Oxfordshire, to murder Arthur Croft, or to London, to murder Viscount Kendrick."

"No!" she protested, unsure whether she was on the verge of tears or laughter. "As tempting as the first option might be, I would hate for you to encounter legal difficulties on account of a man as useless as Sir Arthur. And as for the second option, I don't believe Lord Kendrick deserves such a fate. He seems to have good intentions, and he's … he's …"

As usual, when it came to the subject of Lord Kendrick, her thoughts jumbled, and words failed her. She wasn't at the point of wanting to sing his praises, but she didn't have it in her to disparage him either.

"He's a rake of the worst kind," Edward cut in, finishing the sentence for her. "And whenever he sets his sights on a particular woman, his intentions can hardly be described as 'good.'"

Catherine stiffened. While her brother had been away on the Continent for many years, he'd spent the past months reintegrating with society, occasionally spending time at clubs or events with other gentlemen of the ton.

"Do you know him?" she asked, suddenly aware of the possibility that Edward's knowledge about the disreputable behavior of Lord Kendrick could far surpass her own.

"No more than a passing acquaintance, but one hears all manner of talk …" He trailed off, clenching his jaw. Edward despised few things more than rumors and gossip.

He shook his head with a rueful sigh. "No, I suppose I don't know him. I was acquainted with the former Viscount Kendrick, his eldest brother, prior to my departure for the Continent, along with his middle brother, John. Or Captain Hadleigh, as he became. But as for the current Lord Kendrick, given his youth—he cannot now be more than four and twenty—and his former health complaints, I didn't see much of him in those days. Our paths crossed a handful of times throughout the Season this year, but not enough for me to make a judgment one way or another."

She leaned forward in her seat, her ears nearly buzzing. "What do you mean, health complaints?"

"Kendrick was afflicted by childhood illness. Fever, I believe, that kept him indisposed for a lengthy period well into his youth. However, I know nothing beyond that and really shouldn't speculate further. If the rumors about him hold a degree of truth, poor health doesn't trouble him any longer."

"No," she murmured, "it appears it does not." Her mind drifted to the image of Lord Kendrick, with his thick, dark hair and a face chiseled at all the right angles. She imagined him in the pond with his powerful limbs pushing through the water, and then in the library breathing heavily with Lady Blakely atop his lap, and then in the study next to her, all heat and passion as he kissed her until she could think of nothing but her desire for more. He was the picture of health and vitality. But maybe she'd just uncovered another layer he kept hidden beneath his flawless exterior.

"I hope you realize that you are not obligated to marry him." Edward's quiet words snapped her back to the present. "Eliza and I are not afraid of scandal. We would stand by you no matter what, and you would always have a home here."

"I know, and I thank you." Her throat grew tight, and the corners of her eyes began to burn. She didn't doubt for a second that her brother and sister-in-law would continue to shower her with love and support, no matter the cost. They'd both weathered scandals themselves and were no strangers to finding themselves outside of society's good graces. But now that they'd overcome those obstacles and achieved happiness with one another, not to mention a fragile peace with their place within the ton, the last thing she wanted was to drag scandal to their doorstep once more.

Additionally, even though Edward and Eliza might always welcome her at Highfield Park as though nothing were amiss, what potential suitor would overlook the rumors of her time alone with two men in the Wellesleys' garden? She would certainly never marry, and her dreams of having a family of her own would vanish nearly as quickly as they had come about.

Besides …

"I wish to marry him."

She could hardly believe she'd dared to utter that phrase aloud, although Edward's widened eyes alerted her that she hadn't just imagined it. Her cheeks flamed, and she stared at her lap. But the longer the sound of her words swirled through her head, the more she realized how true they were.

They shouldn't be true. She should have wanted nothing of the sort. And perhaps she wouldn't have, had she never journeyed to the Wellesleys' house party, or had events not transpired so disastrously. However, circumstances being what they were, she could imagine no other way she wanted to proceed. Despite Lord Kendrick's reputation for pursuing women with abandon. Despite the fact he viewed her as frosty.

The thought of reneging on the betrothal left a hollow feeling within her, like some crucial part of her had gone missing. Perhaps the marriage would bring her nothing but disappointment and misery. But, Lord help her, she wanted it all the same.

"Catherine, you've returned to us early. What a delightful surprise."

She turned toward the cheerful voice in the doorway at once. Eliza. Her sister-in-law's muslin skirt was covered with tiny bits of dried leaves, and her auburn hair had come loose from its knot so that long strands, also dotted with leaves, tumbled down her back. Catherine couldn't imagine a more welcome sight. Since the time of their first meeting, Eliza had proven herself a constant friend, offering a steady stream of kindness and encouragement. Furthermore, she, too, had been in the position of wedding a near stranger, and she had successfully navigated the situation to find love with Edward. She was exactly the person Catherine needed right now.

Catherine jumped from her seat and rushed over to throw her arms around Eliza. "I'm so happy to see you." Apparently, the burden of her predicament was wearing down her reservation.

Eliza returned the embrace with a laugh. "Why, I'm happy to see you as well."

Catherine laughed too, and as soon as she did, a couple of the tears burning her eyes slid down her heated cheeks.

"Is something the matter?" Eliza pulled away so she could peer at Catherine, her face clouded with concern. "You must tell me at once."

Catherine stilled herself, trying to muster the fortitude to repeat the unfortunate story, when Edward called out from the middle of the room.

"You have come inside at just the right time, sweetheart. It seems we must prepare for a wedding."

Chapter 10

While Philip had never been overly discerning in the women he chose to pursue, he found it good practice to avoid those with exceedingly protective male relations. Such as the Earl of Ashton, who sat glaring at him, arms crossed, from behind his massive wooden desk.

Philip had known from the moment a taciturn butler escorted him into Lord Ashton's study, and the earl instructed him to sit in a clipped tone, that there was no point in trying to win him over with smooth talk. Instead, he stated his desire to marry Lady Catherine as succinctly as possible. Presumably, Catherine had already apprised him of the details of the situation. He couldn't know for certain, for he'd been brought to the study too quickly to catch even a glimpse of her, and Lord Ashton had answered his inquiries after her health with an abrupt, "She's well."

It appeared that a propensity for silence ran in the family, for Lord Ashton took no issue with continuing to sit there stony-faced, not saying a word. Philip could think of few things more unnerving.

Finally, Lord Ashton shifted in his seat and deigned to open his mouth. "We do not know one another, Kendrick, and I try not to form opinions based solely on rumors and gossip. However, where my sister is concerned, I'm prepared to make an exception."

"I would expect nothing less," Philip said, suppressing a sigh. Of course Lord Ashton knew of his reputation as a rake. Everyone did. It had been well deserved. That is, until Lady Catherine had unknowingly traced her fingers over his face, and he suddenly found himself roaming alone outdoors instead of tossing coins around the card table or seeking a new woman to warm his bed. If he wasn't careful, his reputation would become tarnished in the opposite direction. Untarnished, as it were.

"I have made it very clear to Catherine that she is not required to marry. If we must endure a scandal, then so be it." The lines around Ashton's mouth softened slightly. "However, she says marriage to you is what she desires, and as such, I will not withhold my permission."

Lady Catherine had expressed a desire to marry him? Now, Philip found himself lacking suitable words. Throughout the entirety of his ride to Highfield Park, he had kept replaying the night at the Wellesleys' ball over and over in his mind. Perhaps Lady Catherine had been too shocked to think clearly that evening and consented to the marriage without realizing what she said. Perhaps she had since realized what a horrible mistake she had made and decided she wanted nothing more to do with him. Or worse, that she wished to marry Sir Arthur after all.

He'd told himself throughout the ride that it didn't matter either way. He was under no obligation to fulfill his promise to his mother. If the marquess's health continued to fail, perhaps he would come to the point where he was no longer cognizant of what transpired around him and would forget that he lacked the son and heir he wanted. As for the marchioness, she had already survived so much heartache; surely, she had the strength to tolerate a little more. And in the event Philip's pesky conscience got the better of him again, he could always choose someone else to marry. There would be no shortage of ladies whom he could win over with a few charming words, including the promise of a marquessate.

Except the only woman who filled his thoughts was Lady Catherine. The golden-haired, long-limbed, aloof, frosty, yet oh-so-passionate Lady Catherine.

"But let me also make one thing plain to you." As quickly as Ashton had shown a hint of thawing, his expression turned steely again. "I do not wish the rumors I hear about you now to continue after your marriage. For if I catch even the faintest whisper you have made my sister unhappy ... Well, you had best ensure you do not. That is, if you value your b—"

"Edward!"

The door to the study flew open, and an auburn-haired woman Philip recognized as the Countess of Ashton stumbled inside. Not so quickly, though, that he failed to catch a glimpse of the golden head that was too tall to be concealed behind her. However, only Lady Ashton strolled over to the desk and placed a hand upon her husband's shoulder with a warning look in her eyes. "Good afternoon, husband. And welcome, Lord Kendrick."

The earl gazed up at her, arching an eyebrow. "Eavesdropping at the door, I see."

She flashed him an innocent smile. "Never! Merely passing by."

"Indeed." Ashton shook his head and turned back to the doorway. "I already saw you there, Catherine, so you may as well come in too."

In an instant, Lady Catherine's slender form, accentuated perfectly in a dress of filmy white fabric, reappeared. She approached them gracefully, despite how her cheeks had turned a deep shade of pink, stopping by Philip's chair and dropping into a curtsey. Heat threatened to spread across the entirety of his body, and he dug his nails into his palms, willing the ridiculous sensation to pass.

Ashton eyed them both. "As you seem so anxious for news, Catherine, and in case what I said didn't travel through the door, allow me to inform you that I've granted Lord Kendrick permission to wed you. If you're certain that is still what you desire."

Lady Catherine tilted her chin in a barely perceptible nod, but her assent was clear.

"With some reservations, I admit." He brought his hand up to squeeze Lady Ashton's where it rested against his shoulder. "Yet I know that, on occasion, marriages of convenience can have unexpected consequences that turn out to be exceptionally agreeable."

Lady Ashton grinned at her husband before turning her smile upon Lady Catherine and then Philip himself. "Congratulations to you both. Will you dine with us this evening, Lord Kendrick, so we can toast to your happiness? And you are welcome, of course, to remain at Highfield Park as long as you like."

"No," he blurted out, utterly devoid of charm. He'd achieved what he came here to accomplish and had suddenly turned as awkward as a schoolboy. He'd just become betrothed. Officially. And as a result, he was elated. And horrified. And so perplexed by the foreign sensations within him, he didn't know what to think.

He cleared his throat, attempting to put on his usual mask of nonchalance before he spoke again. "That is, I didn't come prepared for an overnight stay and should venture back to London before the hour grows too late. I came on horseback, so as long as I don't dally, I should make it home before nightfall."

He thought his announcement would relieve Lady Catherine, but instead, her face fell, and she bit the rosy plumpness of her bottom lip until it turned white. Had she possibly wanted him to stay? He was used to having his company desired; however, not by her.

He kept on gazing at her, trying to determine how to best continue, when she pulled herself up a little taller and stepped toward him.

"Would you stroll with me in the garden first? At least while your horse is being made ready?"

"An excellent idea," Lady Ashton said as she shot a pointed glance toward the earl, who appeared on the verge of protesting. "I'll chaperone, of course."

"Lord Kendrick?" Lady Catherine's brown eyes re-garded him so imploringly that he didn't have it in him to refuse.

He offered her his arm, and she let her hand rest lightly atop it, just enough that the sensation trickled through the thick wool of his coat. "Lead the way, my lady."

She guided him to the drawing room and through the French doors that led to the terrace. At the bottom of the steps, an expansive lawn stretched out before them, dotted with trees in their first shades of autumn brilliance, and be-yond that, a glittering lake.

"Shall we stroll toward the water?" Lady Catherine asked without a trace of irony in her voice.

At once, the image of her gliding through the pond in her transparent shift sprang to his mind. How exquisite she'd looked that day as she stood on the shoreline with wa-ter dripping from her exposed skin. He'd been so close to her, the creature he desperately wanted but didn't dare touch. He did his best to shove the memory aside, but he couldn't make himself look away from her now.

He was entirely out of his element here. How much easier it was when he could utter a few pretty words to a lady, have her whisper some to him in return, tumble about in his bedroom—or whatever location proved convenient at the time—with her, and then part ways without a care. But this was different. Lady Catherine was to be his wife. *Forever.* He owed it to her to not make her life miserable from the moment their betrothal became official. In fact, his wish to succeed in this matter filled him with a determination that he'd felt with very few other matters in his life.

Unfortunately, as with most things pertaining to Lady Catherine, his usual self-assuredness failed him, and he hadn't a clue how to proceed. And so, he merely said, "As you wish."

"I just recalled that I must check on something in the herb garden," Lady Ashton said from behind them. "Catherine, would you still like to accompany Lord Kendrick to the lake? Should you need me, I will be *very* close by. Acting as your chaperone, just as I said."

"Yes." Catherine turned back to give her sister-in-law's hand a quick squeeze. "Thank you, Eliza, dear. Shall we, Lord Kendrick?"

He let her lead him over the lush green grass, all the while pondering the fact that, for the second time that day, she had expressed a desire to spend time in his company. And alone, nonetheless.

Something about her was different here at Highfield Park compared to when they had spent time together at Oakwood Hall. Her strides across the lawn were more assured, and she held herself straighter, embracing her full height. Her smiles came easier. Her voice didn't waver.

He caught a glimpse of the woman who existed beneath all those layers of trepidation and reserve. A woman who wasn't frigid in the least. Rather, she heated him to the core. The problem, however, lay in the fact that it seemed far more difficult to encourage that side of her to emerge than to make a wrong move and send her scurrying back into her shell.

He continued allowing her to take the lead, and she brought him to a narrow gravel path where a cool breeze from the lake whipped through his hair and rustled her skirts. He should have commented on the fineness of the weather or offered a compliment on the picturesque scenery at her family's estate. He should have said something, *anything*, to break the silence. But as had been frequently the case of late, his talent for speaking the proper words vanished. Therefore, he said nothing at all.

***

Catherine tried to focus on the scenery before her—the luminous blue of the lake beneath the afternoon sunshine, the scattering of gold and red peeking out against the vibrant green leaves—but her eyes kept darting toward Lord Kendrick. Tiny shocks shot through the hand that she rested against his coat.

Throughout their week at the house party, she'd frequently resented his ability to always know what to say while she stood fumbling. However, she now realized, with remorse, that his suave comments were far preferable to his silence. Had she done something to displease him? Did he regret making his offer of marriage? After all, as she had so fervently told Lavinia, he was a rake of the worst kind. Not the type to settle for just one woman and content himself with a quiet life of marital bliss. Perhaps there was some truth in her words. Nonetheless, she hated that she had uttered them.

The silence dragged her down rather than consoled her, and she couldn't tolerate another second of it. Not with Lord Kendrick. If he refused to start a conversation, she would make an attempt instead.

"I trust all was well in London." She let her eyes rest on him, aiming to adopt some of his characteristic indifference. "Was your father pleased to hear the news of your betrothal?"

Lord Kendrick made a sound almost like a laugh, but there was little humor behind it. "As pleased as he could be, given the circumstances."

Catherine's stomach dropped, and a wave of nausea spread over her. All the comments she'd overheard throughout the Season came rushing back to her.

What a funny creature … it's a shame she lacks charm … everyone knows she's not truly an earl's daughter …

Maybe her many failings were notorious enough to even reach the ears of an ailing marquess. She swallowed down the lump at the back of her throat. "Is he unhappy with your choice of bride?"

Lord Kendrick halted in his tracks and stared at her as if she had just questioned him in a foreign tongue. "Is he unhappy?"

Suddenly, he grabbed hold of both her arms and spun her so they were facing one another. He shook his head adamantly. "God, no. Why would you think such a thing? The problem lies in the fact that the wrong son must carry on his line."

"The wrong son?" She echoed back his words, at a loss for what else to say.

"His heir should have been Charles. The gentlemanly, perfect Charles." Lord Kendrick's bitter smile stabbed directly at her heart. "And if not him, then John. Not, under any circumstances, a rogue who wasn't even supposed to be here."

His fingers dug into her arms, and she gripped him back in an uncertain attempt at support. The pain she'd detected in his mother's gray eyes now shone just as brightly in his, and in this moment, no one could think of him as carefree. But what did he mean that he wasn't even supposed to be here? Edward had let slip that Lord Kendrick suffered from illness in childhood. Could he be alluding to that? Dozens of questions filled her mind, but how could she pose them in a way that demonstrated her caring and not just a desire to pry?

She took a deep breath, silently searching for the right words, when Lord Kendrick spoke instead.

"But never mind that." Somehow, he'd wiped all traces of hurt from his face and regarded her with his usual look of composure. "We should discuss our wedding date. Upon my return to London, I plan to procure a special license so we can be married by the end of the week. I trust that plan is agreeable to you?"

Her mouth fell open, and she quickly bit her lip to prevent herself from gaping at him. How did he always manage to cast away difficulties as if they meant nothing? His eyes now appeared clear and untroubled, and a few unruly locks of hair tumbled across his forehead in the wind, adding to his look of indifference. More than anything, she wanted to return to the previous conversation so she could better understand who, exactly, she planned to marry. However, while his demeanor had become casual, it also suggested that the previous topic of conversation was off-limits.

Besides, the new subject he'd introduced also warranted serious questioning.

"Married by the end of the week?" Once again, she could think only to repeat his words. She took a moment to compose herself. "Isn't that rather ... soon?"

"I think it prudent, if you wish to prevent a scandal from circulating, to go through with the wedding as soon as possible."

He raised a valid point. Yet ... "It's just so soon," she exclaimed, the words tumbling over each other. "I thought we might wait for the banns to be read."

"I see." He raised his eyebrows a shade. "And do you desire a large wedding at St. George's?"

"Not in the least," she rushed to say. She shuffled her feet against the gravel. "It's only that I ... I ..."

Drat her inability to successfully communicate her thoughts! Of course, even her thoughts made little sense right now. A special license would make their wedding faster and easier. Why, then, had she immediately turned it down? She and Lord Kendrick had already agreed to be married; that much was inevitable. Any reluctance she felt could only be due to her familiar old companion: fear.

"We shall wait if that is your preference." His mellow voice broke through the silence. "Your wish is my command."

How comfortable he appeared standing before her in his tan riding breeches and his smart blue coat. His handsome features made it difficult for her to stop looking at him, and his easy smile drew her in, promising her things she couldn't fully understand. Yet something, some barely perceptible little detail about him, didn't seem quite right. Perhaps it was that he held his shoulders with a hint of tension. Or that the light from his smile didn't shine through his eyes. Whatever the case, something looked to be slightly amiss.

A troubling idea hit her like a slap across the cheek. By asking to postpone the wedding, had she disappointed him? Surely, such a minute point would never bother Lord Kendrick. If anything, it should make him glad. Still, she couldn't shake the feeling that something between them hung off balance.

She suddenly became aware that her hands had never left his coat. Her silk-gloved fingers grasped his arms, and he, in turn, continued clinging to her. In fact, throughout their conversation, they must have unthinkingly drawn closer to one another, for their bodies almost touched. Her heart rate quickened, turning into a persistent thump that pounded against her chest. Could he detect it? She nearly pulled away; it wouldn't be fitting for him to notice her all aflutter.

Instead, her body moved forward as though not her own, pressing itself fully against him so the warmth of his chest heated her, and the brisk rhythm of his heartbeat vibrated through her. Then, with newfound boldness, she released her hand and brought it to cup the side of his face. The rough stubble and sharply angled jawline enthralled her, just like the first time she'd run her hands over him, but this time, it wasn't enough.

She'd lived her whole life with restraint and still managed to find herself on the brink of ruin. Now, she had nothing more to lose. That knowledge made her powerful. It enticed her to tilt her chin upward so she could press her lips against his.

His mouth covered hers at once, providing the pressure she so craved, the sensation she hadn't stopped thinking about since their evening in the study. One of his hands ran through her hair while the other pressed into her back, holding their bodies together as his tongue circled over her lips. She allowed her tongue to slide out to meet his, absorbing his heat and tasting his essence. She had no idea what she was doing, but somehow, it felt right.

On the other hand, he knew exactly how to circle his tongue, exactly how to trace featherlight caresses over her skin, to leave her aching for more and feeling like her body couldn't get close enough to his. Undoubtedly, many a woman had lost her heart to him this way, and it seemed inevitable that she would follow suit. It didn't matter. Some hazy part of her brain alerted her that Eliza still lingered nearby, but she couldn't make that signify either. Her desperation for him overruled all else, and she never wanted this connectedness to stop. No matter the consequences.

He pulled away. The rake who supposedly had a different mistress in his bed each night stepped away from her, leaving her body cold and screaming in protest. It occurred to her that she was holding her breath, and she forced herself to exhale as she tried to process what had just transpired. Did he not desire her? Did he find her deficient in some way? Her cheeks heated, but when she dared to meet his gaze, his eyes blazed too brightly to suggest a lack of interest.

"I should take my leave. I'm sure my horse has been made ready by now." Even the silver-tongued Lord Kendrick couldn't utter the words without his voice wavering. He smoothed his rumpled cravat and waistcoat with clumsy strokes and pushed the errant locks of hair away from his face.

"Let's walk toward the house, then," she said, miraculously retaining her ability to speak. Once again, he held out his arm to her, and she placed her hand upon it so they could saunter back in the direction from which they had come as though nothing had happened.

Except that something very much *had* happened. Perhaps this encounter was no different than a typical stroll in the park for him, but it left her insides in knots and her heart racing. She had no idea what this all signified and whether she should be appeased or terrified. But of one thing, she had no doubt.

"Lord Kendrick?"

He turned to her at once, his mouth set in an even line but his eyes still burning. "Yes, love?"

She tightened her grip on his sleeve. Not enough to pull him to her, but just enough to remind herself of his warmth and of the heat and power that must exist underneath that thick layer of wool. "I've reflected upon what you said, and I now see that you were correct. We should be married by special license. Within the week."

Chapter 11

Their wedding took place six days later, in the drawing room at Langley House in London. Philip hadn't dared to venture back to Highfield Park during those six days, not after what had transpired between him and Lady Catherine the first time. It made her appear all the more alluring when she stepped into Langley House, her brother and sister-in-law in tow, wearing a silver dress that hugged the slender lines of her body and glittered as it caught the morning light streaming through the windows.

She was visibly nervous, as he'd known she would be, yet she didn't once turn her eyes away from him as she recited her vows. Whatever he could make of that. At the very least, he could assume she no longer hated him entirely.

And then, just like that, they were married. Lady Ashton embraced her sister-in-law. Lord Ashton offered reluctant felicitations. And from the wingback chair in the corner, his father, who had donned a respectable suit of clothes atop his withered frame and been escorted downstairs for the occasion, observed, giving him a slight nod at the completion of the ceremony. His mother stood regally with her hand upon the chairback, inclining her head and drawing her lips into a hint of a smile.

Perhaps he could take that to mean he had pleased them. An unimaginable feat indeed, but here he was, a rake turned husband, just as they'd desired. Then again, he could sire ten heirs, and it wouldn't take away the sting of the knowledge that he wasn't Charles. Or John. That he wasn't the son they wanted to carry on the line, and nothing he did could change that.

He didn't know how they felt, and there was no use trying to decipher meaning from their expressions. He had the sense that he didn't know anything anymore. Even his own feelings on the matter—including the realization that he was an unattached rake no longer—churned about in a jumble, too bewildering for him to decipher.

He told himself it would get better once they departed Langley House after the wedding breakfast and made their way to the country. And it did, in a way. Once in the carriage, he had no one to think of but Lady Catherine, and as they exchanged only vague pleasantries before her eyelids grew heavy and she pressed herself into the corner to sleep, he was left to his own devices. He could close his eyes as well and let the motion of the carriage calm him as he tried to concentrate only on the journey ahead.

He hadn't visited Clifton Manor, the family seat in Hertfordshire, in several years. After all, it was his parents' home. Charles's home. He far preferred London or passing time at a friend's estate, and when that grew tiresome, he usually opted for Ravenfield, the family hunting lodge in Norfolk. However, Ravenfield, with its gloomy interior and perpetual dampness, didn't seem right for Lady Catherine. With its airy rooms and multitude of windows overlooking the gardens, Clifton Manor was the proper place for her. Why, it even had a lake. As for any unwanted memories the property invoked in him, he would try casting them aside if the location brought her contentment.

And she did appear happy—or at least, not unhappy—upon her arrival to Clifton Manor. She walked arm in arm with him as if they had been married for years, greeting the servants and bestowing several quiet compliments upon the estate. She carried herself stiffly, not quite comfortable with her new surroundings. But she also didn't appear in imminent danger of fleeing.

Up to this point, the day had gone as well as could be expected. Except now, Philip had a glaring problem. A beautiful woman stood in the entrance hall of his home, awaiting his direction, and for the first time in his life, he hadn't a clue what to do with her. For this wasn't any woman. This was his *wife*.

"We'll have dinner at seven. From what I recall, the cook here is quite good. The staff is prepared to serve us a full five courses in the dining room, although after the wedding breakfast, we could also opt for something lighter if you prefer." Why he'd chosen their evening meal as a topic of conversation as soon as the servants had scattered and left them alone, he really couldn't say. And why was he rambling so nonsensically?

Fortunately, his ineptitude didn't appear to bother Lady Catherine, for she regarded him placidly. "Perhaps just something small this evening. In fact, the staff needn't trouble themselves with setting out a meal in the dining room at all, at least not on my account."

"As you wish." Did that mean she'd experienced enough of his company for one day and wished to shut herself upstairs? It could be she simply felt tired, although her upright posture and alert face didn't show hints of fatigue. "Would you like me to show you to your room?"

"Yes. Thank you." Her voice had lowered to a near whisper, but he still didn't detect that startled expression in her eyes that made her look like she was about to bolt. Rather, she strengthened her grip on his arm, urging him to lead the way.

He started up the curved mahogany staircase, trying to think of some comment regarding the history of the house or even the weather, if it came to that. But he couldn't. With each heavy footstep that brought them closer to the upstairs corridors, he could only focus on the inanity of the fact that he led a woman to her bedroom but had never felt more lost.

This must be what came of trying to deny his true nature. This was the result of him neglecting to seek out entertainments during his days—and his last few days of bachelorhood, at that—in London, instead passing the time with only himself for company. Upon his arrival in the city, he'd wasted no time in driving past the theater where he could seek out the company of Lucia or another eager actress. But it hadn't felt right. He hadn't wanted those women. The carriage had turned back, passing familiar gaming hells and gentlemen's clubs as it went, and still, he hadn't gotten out. He couldn't risk encountering Sherwood or another acquaintance who happened to remain in London, for that would only lead to a night of trouble. Instead, he'd returned to the sparse loneliness of his bachelor lodgings and spent the rest of his time there as celibate as a monk and as disoriented as a lost puppy.

A trend that showed no sign of cessation even here at Clifton Manor.

They reached the end of the east corridor, the location of his former bedroom. The housekeeper, Mrs. Shaw, had seen that the bedroom across the corridor from it was prepared for Lady Catherine, and he pushed open the door to survey the scene. Seeing that the bed had been made with a thick flowered counterpane and topped with a row of fluffy pillows, a vase of fresh-cut lilies stood on the nightstand, and a fire burned invitingly in the grate, he gestured inside, careful to keep his feet planted against the floorboards in the corridor.

"Here you are, my lady. I hope this is to your liking."

She released his arm so she could take a few steps inside and glance around. "The room is lovely. Thank you."

He should have taken his leave immediately, but his eyes kept darting to the bed and then to her. She stood with her back turned to him, so he had a perfect view of the golden ringlets that kissed her neck and the row of buttons that made its way down her pale blue traveling dress. If he stepped forward, he would be able to reach out and touch the silky skin beneath the curls and inhale the sweet orange scent of the perfume she favored. And then, if he were that close, he could use his hands to spin her to face him, and press his lips to hers, and lower them until he had kissed every inch of her body, and—

Damn it, he wasn't supposed to be thinking these things. Not right now. Not when this surprise marriage had just descended upon them, and one wrong move could send his wife slapping his cheek and running from him again. Having to keep her at arm's length, at least for now, was torture enough. But moving too fast and having her resent—or worse, fear—him again was more than he could bear.

"I'll leave you now," he said, taking a step backward. "If you need anything, you have only to ask. The staff will be happy to assist you."

She turned around, her mouth twitching uncertainly. "Are you not coming in?"

Her question caused all his muscles to abruptly tense while a surge of longing coursed through his veins. How the hell could he prevent these futile internal sensations from taking hold? He would need to go outdoors and jump in the lake.

He kept himself very still as he stared at her face, trying to decipher meaning from her expression. Had she posed the question because she feared he would intrude upon her newfound sanctuary? That he would live up to his roguish reputation and ravish her on the spot? Maybe, but he didn't detect concern upon her face. Rather ... could her lowered head and pinched lips signal disappointment?

Surely not. He'd spent so much time turning over thoughts of her that he began to see things that weren't really there. Fool that he was.

"No," he said brusquely. "No, I should bid you farewell for now and leave you to get settled."

In his haste, he—the unflappable Philip Hadleigh—actually stumbled over his own feet as he spun back in the direction of the stairs. He had to get away from here. Perhaps he could fetch a horse and go for a long, intensive ride. Or go below stairs and ask Mrs. Shaw to have a different bedroom made up for him at the opposite end of the house. He just had to go *somewhere*, far away, before he did something they would both regret.

He managed only a few steps down the corridor when her soft voice called out to him.

"Wait."

***

With each thump of Lord Kendrick's boots against the floorboards, Catherine's heart gave a painful heave. She was in a new home as a new bride whose new husband walked away from her as she stood waiting for him in her bedroom. How had they gotten to this point? She'd spent nearly all day with Lord Kendrick, yet the suave, confident viscount to whom she'd become accustomed was nowhere to be seen. Why, if she hadn't known better, she would have thought him anxious.

Or, more likely, he had become withdrawn due to the unwelcome knowledge that he was now a married man.

Even the comfortable traveling dress she wore grew tight against her torso, and she felt her shoulders droop. After an already eventful day, the easiest thing would be to burrow into the comfortable-looking bed and allow herself to wallow in discontentment. But at the same time, what would that accomplish other than bringing her more misery? Once more, she had nothing left to lose. So, she called out to him.

"Wait."

The word came out as little more than a quiet murmur, but he turned around instantly.

Her skin heated under his gray gaze, and she stood open-mouthed and silent. She should have planned what she wanted to say beyond that lone word. But how did one even phrase such matters delicately?

Ever since her arrival at the Wellesleys' house party, her thoughts had swirled about in a tangled web, and the days leading up to the wedding had only caused her to feel increasingly more off-kilter. As she'd prepared for bed the previous night, Eliza had come to her room for a private conversation, wanting to ensure she knew the details of what transpired on a wedding night. And after she'd fallen asleep with that information floating through her mind, her familiar dream returned.

Lord Kendrick lounged in an armchair in the darkened library, holding Lady Blakely against him, pressing kisses into her neck. Except suddenly, the woman wasn't Lady Blakely. It was her, Catherine. Her skin tingled and burned as he pulled at her bodice, her nerve endings screaming for something she didn't understand yet desperately needed. A hot sphere of sensation gathered between her legs, and his hand traveled up her thigh, leaving sparks in its wake as he drew nearer to the place where she ached for his touch. He was so close, his skilled fingers nearly at her peak, and she cried out, urging him on ...

And that was where she'd awoken, breathless and covered in a thin layer of perspiration. That was what had kept her awake most of the night and then made her exhausted enough that she fell asleep against the carriage window before they even departed London. Only to awaken to a reality in which her husband wanted nothing to do with her.

"Do you not desire me?" The question burst out before she could stop it. Her cheeks burned, and she momentarily considered slamming the door and jumping beneath her counterpane where she could pretend she'd never uttered something so forward. However, she couldn't back away now. Not with the puzzle of why the cad who pursued women for sport wouldn't even set foot in the bedroom of the lady he could take without obstacle.

She would bring as much warmth to my bed as a chunk of arctic ice. She'd come to believe he regretted those words, and that the events that had transpired since that day had enticed him to feel differently. Had she been wrong? Did he find her so lacking that he didn't feel even a faint stirring of attraction?

Her jaw clenched, and she forced it apart so she could speak, her voice coming out as a low, steely whisper. "Do I not appeal to you as Lady Blakely does? Or any of the countless others?"

His entire body stiffened, and he took an abrupt stride through the doorway, planting himself in front of her. "*What* did you say?"

"I saw you," she cried. "I saw you with Lady Blakely." A note of frenzy crept into her voice, but now that the shameful secret she had concealed for so long began pouring out, she couldn't hold it back. "At Lady Whitmore's musicale. In the library. I *saw* you."

His eyes widened into huge gray orbs. "You do not understand …"

"I saw you," she repeated, her hands clenching into fists that began to shake, "and if the rumors hold any truth, she is far from the only one with whom you've been in that position. Why, though? Why her? Why all the others? And why not me?"

His look of surprise vanished as his eyes narrowed and the muscles in his face tightened. "How right you are, Catherine. About the rumors, I mean. Whatever you saw me do with Lady Blakely, I can assure you, I've done many times before, with more women than I could possibly name. I'm a careless rake, after all, with a reputation to uphold. And when the only thing a rake like me desires is a quick fuck in the dark, one woman is as good as another."

The cold bite of his words hung heavy between them. Did he *want* her to slap him and go scurrying from the room? Her palm twitched, aching to connect with his cheek in a

stinging blow, but she forced her hand to her side. She refused to let him rob her of her composure any further.
Moreover, she absolutely would *not* back away. Not until he
answered her question once and for all.

His chest heaved in and out as if he fought for air, and
suddenly, he took another step toward her, bringing him
close enough that she could detect wisps of his breath upon
her face.

"That's the way it should be," he said, his turbulent eyes
boring into her as if he could see right to her soul. "That's
the way it always was. But then, something very peculiar
happened. You stumbled into me in the Wellesleys' library,
and suddenly, all I could think of was your hands upon me.
I should have wanted nothing to do with you, and I might
not have, had fate not been determined to keep throwing us
together. Perhaps I should have taken it as a sign that you
were mine to pursue, just like any other woman. The problem lies in that you are *not* just like any other woman I've
known. You're an innocent, Catherine, and I know you've
often held me in contempt. I haven't the faintest notion of
how we're to navigate the rest of our lives together. All I
know is that I cannot risk doing something that will earn me
your eternal scorn. Even if I go half-mad with longing for
you in the meantime."

Her ears buzzed as her brain attempted to process everything she'd just heard. No small feat when all she believed
had been turned on its head. Her throat had gone far too
dry to manage words, and in any case, what would she say?

Instead, she reached out her hand, letting her fingertips graze the hard surface of his chest. His quickened heartbeat throbbed beneath them, and he gave a sharp inhale.

She swallowed heavily. "Philip." She tested his name as a whisper, surprised to find how smoothly it rolled off her tongue. It gave her the momentum to keep speaking. "I think I made judgments that I had no place to make. I do not despise you. I do not want you to keep me at a distance. I want to be your wife. In every way."

Without breaking his gaze, he placed his palm upon her chest, resting it against her pounding heart just as she did to him. She made herself stay very still, though her breasts had grown tight against her bodice, and she longed to press herself into his hand and absorb more of his touch.

He bent his head so that his mouth lingered beside her ear. "Are you certain you know what you ask for?"

The heat of his breath sent a shiver rippling through her, and every inch of her skin tingled. Her mind had gone cloudy, consumed with a desire that ignited like kindling. Forming a coherent sentence was now beyond her, although she made a low sound in her throat that came from a place of sheer need. And in case that wasn't enough, she nodded, for she needed him to understand, beyond a doubt, her overpowering desire for him.

The motion of her head caused his mouth to connect with her earlobe, and his tongue traced over the sensitive skin. Another low cry emerged from her throat, and she managed to utter his name, although it sounded more like a plea. "Philip."

He pulled away from her ear, bringing his forehead to rest against hers. She closed her eyes, waiting, for his lips were so close yet not close enough. She felt a little twitch that made her think he must have turned his mouth up in a smile.

"If you are sure, love." Ever so slowly, the hand resting against her chest began inching downward, and his mouth hovered just a trace closer, bringing the promise of imminent pleasure. "We shall do as you wish."

Chapter 12

Philip crushed his mouth over Catherine's, unable to wait another second to twine his tongue with hers and drink in the sweet taste that belonged to her alone. This wasn't their first kiss, but it was the first time he had her within his arms while knowing she wasn't on the verge of running away with disdain. She'd grown more confident with her caresses since that first time, pressing her mouth to his without hesitation and encircling her hands about his waist to hold him close to her.

She was flawless. Soft, heated perfection that set his body ablaze in a captivating and thrilling way.

He ran his thumb over the gentle curve of her breast before sliding it over to circle the hardened nipple pressing against the fabric of her bodice. She moaned again, soft and needy, pushing herself into his hand and sending an extra jolt of sensation to his rampant erection.

It was no longer enough. In one swift motion, he scooped her into his arms, breaking their kiss just long enough to settle her against his chest. He made it to the bed with her in four brisk strides, depositing her atop the plush counterpane.

He blinked, long and slow, trying to ascertain that the scene before him was more than just a dream. For there was Lady Catherine, with her golden hair beginning to fly free of its knot and her dark eyes blazing, lying in bed, awaiting his touch. Not frigid in the least. But wearing entirely too much clothing.

"Turn over," he murmured, giving her a soft nudge as he seated himself beside her on the bed.

Wordlessly, she obeyed, rolling onto her stomach and exposing the row of buttons at the back of her dress. How ironic that they found themselves in the same position as on that day by the pond, except this time he undid buttons rather than fastened them. An entirely more enjoyable task. Furthermore, last time her skin had been freezing and her posture rigid. Now, she lay heated and pliant, welcoming his touch. Making him yearn to end his torment and plunge into her depths, yet he'd be damned if he would rush a single second of this encounter.

With the pale blue fabric of her dress gaping open and her stays unlaced, he leaned down to brush a kiss against her nape. "That's better. Turn to your back again for me, love."

She did as he asked in one seamless movement, and he wasted no time in sliding the dress from her shoulders, easing her up slightly so he could pull it down her body and cast it to the floor, followed by her petticoat, stays, and stockings. However, now that she lay sprawled out in only her flimsy shift, her eyes took on a hint of trepidation.

"Is something the matter?" He stilled the hand that had been working to untie her shift, instead bringing it up to brush a tousled curl away from her face. "Because if you have changed your mind and no longer wish to continue, you need only say the word, and we can stop."

It might kill him, but he would assuredly stop.

"No, I haven't changed my mind." She reached for him, her touch searing his neck as she idly toyed with his cravat. "It's only … why must I be bared to you when you remain before me fully clothed?"

Relief washed over him, and a smile began tugging at his lips. "I suppose it's on account of my eagerness to take in your beauty. All of it. But rest assured, the act we're about to perform requires me to be divested of my clothing along with you."

She folded her arms across her chest, shielding the tempting shadow of her nipples from view. "I would like you to divest yourself of your clothing first. For I want to look upon you as well."

Her request made him momentarily freeze. Once again, had he possibly transcended reality and entered into a dream state? But no, Catherine still lay before him, unwavering, with her eyes holding a hint of challenge.

He shrugged as though her request hadn't surprised him in the least. "As you wish." He pulled at the knots in his cravat until it fell away and his shirt hung open at the neck, while Catherine's gaze remained fixedly upon him. He bent over to remove his polished top boots, and when he sat back up, she was still watching him carefully. She continued to do so as he shrugged off his tailcoat and white silk waistcoat. He observed her, too, gauging her reaction as he discarded his shirt, leaving his chest bare. The candles and firelight, combined with the evening's final rays of sun peeking through the window, illuminated them both clearly, and he half expected her to shy away from the sight and ask him to cease. She didn't, though. Her mouth gave the tiniest twitch, but other than that, she remained still, watching and waiting.

It was just as well, for his arousal strained uncomfortably against his trousers, desperate for release. He stood so he could tug at the buttons of his fall front and then at the waist of his smalls, pushing both garments to the floor. Leaving himself entirely exposed to her as she regarded him, wide-eyed. He'd been in this position countless times before, but he could have thought himself a green boy with the way his stomach fluttered as he lay upon the bed to face his wife.

He longed to connect his body with hers, but he kept himself at a slight distance, close enough to feel her heat but not close enough that any parts of them touched. "Does this please you?"

She placed her hand upon his chest, the sensation so much more intense now that layers of fabric no longer created an obstacle. "I … you … yes. You're splendid."

He needed no further encouragement. He pressed his mouth to hers again, savoring the plumpness of her lips before moving down to kiss the silky skin of her neck. "*You* are splendid," he said, bringing his hands back to the loosened ribbon at the neckline of her shift. "I trust I can now remove this?"

Mercifully, she nodded, pulling her clenched arms away from her chest.

"Good." He wrenched the ribbon a final time so that it came undone. At last, he could pull away this remaining unwanted layer and look upon the sight he craved more than anything.

She shifted, her hands creeping back toward her exposed breasts, but he grabbed hold, gently pinning her arms to her sides. "Please, do not feel anxious. I want so much to look at you, for you are beyond glorious." His breaths grew heavy as he glanced at the rosy nipples and then down to the dark gold covering of hair that stood out against the milky white of her skin. "You are flawless."

She tilted her chin toward him, nodding her assent, before placing an uncertain kiss upon his throat. "I suppose I must oblige you, then." She kissed him again, her fingers wriggling, and as he slackened his grasp upon her, she reached over to caress his hips. "I'll try not to feel anxious any longer. And I do feel ready for you. And I want you to ... to ... enter me."

His throat instantly went dry, while another rush of sensation pulsed in his groin. He was supposed to be the expert at this, always in control. Yet Catherine's eager innocence was entirely new to him. She never ceased to throw him off balance.

"Patience, love." Her fingertips created sparks against his skin, and he couldn't help but imagine doing what she suggested and entering her without a second thought. That, however, was not how he envisioned the evening going. She still had an abundance of things to learn, and he had every intention of acting as her diligent teacher.

He swung his legs to each side of hers and raised himself up, bracing himself with his arms so he hovered above her. "We have much to do before we reach that point." He shifted against her, letting the tip of his arousal brush against her sex.

She thrust her hips upward, seeking more of his touch. "But why, when I desire you now?"

"Because," he murmured, shifting against her again and lowering his head until it rested just above her breast, "the desire can grow so much greater when you give it time to linger. Why rush the pleasure? We have all night. All week. All our lives. And I mean to show you a thing or two."

Before she could utter another word, he brought his mouth to her nipple, laving the tightened bud as his fingers rolled over her other breast.

She arched her back, raising herself to him with a low, longing cry. Who would have thought Lady Catherine would be so receptive to his every motion? She surpassed even his wildest imaginings.

He lifted his head, earning him a whimper of protest as her eyes flew open. "Why did you stop?"

He flashed her a sly smile and let his fingers begin working their way down her torso. "I would be remiss in focusing all my attention on merely one part of you. There is so much left for me to explore. I imagine I could find other areas in want of attention."

His hand reached the apex of her thighs, and he traced a lone finger through the wiry curls, traveling down until he reached the hot wetness of her entrance. She gave another cry, louder this time, her usual restraint entirely vanished.

"I want to know every inch of you." He moved downward with his mouth, dropping delicate kisses against the underside of her breasts, then her belly. "The feel … the scent … the taste …"

Without interrupting his trail of kisses, he used his free hand to nudge her legs farther apart, giving him unrestricted access to her. He made his way below her navel, his mouth now so close to its destination that his brain had grown fevered and all he could think of was pleasure, both his and hers.

"Philip," she choked out, her eyes flying open again, "are you certain—"

He connected his mouth to her, making his kiss fall upon her sensitive peak.

"Philip!" This time, his name left her mouth as a moan, and a quiver shot through her body.

He repositioned his hands at her hips, holding her steady against the mattress. "Quite certain." He raised his head just a shade so that his breath still connected with her sensitized flesh even though his mouth did not. "Are you wary? For I'd like to make you certain as well."

He tried again, rolling his tongue over her in a gentle circle. She cried out, digging her nails into his shoulders.

"This cannot be … proper," she managed to utter between heavy breaths.

"Oh, decidedly not." He stayed close, allowing his heated words to travel across her skin. "I see no reason why we should let that impede us."

She gazed at him another instant before screwing her eyes shut and tossing her head back against the pillow. "As you say, then. For I'm certain, I do not wish you to stop."

That sight, and those words, brought him beyond bliss. He continued caressing her with his mouth, each kiss and lick eliciting a tiny mewl from deep in her throat. He didn't wish to stop either. Not when he could look upon the exquisite sight of his willing wife, whose face slackened with desire as he drove her higher and higher. Her body became tense and her cries more urgent. And then, she came apart, shuddering against his mouth as he continued lapping at her, drawing out each surge of pleasure until she lay still and sated upon the mattress.

Only then did he realize how painful his arousal had become. How his immeasurable desire had somehow amplified.

"Catherine?" His voice came out as a husky murmur as he began tracing circles over her thighs. "Do you still feel ready for me?"

Her eyes widened, and although she had just reached her climax, a bright flicker crept into them that looked rather like desire. "Yes."

She spoke confidently, with none of her former trepidation. In fact, the word held the same note as her earlier cries of yearning.

Because apparently, he had become the luckiest man in existence.

He eased himself over her again, brushing his hardened length against her thighs on his way to settle himself at her entrance. Despite his desperation, he vowed to take things slowly. He had to. For her. Even though his restraint now walked a thin line.

"Philip?" Catherine's soft voice grounded him. "Does this—act—feel the same for you as for me?"

He edged forward slightly, allowing just his tip to enter her before forcing himself to withdraw. "That depends." Somehow, he'd retained his ability to speak an intelligible sentence, even though all his nerve endings demanded more. "To answer accurately, I would need to know how the experience thus far has felt for you."

He pushed forward again, a little farther this time, and she grasped his hips to prevent him from making a full retreat. "Wonderful," she breathed.

He pushed forward again as she wriggled her hips beneath him.

"Enchanting." Her breath caught on the end of the word as she absorbed the sensation. "Heavenly."

"Then yes, it is the same for me," he said, bringing his face close to hers while sliding into her another inch.

"Sensational. All-consuming. Although I'm very sorry if this next part causes you discomfort."

"Do not be sorry." The desire on her face was now mixed with staunch determination. "I told you, I'm ready."

He could hold back no longer. After placing his mouth upon hers in a gentle caress, he pushed forward the final distance, letting himself become fully absorbed by her tight, welcoming warmth. She flinched beneath him, letting out a gasp.

He pulled away at once, despite his body's shouts of protest. "Catherine, I apologize if I hurt you. I promise, this is the one and only time you'll experience pain. But if you're unhappy—"

"No." She set her mouth in a firm line, tugging his hips back toward her. "You needn't apologize. For it's my understanding that the pain gives way to pleasure."

"Oh, it does." He kissed her again before easing back into her, his length now gliding more smoothly. "I'll see to it that it does."

He tried a few light thrusts, studying the little twitches that crossed her face as she adjusted to the intrusion. And then, as he moved forward again, her hips rose to meet his, and she let out another of her quiet moans.

He moved faster now, no longer able to deny the urgency that rushed through his blood like fire. How could an act he'd performed countless times before suddenly feel new? For each sensation had become more acute, each stroke bringing pleasure with an intensity like he'd never known.

She closed her eyes again, her face awash with longing as she propelled her hips upward in time to each of his thrusts. It was too much: The sight of her lying beneath him in unrestrained bliss … the feel of her blazing intimate flesh …

Release hurtled toward him at an unstoppable pace. Meanwhile, insistent, yearning sounds escaped Catherine's lips, and her body grew taut once more. Her own climax had to be approaching, a fact that only increased his frenzy. With what little coherence he still possessed, he dragged his hand across her breast, rolling her hardened nipple as he gave one more powerful thrust.

Her muscles pulsed around him as she came with a throaty sigh, and he swiftly followed her, his days of pent-up tension dissolving into wave after wave of ecstasy.

As much as he didn't ever want to withdraw from her, he finally pushed himself away and rolled to his back, taking a moment to catch his breath. The world seemed hazy, like he couldn't quite make sense of it. But Catherine lay beside him, and right now, that was all that mattered.

Eventually, he became aware that she lay on her side gazing at him, and he turned to her, stroking a finger against her cheek before encircling her in his arms. "Are you pleased, love?"

He couldn't recall ever asking that question before. After all, he could usually tell by a woman's relaxed body and languid grin that she was satisfied. Catherine currently displayed both these features. Nonetheless, he felt an inexplicable need to have her say the words aloud.

She nuzzled her head into his chest, her golden hair deliciously tickling his still-sensitized skin. "Very. I hardly think you would possess a reputation as a rake if you lacked skills."

He burst into a laugh at her bluntness, although the sound quickly dissipated into a hollow grunt. Did she think he viewed her as merely another of his conquests? There were so many things he should try to explain to her, yet how could he when he didn't possess the words himself?

"Do you require anything?" Rather than focus on matters beyond his comprehension, he changed the subject. "I could ring for a bath if you'd care for one after our day of travel. Or are you hungry?"

Never in his life had he rambled as maladroitly as he did this day. He sincerely hoped this wasn't the beginning of a trend arising from his newfound status as a married man.

But Catherine merely tilted her head to smile up at him. "I require nothing I don't already have. I wish only to lie here with you."

"Of course." He managed a genuine chuckle at that comment and then quirked an eyebrow at her. "You'd best rest and recover your strength, for you may require it later."

Although her eyelids had grown heavy, a sudden light flickered within the brown irises. "I certainly hope so."

It was enough to make his cock stir again, although he closed his eyes, trying to make the sensation pass. As much as he wanted her, his previous words to her remained true: There was no need to rush things. Right now, it would benefit them both to sleep. Perhaps then, he could awaken revitalized instead of fumbling.

He hugged her to him more tightly, stroking her back as she resettled herself against his chest. Her breathing slowed, turning into a series of quiet inhales and exhales, and he used the rhythm to lull himself into a state of tranquility.

"Philip?" she mumbled suddenly, her hazy voice suggesting she lingered somewhere between wakefulness and sleep.

"Yes, love?" He spoke softly and continued his light caresses, just in case she was about to drift into a dream.

But Catherine managed to speak again, though her tone grew more faraway. "Will I be enough for you?"

He froze, the question beating at his heart like a sledgehammer. He opened his eyes, half expecting to be met with her inquisitive stare, but she remained cuddled into him, on the verge of sleep. With great difficulty, he forced his hand back into action, not wanting to rouse her with an abrupt pause in his strokes.

Up until the previous week, he would have laughed mockingly at such a question. Of course he would never content himself with only one woman.

But then, Lady Catherine had come traipsing into his life, and everything changed. He had no idea of the reason for it. Her innocence? Her hidden layers of passion? Whatever the case, he began imagining things he had never allowed himself to consider or want before. A wife ... a partner ... someone he could settle with ... someone he could confide in, who knew every facet of him and would still view him as enough ...

"Yes," he murmured, even though such a thing was likely just a fancy. Everyone knew they were direct opposites: an aloof debutante and a shameless cad. They could never achieve an undying state of happiness together ... could they?

Catherine's mouth turned up in a smile. "Always?"

The question terrified him, and the concept was almost too difficult to grasp. But in the far reaches of his brain, he envisioned a future in which he didn't feel the need to patch the hole within him by constantly striving for more and better. A future in which he could take what he had and simply feel content. For that gaping, ugly hole would be filled by— dare he think it?—love.

He planted a kiss atop her head, although she had gone so still, and her breathing turned so shallow that she had to be fully asleep.

That's how he knew it was safe to whisper to her. "Yes."

Chapter 13

Not until late the following morning did Catherine and Philip finally leave her room so she could receive a tour of Clifton Manor. Even then, the effort of rising from their tousled bedsheets felt gargantuan. However, with much reluctance, he'd helped her into a white day dress, and she'd twisted her hair into a simple knot so he could take her below stairs and get her better acquainted with the housekeeper, Mrs. Shaw. A necessary task, after all, even if they could both think of a more pleasurable way to spend the remainder of the day.

She couldn't recall ever staying abed for such a long time, except perhaps on an occasion or two when she'd been ill with a head cold. But while her skin had often felt feverish over the past day, it was most definitely not on account of a routine illness. No, this was due to a different matter entirely, one that caused her to *want* to burrow beneath the counterpane and not get up for a very long time. That is, if Philip remained beneath the counterpane with her.

For she'd come to realize something peculiar about lovemaking. They'd lain together prior to falling asleep last evening … and then at the first traces of dawn … and once more after ordering a breakfast tray and realizing they weren't hungry for food after all … and still, the sparks that flared low in her belly wouldn't dissipate. On the contrary, the more time she spent enveloped in Philip's embrace, the more she craved it.

Her cheeks reddened at the thought, despite how she'd been trying to concentrate on Mrs. Shaw's lengthy description of menus for the week. However, it wasn't the sort of flush that made her want to lower her head and flee. Rather, it was a tingling heat that made her envision Philip's skilled fingers upon her, and it enticed her to subtly brush her hand against his as they both sat ceremoniously in Mrs. Shaw's sitting room.

"Mrs. Shaw!"

A young housemaid peeked through the open door, interrupting the housekeeper's explanation of sauce choices for tomorrow's salmon and Catherine's reverie about Philip's caresses.

"Pardon my intrusion," the housemaid uttered, dropping into a curtsey as she spotted the visitors on the housekeeper's settee. "But the new chambermaids you requested arrived early, and no one is certain what's to be done with them."

"By all means, attend to them at once," Philip said to the housekeeper as he rose from his seat. "I'm pleased you were so efficient in hiring additional staff now that my wife and I will be here for a time, and I'm sure Lady Kendrick would be agreeable to continuing the tour at another time. Perhaps tomorrow."

"Of course." Catherine accepted Philip's proffered hand and rose to her feet. Already, he inched them toward the doorway.

Mrs. Shaw's weathered face lit up in a smile. It seemed even the housekeeper wasn't immune to her young master's charms. "Thank you, my lord, for your understanding. We're so pleased to have you here again."

After seeing them out of the sitting room, Mrs. Shaw bent into a polite curtsey and hurried away, leaving Catherine and Philip alone in the corridor.

All of a sudden, Philip's arms encircled her waist, and he spun her toward him, dropping an appreciative kiss upon her lips. "Would I be remiss in saying that I care far less about menus than I do about being alone with you again?"

She giggled, relishing the fact that she could now run her hands over him freely. "I hope not, for I must confess, I feel the same way."

"Good." He kissed her again, clasping her hand where it rested against his chest. "Well, you've seen the kitchens, cellars, and servants' quarters. As Mrs. Shaw is no longer available, perhaps I should give you a tour back to your bedroom. Just in case you've forgotten the way."

His knowing grin caused the heat in her belly to augment. But instead of giving in to the urge to press her body against his and then run without stopping until they reached her bedroom, she pulled away slightly, trying to focus on something beyond Philip's delectable embrace.

"A clever idea, but maybe we could make a few stops along the way. I would like to have a general idea of the house's layout beyond only my bedroom. For I assume I'll leave it at least on occasion. Besides, I thought you said it was better if we didn't rush our intimacy."

"Surely I never said anything so idiotic," he grumbled, his mouth turning down in a mock scowl as he placed one more kiss upon her throat. However, he led her back up the servants' stairs and to the main corridor, made bright by the sconces that lined the walls.

The house had clearly been expanded upon throughout the years, for additional corridors with assorted floor coverings and paneling jutted off in every direction, rather like a maze. A tour would indeed be necessary if she was to have a hope of successfully traversing her new home.

"Come this way first," Philip said, casting open a sturdy carved oak door. "The gallery wing."

Sunlight flooded the long, narrow space, for the displays of family portraits upon the walls were interspersed with tall, uncovered windows. Catherine stepped inside, peering up at the gilded ceiling that was adorned with a fresco of cherubs.

"Lovely," she murmured, taking in the opulence that rivaled what she had grown up with at Highfield Park.

"I haven't entered this space in years." Philip's eyes scanned the room before returning to rest upon her. "But I thought you might like it. These windows provide the best view of the lake from anywhere in the house."

Catherine's mouth spread into a rueful grin despite herself. Philip would certainly never let her forget the incident at Oakwood Hall's pond. A lake of flawless cerulean, smooth due to the breezeless day, shone in the distance. Perhaps they could make new memories there—at least once the weather warmed—ones in which she floated through the water while melting into his touch rather than fighting it. However, a portrait on the far wall caught her attention and prevented the idea from fully taking hold.

She released Philip's arm so she could saunter over to it, the pristine faces drawing her in. The woman who sported an elaborate black coiffure as she sat grandly upon a bench could be no other than Lady Langley in her earlier years, and the robust, dark-haired man standing beside her had to be the marquess before poor health had made him stooped and frail. But what truly captivated her attention were the two dark-haired, solemn-faced youths who sat beside the marchioness, and the little boy, who couldn't be more than three or four, reclining near her feet.

"Why, Philip," she exclaimed, "is this your family?"

"Indeed." He crossed the room to stand beside her, but his tone had become strained. "My parents, as you probably know. And Charles, and John … But it was painted a very long time ago."

He abruptly spun away from the portrait and strode toward the nearest window, gazing aimlessly at the scenery.

Had she done wrong by bringing it to his attention? She'd merely wished to catch a glimpse of the little boy he'd been before time and circumstances had changed him, and to lay eyes upon his brothers whom she could never know otherwise. For on that subject, there were so many matters of which she remained unaware. Had Philip been close with his brothers? And beneath his cool facade, did he still mourn their deaths? If she could only make him trust her enough to let down his guard and tell her his true feelings on the matter ...

But as she racked her brain for a suitable comment, her eyes fell upon another portrait at the edge of the wall, and she shuffled over to gaze at it. The scene was much the same: the marquess, gray-haired but still robust; the marchioness, ever lovely despite the passage of time; and the two dark-haired youths, who had now become young men. One had deep brown eyes, and the other had a wider face and hair that curled wildly atop his head, but aside from those differences, they bore a striking resemblance to Philip as he was now. It was a stately portrait, befitting of the marquess and his family, except it lacked one key element.

"Philip, why were you not painted in this one?"

Perhaps it was an indelicate question, but his absence struck her as so unusual that she couldn't help but remark upon it.

He glanced over his shoulder without really looking in her direction before turning back to his view out the window. Clearly, he had no need of peering at the wall to realize of which portrait she spoke.

"I was ill at the time. Not worth painting." He rushed the words like they held little significance, but the note of hurt in his voice was undeniable.

She pulled her eyes away from the disconcerting portrait and tiptoed toward Philip, as cautiously as if *he* now presented a risk of fleeing. However, when she came up behind him and placed a hand upon his shoulder, he stayed just as he was, unmoving.

She pressed her fingers into the fabric of his coat, kneading the taut muscle beneath. "Will you tell me about it?"

"Why would you wish to discuss such a maudlin subject?" He whipped his head around, and this time, his gaze rested upon her, his eyes as cold and hard as granite. "We should continue our tour, and while doing so, surely we can come up with a more pleasant topic of conversation."

At one time, a speech such as this might have left her cowering and silent. But not right now. This was far too important for her to back away from.

"I wish to discuss it because I would like to know more about you." She stepped forward and turned, placing herself between him and the window. "We are married, yet so many aspects of ourselves remain concealed from one another. I wish I could understand more. I ask not because I wish to meddle, but because I care."

He sighed heavily, but the steeliness in his eyes softened. "I must brace myself for future difficulties, for I seem to lack the ability to deny you anything."

He dragged a hand through the dark locks that had spilled over his forehead, taking in an unsteady breath.

"Very well, then. If you truly wish to know, I contracted scarlet fever at the age of eight. A rather difficult case."

"I'm sorry." Her chest constricted, and she placed her hand against his shoulder again, reminding herself that the man who stood before her was strong and full of life. Meanwhile, her eyes drifted back to the portrait, for based on the apparent ages of the painted figures, something still didn't seem right.

"Philip? Wouldn't you have been a great deal older than that at the time this portrait was painted?"

"Yes. Fifteen, if my memory serves me correctly." He stared straight at her, never once turning toward the artwork in question. "The effects of the illness lingered for some years, I'm afraid."

"How terrible. For both you and your family." It was an inane thing to say, but his revelation made it difficult for her to think clearly. Despite how Edward had alluded to these circumstances, she found it nearly impossible to imagine someone as dynamic as Philip waylaid by illness for years.

"Indeed." He gave a smile that was cloaked in bitterness. "Then again, third sons are expendable. Or at least they should be."

Despite her efforts to remain still, Catherine couldn't contain her flinch. She'd grown up with no mother and a father who didn't seem to care about her existence one way or another. But to hear that Philip, too, felt like he didn't matter to his family … She thought back to the way the marchioness had regarded him so carefully throughout the house party and how the marquess, despite his frailty, had done the same at their wedding. Surely, Philip was incorrect in his assumption. Wasn't he?

"But there's little use debating the subject," he said, seeing her about to protest. "The fact is, I didn't succumb to the illness, did I? After all those years of watching life through doorways and windows, after being so feeble that I lacked the ability to even climb a damn set of stairs without getting winded, I decided I couldn't carry on that way. One morning, at the first light of dawn, I slipped from the house so I could run about the grounds. I made it about as far as that tree"—she turned as he pointed to a towering golden beech tree at the near side of the lake—"before I collapsed."

Catherine shuddered as she envisioned his limp body on the neatly kept grounds before her, and she spun back to face him, no longer able to look upon the scene out the window.

He shrugged as if it didn't matter. "It didn't stop me from trying again the next day, and then the day after that. I had come to a decision. I would either recover from the illness or let it kill me. I would *not*, however, keep only halfway living. As it turned out, I wasn't damaged beyond repair, for the task got a little easier each day. After about a month, I made it to the far side of the lake. A month after that, I got to the woods beyond. Eventually, I was able to leave the estate. To journey to London, and elsewhere. I even made an attempt at Oxford, as by that time, I had finished instruction with my tutor, and as a third son, I should have been destined for the church. Can you believe?"

He laughed, although the sound rang hollow. "I imagine that the second I stood at the pulpit to preach a sermon, I would have burst into flames. No, I had other plans. Life had been restored to me, and I wanted to … well, live. After spending so many years as a nonentity, I couldn't see how my actions would matter one way or another. I was neither heir nor spare. Except by that time, John was on the Continent, and then news came from Waterloo that he was … that he had been … killed."

Catherine blinked away the tears that began forming in her eyes. Although he spoke evenly, she would have to be blind not to recognize how delivering this information affected him. "What a horrible tragedy."

"Yes, horrible. Devastating." His features became pinched, and she could notice the effort behind his nonchalance. "But at least all hope was not lost. Not with Charles as the ever-dependable heir, always eager to learn about estate business or roam London in search of the perfect wife and future marchioness. Even when Charles caught a chill and took to his bed, no one thought anything of it. Prior to that time, I cannot recall him being afflicted by so much as a headache. He was in the prime of his life. The illness that dared mar his perfection should have been nothing more than a passing annoyance. Of course, circumstances transpired quite differently, until suddenly, all that remained was a dissolute third son who should have been dead ten times over."

"Philip …" She fought back the urge to launch herself into his arms and cling to him as if by doing so, she could absorb some of his hurt. However, given his visible discomfort at having spoken so openly, she approached him carefully, stroking her fingers over his arm. She ached for him. For his stolen youth. For him having his return to health followed by unthinkable tragedy. And for his apparent belief that he was wrong to be alive while his brothers were not.

"Come. We're turning far too morose." The pain etched across his features vanished as if by magic, and he spun toward the doorway. "If you wish to see the remainder of the house, I suggest we continue the tour. At this rate, it will take us into next week to finish it."

She stared at his retreating form, dumbfounded, before forcing her feet to catch up with him. How could he walk away as though everything he'd just told her meant nothing? Her mind reeled with all the things she wished to say to him once she managed to gather her thoughts.

Yet here he was, strolling back through the corridor like their conversation in the gallery hadn't even taken place. Except it had, and she couldn't simply brush away the hurt he had dared to reveal, however briefly. She now knew, without a doubt, that his air of carefreeness came only from his skill at hiding his inner turmoil. Which is why she needed to find a way of offering comfort. She couldn't allow him to go on thinking his existence was a mistake or that it didn't matter one way or another. Not when she already felt things for him that she never could have dreamed.

"Philip ..." She tried his name again, uttering it softly as he turned down a corridor near the stairs.

"Here we are. The library." Either she had spoken too quietly or he had deliberately chosen not to hear her, for he cast open the first door they came to and beckoned for her to join him in the darkened room without offering an additional response. Whatever the case, one thing was abundantly clear. The subject she wished to broach with him was no longer up for discussion.

Chapter 14

Catherine glanced around at the mahogany shelves laden with books that stretched to the ceiling, but she couldn't truly take them in. The weight of everything she'd just learned, and the predicament of what to do with that knowledge, bore down on her. The curtains were drawn, leaving the room in shadows, but she could still discern a wide wingback chair, covered in plush blue velvet, near the window. "Would you mind if I sat for a moment?"

Wordlessly, he took her hand and led her toward the chair, his placid expression betraying just a hint of concern. She smoothed her skirts, preparing to sit, when suddenly, Philip flopped down on the velvet surface, and she found herself sprawled atop his lap. He cupped her face in his hands, holding her close to him, and pressed a soft kiss upon her lips before withdrawing slightly so he could look at her again.

His name rose in her throat once more. *Philip.* She had to speak to him, to make him understand. However, there was something in his stormy gray eyes that stopped her. They shone with a light she had come to know as desire, but there was something else there. A wordless, vulnerable plea that implored her to simply *be* with him without delving into painful memories.

"You're so lovely." He pushed his lips against the throbbing pulse point in her neck. "I cannot stop wanting you."

More than anything, she wanted to find the words that would convince him of his own worth. But with each caress, it became more difficult for her to think logically, her melancholy for him giving way to the stirrings of her desire. Despite everything, the reality of their present circumstances hadn't escaped her. He sat entwined with her in a darkened library, just as she'd seen him do with Lady Blakely. Just as she'd imagined herself doing with him.

His mouth traveled lower, skimming the swell of her breasts as he worked to pull away her bodice. It was exactly like the dream she'd had so many times and then tried desperately to forget in the morning. However, she now wanted nothing more than to embrace every modicum of the pleasure he sent rippling through her body and sear it into the deepest recesses of her mind.

He succeeded in wrenching down the bodice and underlying shift, and a rush of cool air hit her bared breasts before his mouth connected with her nipple, encasing her with his heat. She grasped the hair at the back of his head, shamelessly holding him against her so he would continue with the exquisite laps of his tongue. Dampness accumulated between her legs, and as he turned his attention to her other breast, she became vaguely aware that he tugged at his falls.

He pulled his head away so he could face her again. "Put your legs to either side of mine and raise your skirts."

She gathered the folds of muslin and obeyed without question, for all she could think of was how her skin tingled and ached for more of him. She watched as he released the final button of his falls and his arousal sprang free, and she moaned as the tip swept along her sex.

"Good." His voice had gone ragged, and his eyes smoldered so that they looked almost black. "Now, come to me."

He grasped her hips, urging her toward him, and as she brushed against his shaft again, he pushed forward the remaining distance to bury himself within her. A hint of an ache remained in her until-recently untried body, but the sensation was nothing compared to the pleasure that now came from having him fill her. Especially in this novel position, at this different angle, where he seemed to penetrate her even more deeply.

She kept her hands fisted in his hair, anchoring herself against him as he guided her up and down his length. Despite her lack of experience, her body seemed to know what to do, and she quickly developed her own rhythm, desire shooting through her each time she sank down and he rose to meet her with a slight thrust. She had always been known as the silent type who lacked things to say, but when she was with him like this, drawing ever closer to release, heady cries escaped her throat without effort. This intimacy—and this yearning—far surpassed her fleeting dreams on the subject. She tried to hold back her flood of desire and prolong the experience, just as he'd insisted upon that first time, but then he let go of her hip, and his fingers slid between them, caressing her in just the right spot between her legs. She could contain it no more. Pleasure burst through her, sending her intimate muscles spasming around him, and with a final thrust, he groaned with his own release.

He clung to her as the waves of bliss washed over them, resting his head atop her bare shoulder. She buried her face in the earthy scent of his hair, planting her arms firmly against his back. Only when his chest no longer heaved with each inhale and exhale, and her own breathing had returned to a tranquil rhythm, did she lift her head to gaze at him. His face had gone slack, his lips curled in a suggestion of a smile, and his eyes were their usual clear, striking gray.

Somewhere in the back of her mind, she recalled her former desire to continue their conversation from the gallery. Yet seeing him here like this, calm and sated, as her own limbs turned boneless, made her think that maybe she didn't need to. Maybe simply *being* together was enough, after all, to let him know how much she valued him. Unlike Philip, of course, she didn't have any past experiences to compare this to, but she didn't see how two people could share this level of closeness and not realize how they meant something to one another. Without a doubt, any bond they built would never erase the suffering of his youth or the painful losses he'd experienced in adulthood. However, she could hope it would show him that his survival was more than an accident and that he deserved to have a future filled not just with mindless entertainments, but with things that were fulfilling and real. Whether he was correct or not about his parents' indifference, one thing was certain. He had already won her esteem. And though part of her feared she was very foolish for relenting so easily, he was well on his way to capturing her heart.

She lowered her head to his again, and after that, she stayed just as she was, seated in his lap with him still inside her as she clung to the back of his coat. She felt as though she could stay like this with him forever, silent but at peace.

For she knew as well as anyone that not all emotions required words.

***

Philip passed two blissful weeks with his wife at Clifton Manor before the letter came that changed everything.

It was ironic, really, how perfect those couple weeks had been, given that they resided in the house he wanted no claim to with only each other for divertissement. Yet, as had been a recurring theme with time spent in Catherine's company, he discovered something curious about himself. He didn't miss the incessant whirl to which he'd grown accustomed—the clubs, the parties, the sleepless nights in pursuit of pleasure—which had reminded him that he was alive and strong and in control. Somehow, passing quiet days—and passionate nights—with Catherine provided fulfillment in a way those other diversions had not. So much so that, on occasion, he envisioned them living there well into the future. Together. Sometimes, he even imagined the patter of tiny feet and joyful shrieks from the children she wanted. And the more times that thought crossed his mind, the more he began thinking that he wanted them too.

He was becoming a sorry rake, to be sure. Surprisingly, that knowledge troubled him very little.

They'd grown accustomed to passing evenings in the drawing room—that is, when they didn't leave the dinner table and retire immediately to his bedroom—and this evening proved no different. As usual, he brought a book with him so that Catherine didn't become disconcerted by the extra attention upon her, but in truth, his eyes often rose from the pages so he could watch her as she played the pianoforte. Her fingers glided over the keys so effortlessly, and her body swayed with the music so lithely that it was difficult to look away. A grin crossed his lips as he thought back to that stormy evening last week when he'd slid beside her onto the bench and pulled her into a kiss, and suddenly, he found himself claiming her against the pianoforte, rain beating against the windows as her thighs hit the discordant keys.

However, the abrupt entry of a footman carrying a letter atop a silver tray pulled him from the idyllic memory.

"This just arrived for you, m'lord."

Philip accepted the proffered letter, tearing at the seal as an unsettling tightness pulled at his chest. There were a number of unnerving possibilities as to why a letter would arrive for him well into the evening, and as he scanned the contents of the single-paged missive, he at least determined the news wasn't dire. Still, he couldn't help but let out an exasperated huff as he reached up to squeeze his temples. His days of uninterrupted bliss with Catherine were over, at least for now. He shouldn't have been so shortsighted as to neglect considering what would happen when this matter came up. Because it always did, sooner or later.

He became aware that the cheerful notes of her minuet had faded away, and when he turned in her direction, she was staring at him, her brows knit.

"Is something the matter?"

He shook his head, scrunching the paper in his fist and walking over to throw it in the fire. "Merely a letter from London."

Catherine leaped from the bench and was at his side in an instant. "Is it your father?"

"No. Nothing like that," he rushed to assure her. On the contrary, his mother had sent a letter several days prior saying that the marquess had regained a little of his strength in the time since the wedding, so much so that he felt he might finally be up to departing London and spending the rest of his days in the comfort of his beloved Clifton Manor.

He sighed, pondering what should come next. In a way, it would be so much easier to lay the truth of the letter out before her. She was his wife, after all, which had come to signify more to him than he ever imagined. Then again, alluding to the letter's contents would keep them in the drawing room discussing subjects he wanted no reminder of for far longer than he would like, notwithstanding the fact that he'd been sworn to secrecy.

"It's a small matter of business pertaining to the family that necessitates my attention," he settled on disclosing, not oblivious to her slight frown. "I'll need to journey to London to attend to it, unfortunately, but not for more than several days, or perhaps a week at most."

Surprisingly, even the thought of that brief separation from her caused a gnawing in his gut, and he reached for her, clasping the softness of her ungloved hand. Her mouth twitched as a flood of unanswered questions flashed across her face, and he braced himself for the half-truths he would need to give.

Ultimately, though, she peered at him with clear eyes, squeezing his fingers against her own. "Let me come with you."

He blinked slowly, trying to contain his surprise at the request. "But I thought you disliked London."

"I do. But I dislike the thought of being parted from you even more."

He should have refused outright. Having her there would complicate matters in numerous ways, starting with his ability to return to his bachelor lodgings. Yet if he was being honest with himself, the idea of returning to those sparse rooms, which he had once relished for the freedom they provided, now appealed to him as much as another frigid dip in the Wellesleys' pond. Not that he had a desire to frequent Langley house either, but with Catherine by his side, the whole affair could be almost ... well, tolerable.

Besides, she said she *wanted* to be with him. He craved her company too, and if he could deal with the task at hand while knowing he could return to her each night, perhaps the matter requiring his attention would become more tolerable.

"If you're certain that's what you wish." He paused, giving her the opportunity to rethink and refuse. Their infatuation aside, she really would be better off remaining in the country. However, she didn't waver for an instant.

"I'm quite certain."

He rose to his feet, pulling her against him. She smelled so good, her sweet orange scent welcoming him just as her arms wrapped around his back, returning his embrace. She deserved so much better than a cad for a husband, and one who kept secrets besides. Maybe he should just tell her and have it out in the open where it could no longer stand between them. But many months ago, he'd made a vow, and amongst his streak of careless debauchery, he'd managed to do the decent thing and keep it. Whether keeping it now remained the decent thing, he couldn't entirely say, but in any case, it seemed prudent to hold onto the secret for now as he tried to solve this quandary.

"I hate having to end this time alone with you at Clifton Manor." He rested his chin against her shoulder, reminding himself that there was no need for sentimentality when they would travel to London together and could journey right back to the country after he conducted his business, if they so chose. Regardless, something about this embrace felt rather like a farewell, which left his limbs heavy and his throat tight.

It made pulling away from her and speaking his next words especially difficult. "However, I suppose all good things must come to an end sooner or later. We should go see that our things are packed. We'll need to depart tomorrow."

Chapter 15

Philip was correct about Catherine's distaste for the bustle of London. She strolled along Bond Street, trying to muster enthusiasm for the various displays of fabrics, hats, shoes, and jewelry that aimed to entice behind shop windows. However, she already had an ample supply of all these items, and shopping didn't appeal to her enough to provide a sufficient distraction. At least her excursion had the advantage of being uncrowded, unlike during the height of the Season when she couldn't make it from one shopfront to the next without encountering an acquaintance and being forced to stop and make small talk. Nonetheless, the unsettled sensation she'd experienced while traversing these crowded streets several months ago continued to plague her even in this day's relative quiet.

It was an absurd feeling, and one she'd chastised herself for time and again. The feeling had no truth behind it, obviously, and was born only of her silly discomfort with crowds and commotion. Unfortunately, that knowledge did nothing to quell it. As she roamed throughout London, she couldn't shake the sensation that eyes rested upon her. Watching her. Judging her.

A shiver ran up her spine, and she gave her head an abrupt shake, annoyed at her relentless anxiety. Regardless, she'd done more than enough shopping for one day, and she began glancing around for the coach displaying the Langley crest. Luckily, the driver remained with it just a short distance up the street, and she hurried over to the gleaming black vehicle, bursting through the door the instant the accompanying footman opened it for her.

At last, she could sink into the velvet seat cushions and breathe a little easier, certain that she sat alone and unobserved. What had come over her on the street to make her suddenly so apprehensive? It likely had nothing to do with the shopping excursion itself but instead was the result of events of the past couple of days. Philip's mysterious letter … their unexpected trip to London for reasons she still didn't understand but was reluctant to inquire about further. There was little point when he had already shown his skill at burying matters he didn't wish to discuss.

Everything had gone so well at Clifton Manor once they'd fallen into a routine and grown comfortable with each other. Leaving it behind gave her a feeling akin to the one she'd experienced as a child each time Edward had departed Highfield Park to return to school, leaving her alone and friendless in an echoey house. She wasn't alone now, of course, for Philip remained nearby. Yesterday, their first in London, he'd arrived home in plenty of time for dinner, and he'd assured her with one of his easy smiles that today would be no different. Nonetheless, the spell that had come over them at Clifton Manor, the one that caused her to forget the circumstances of their union and the rumors of his past, had been broken. She couldn't help but feel that they'd been thrust from a state of bliss into the real world, and matters between them would never be so easy again.

The heaviness that had fallen over her was replaced by a light flutter in her abdomen as the coach pulled up before Langley House. She envisioned Philip, lounging upstairs in their bedroom, ready to welcome her home. However, no sooner had she removed her pelisse in the entryway than Swift, the family's butler, informed her that Lord Kendrick had not yet returned. She should have known that, really, for it was only midday. Likewise, it turned out that Lord and Lady Langley had departed for Clifton Manor just that morning, the marquess having mustered a burst of strength that finally left him able to undertake the journey.

No wonder the house was so quiet, then, when she was its sole occupant aside from the servants. But perhaps it was just as well. She retreated to the drawing room, letting her weight sink into the wingback chair nearest the fireplace. She wouldn't be good company right now anyway. Maybe an hour or two alone was just what she needed to pull herself out of this ridiculous slump she had gotten herself in and restore her good humor prior to Philip's arrival.

Amidst the silence, a quiet rustling noise came from the doorway, and she turned to see her lady's maid peering at her eagerly. "Would you care for some tea, my lady?"

"Yes, that would be nice …" She trailed off, her eyes fixing upon something she hadn't noticed before as she turned back toward the fire. On the end table next to her rested a single sheet of folded paper, addressed with a sprawling, ragged script. *Catherine, Viscountess Kendrick.*"

"Yes," she repeated, clearing her throat and prying her eyes away from the mysterious page and back to the lady's maid. "Betsy, did a caller come while I was away?"

Betsy pondered a moment but then shook her head. "Not that I know of, my lady. Were you expecting someone?"

"No." Her voice cracked, and Betsy remained shuffling in the doorway, looking her up and down as if trying to solve a riddle. Catherine managed a partial smile, praying that the apprehension that knotted within her didn't show upon her face. "I have no need of anything further. Just the tea, if you please."

After one last bewildered glance, Betsy curtsied and went on her way, her footsteps echoing down the corridor. Once they became faint thumps, Catherine grabbed the paper, turning it over in her fingers as if it were a foreign object. It had no stamps or even a wax seal; it couldn't have come in the post.

There were few things more mundane or innocuous than a letter. Some high society lady who remained in London had probably sent her an invitation for tea or some such entertainment, too eager to lay eyes upon the new and unlikely Lady Kendrick to be proper with her correspondence. Why, then, had the unsettled heaviness from earlier returned to her with full force? The feeling wouldn't leave her, despite how she now sat safely at home, and whether that signified anything beyond her tendency to overreact and fluster easily, she really couldn't say.

She would gain little by continuing to wait and letting her thoughts get the better of her. Instead, she unfolded the single sheet of paper so its contents were bared to her.

Dear Catherine,

Forgive my impudence, but while I may be unknown to you, I can assure you, you are very well known to me. We have not yet had the pleasure of a formal introduction, and I feel it is high time we remedy that. As the matter of which I wish to speak with you is of some significance, I propose we meet today, at three o'clock, in St. James Park. I cannot emphasize enough the importance of this meeting, so let me only say that it will be of immense benefit to us both, especially insofar as to prevent blemishes from staining your newfound status as Viscountess Kendrick and the future Lady Langley. I shall await you by the Chinese bridge and will count on your prompt arrival. I trust I need not state the necessity of your absolute discretion in regard to this meeting.

She screwed her eyes shut, her rapidly pounding heart feeling like it had sunk low in her stomach. She wanted to read no more. Or better yet, to turn back time and never have looked upon a single word of the letter in the first place. However, it was too late now. Only the signature remained. What use was there in cowering in ignorance any longer? She forced one eye open, the final lines of black ink confronting her like a death sentence.

Sincerely,
Your devoted father

And there it was, the truth staring her in the face in an untidy scrawl. The air rushed from her lungs, and she found herself struggling to take another breath.

"My lady?" Betsy's voice called to her from across the room, and in an instant, the lady's maid was at her side, casting the tea tray to the end table with an undignified rattle. "My lady, whatever is the matter? Do you require smelling salts?"

Catherine forced a ragged inhale. "No, I'm quite all right," she said. At least, she thought she uttered those words. She could barely focus above the grating hum of her thoughts.

She supposed she should have known all along, and in a way, perhaps she had. There were numerous pieces of supporting evidence, if she cared to focus on them. The former earl's lifelong indifference to her ... the loudly whispered rumors surrounding her mother and, in turn, her. *Everyone knows she's not* truly *an earl's daughter.*

Which led to another crushing realization that once more threatened to take her breath away. That unnerving feeling of eyes upon her in the street, that feeling that caused her to question her soundness of mind—had it been more than paranoia? How else could this letter have arrived for her, perfectly timed, despite Betsy's claim of a lack of visitors? What if this man—her so-called *father*—had always known about her too? Maybe he knew her far better than she imagined ...

She shuddered, her body quivering from her head down to her toes.

"Did you receive distressing news? My lady?"

Betsy's questions snapped her out of her trance, and she became aware that the lady's maid now knelt beside her chair, her youthful face etched with concern as she motioned toward the letter clutched tight in her mistress's grasp.

"All is well," Catherine bit out, her voice a tight rasp that suggested anything but. She jumped from her seat, crumpling the offensive piece of paper. What a fool she was, sitting idly, pondering, while this damning evidence rested beneath her fingertips. She tossed the wrinkled ball into the fire, watching as the flames licked at the page, turning it into smoke and ashes. No one else would read those words. But that wouldn't erase them from her memory.

Betsy pushed herself to her feet, not quite able to contain her sigh. "If all is well, then won't you sit and drink your tea?"

"No." She stayed peering into the fire, not yet able to meet Betsy's gaze. "That is, I have decided to go out once more."

"Shall I call for the carriage again?" Betsy's face was awash with bewilderment.

Catherine shook her head. While the letter writer might already know all too well who she was, the last thing she could do was show up to their meeting in the coach proudly displaying the Langley crest, announcing her whereabouts to all. "I'll hire a hackney. Or walk." After all, St. James Park wasn't much more than a mile away.

"St. James Park?" Betsy squeaked. "Begging your pardon, but I cannot understand the urgency to travel to a location that's no place for an unaccompanied young lady such as yourself."

Drat, she hadn't really uttered the location aloud, had she? Yet by the way Betsy rushed to her side again and stared at her with brows raised in disbelief, it would seem Catherine had, in fact, managed this blunder.

She held her maid's gaze, abandoning her failing attempts at nonchalance and letting her desperation break through. "I must go, and undetected. Please do not ask me to explain the reason. Please."

She waited, preparing for further protests from the maid who had been her constant companion for close to a year now. However, Betsy merely nodded. "I'm going with you, though, my lady." She raised her hand, staying the protest that began forming on Catherine's lips. "I grew up in St. Giles and can hold my own. But it's for your safety, my lady, that I cannot let you go alone. Lord Kendrick would have my head if he knew I hadn't prevented you from taking such a risk. Indeed, my lady, couldn't you wait for his return and then—"

"You may accompany me." Catherine had no more time to argue the matter, not when three o'clock would arrive all too quickly. Besides, Betsy was correct about the dangers that lurked. She could pretend all she wanted that she was about to embark on a pleasant stroll through the park with someone who had long wished to meet her and would shower her with the fatherly affection she'd always lacked. It wouldn't change the truth: that she was about to travel to a location rife with debauchery to meet the man whose brief missive contained a subtle threat behind the words.

Her mind flashed to Philip, and for just a moment, she imagined doing as Betsy suggested and waiting for him so she could lay the unfortunate truth at his feet. He seemed to know how to handle any situation without getting so much as a hair out of place. Yet her face burned at the thought of him knowing her shame. He wasn't usually the type to be appalled by scandal, of that she felt certain. However, how could he help but be shocked to learn that his innocent wife—the earl's daughter whom he'd chosen to help him carry on the family line and prove himself a worthy heir— was really an illegitimate pretender?

The revelation could cause disgrace to fall upon them both, and she knew she couldn't share the contents of the letter. At least not yet. Presently, this conundrum belonged to her alone, and aside from some distant supervision from Betsy, she would face it unaided. She could only hope she possessed the wherewithal to manage it.

Chapter 16

Catherine stood beneath the sprawling branches of a mulberry tree, scanning the visitors to St. James Park from beneath her silk veil. A scattering of people strolled alongside the canal and atop the ornate bridge that stretched across it, all seemingly engrossed in their own affairs. Still, she could *sense* eyes upon her, just as before. She turned back to where Betsy remained on a bench near where the hackney had dropped them off, bent over as if engrossed by interesting wildflowers amongst the grass. In truth, Betsy had a kitchen knife tucked into her boot, "just in case," and she likely wanted to ensure it remained in place and ready for use. Catherine hadn't bothered mentioning that her predicament seemed an unlikely one to be resolved with the wielding of a weapon.

No doubt Betsy continued to keep an eye out for her, but Catherine felt certain that wasn't where her sense of being watched came from. She reached up to the plain straw bonnet she'd borrowed from Betsy, ensuring her shock of golden hair remained concealed beneath it, and ventured a step forward. When nothing happened, except for a gentle swishing as the breeze brushed through the dried leaves upon the ground, she took another step, and then another. All the while, she did her best to move gracefully and appear composed, but she couldn't stop her eyes from darting around wildly, on high alert for danger. Or whatever awaited her. She'd worn her plainest frock, a nondescript gray muslin left from her half-mourning period, but that didn't stop her from feeling as though she stuck out like a lantern in the dead of night. She adjusted her veil, as if that flimsy scrap of fabric could somehow protect her, and continued her search, looking for any sign of the person who sought her in return.

She knew him the instant he stepped out from behind the bright yellow pillar on the other side of the bridge. Not because they'd ever been formally introduced or even encountered each other in passing, for she was certain she'd never laid eyes upon him in her life. Rather, through some dark, sickening sense, she just *knew*. And despite her unremarkable clothing and concealed features, she could tell at once that he knew her too.

She shuffled toward him, her legs turning heavy, eying him as he started across the grass in her direction, looking to meet her partway. His clothes—the black leather breeches, the smartly cut black coat, the distinguished beaver hat—gave him the appearance of gentry, except that each garment had a look of wear and dishevelment to it. As for the man himself, while his tall, lean figure and even features suggested that he could have been handsome once, the years hadn't been kind to him. Deep grooves surrounded his mouth and eyes, his skin had taken on a sallow tinge, and the gray-streaked hair beneath his hat hung limp and unkempt.

"Good day, Lady Catherine. Rather, I should say Lady Kendrick. And perhaps before too long, Lady Langley." He greeted her in a pleasing voice, as naturally as if they were two old acquaintances who happened upon one another while out for a stroll.

Despite her need to study him further, just as a cornered animal stares at its hunter, she shifted her gaze back and forth, ever cognizant of the people meandering nearby.

"We cannot speak here," she hissed, reluctantly stepping closer to him as a pair of gentlemen crossed the bridge, passing right beside them. "I came here as you requested, but I will not stop and hold a private conversation where anybody could come by and hear."

"Of course." He flashed his yellowing teeth in a smile, the picture of agreeableness. "We can speak wherever you feel comfortable. Lead the way, and I will follow as your humble servant."

If his words were intended to reassure, they failed miserably. But what else could she do? Silently, she turned away from the bridge, crossing the grass toward a group of oak trees and slipping behind the trunk of one that still retained many of its leaves. The area sat deserted, just as required, but at least she could still spot Betsy in the distance.

Her fa—that *man*—halted beside her, also concealed behind the thick trunk. After scanning the area to confirm for himself that they remained unobserved, he inclined his head to her. "That's better. But let's not waste time. Shall I introduce myself? Or do you already know who I am?"

Her mind screamed at her to turn and run and not look back. Nothing required her to listen to another word he said, and perhaps she'd been wrong to put so much credence in his letter. After all, he could be half-crazed.

However, one unavoidable fact stopped her. She'd been told all her life how much she looked like her mother, and the people who made this statement weren't wrong. They merely overlooked one small detail. Georgina Adderley's portrait showed her eyes to be a bright, sparkling blue. Much like Edward's eyes. Not so different from the former earl's eyes, which also contained a blue tinge, only paler. Catherine, on the other hand, had deep brown eyes fringed with dark lashes. Just like the man who stood before her.

"I'm afraid I don't know your name." Somehow, she managed to speak despite the choking dryness in her throat.

"Forgive me." He lowered into a deep bow and tilted his hat, gestures bordering on ridiculous from the way he exaggerated them. "My name is Lawrence Holbeck, and I'm most pleased to meet you at last. Do you have any questions for me, Lady Kendrick? Daughter?"

She staggered backward, his final word hitting her as if he'd slapped her. Up to this point, a naive part of her, however small, had held on to the faintest shred of hope that it was all a nightmarish misunderstanding. Those two syllables brought the truth into glaring focus, robbing her of her ability to pretend.

Of course she had questions. Dozens of them. But how did one begin making inquiries about the matter that turned one's life on its head?

"Did you and my mother love each other?" Of all the thoughts whirling through her head, this silly, insignificant musing was the one that popped out.

He burst into laughter, a deep, resonating sound that sent her eyes flitting around, seeking any sign that he'd attracted notice. Fortunately, the area remained deserted. Under any other circumstances, her face would have heated, and she'd have dashed away after receiving such a response. Right now, she lacked the ability to move, and her face felt bloodless. Her whole body had turned to ice.

He cleared his throat, forcing back his chortle, but the smirk remained upon his lips. "Dear child, no. But we enjoyed each other's company nonetheless."

It didn't matter. All that signified now was deciphering the bare facts and the purpose of this meeting. She tried again. "Did you always know about me, or was this only a recent discovery?"

"Of course I always knew." He regarded her with a look that, in another, she might have considered affection. However, she didn't trust him nearly enough for that. "Many years ago, Georgina and I attended the same house party at a time when the earl was off on a separate hunting excursion. Not that they were ever seen together in any case. More's the pity for the earl, I would say. Georgina was such an enchanting, eager—"

"Never mind that." Catherine cut him off, not able to tolerate another second of the way this conversation was headed. "I only wish to know the reason for your sudden desire to become acquainted with me after all these years."

"I would hardly interfere when old Ashton was still alive." He widened his heavy-lidded eyes as if it were obvious. "I have more sense than to come between a possessive earl and what he views as his property. I thought of doing so when the new Ashton and the chit he wed to fill his accounts had you traipsing about London, but you were there for such a short time, and you were still little more than a girl. Now, matters are different. You did well to marry Kendrick, and while you may still be a child in many ways, in others, you are a very wealthy and powerful woman."

The insults he'd delivered to them all—her unknown mother, her beloved brother and sister-in-law, and Catherine herself—stung her to the quick, but she had no strength left to defend against them. Not when the truth of what he wanted had arrived to confront her. "So, this is a matter of money?"

He clutched his chest as though deeply wounded. "Can you not believe that I'm a faithful father seeking to know his dear long-lost daughter?"

"No." She wouldn't dignify his question with any response beyond that.

He chuckled again, a sound that grew increasingly more unpleasant as it flooded her ears. "I suppose even *you* are not that innocent. Very well. As a fourth son who didn't have the good fortune to work his way up to a title as your rakehell of a husband did, I find myself lacking in funds. My allowance is next to nothing, and certain ... entertainments in which a gentleman engages cause him to accrue debts. As your station has become elevated of late, and mine grows increasingly dire, I thought you could find it within your heart to assist your only surviving parent. I do not ask for much. A mere two hundred pounds."

She peered at him, forcing any trace of emotion away from her face, for he stood so close that he could likely make out her features through her veil. Meanwhile, her pulse raced as anger simmered deep within her. She recalled the day, several months after the earl's death, when Edward told her that their father—at least, the man she'd viewed as her father—had nearly bankrupted them with his careless gambling. Was it true that the man who stood before her—her actual father—had been reckless enough to do the same and now expected his stranger of a daughter to get him out of his bind? It was beyond bearing. Not to mention how he'd insulted Philip besides. Despite her best efforts, her lips tightened, and she felt her eyes narrow.

The man frowned at her in return. "Really, Catherine, I didn't view you as the sort to behave so ungenerously. Perhaps I should explain myself differently, then. As you can see, our meeting today has been discreet. You can return to Langley House with no one any the wiser for it, and in the eyes of the ton, you'll still be the Earl of Ashton's daughter, as has always been your station. With that said, as the daughter of a beautiful, voracious mother who openly disdained her husband, you shouldn't imagine yourself completely above rumors. I would hate to think that it could come to light, in a very public manner, that the rumors are indeed true and that the illusion you've clung to for so many years would suddenly be shattered. I doubt Lord Kendrick would be pleased to learn that he'd chosen a by-blow as his future marchioness. And as for the marquess, who I hear is in increasingly poor health after suffering numerous devastating misfortunes—well, this could be the blow that finishes him altogether. Two hundred pounds is but a small sum to rid yourself of that terrible possibility."

Catherine's hands began trembling, and she clenched them into fists, digging in her nails until she detected a warm trickle of blood against one palm. This man already viewed her as an innocent, easily manipulated girl. She refused to display additional signs of weakness before him.

However, he had her cornered, and he knew it. He threatened her with precisely what she'd married to avoid—a scandal—and now, her own reputation was far from the only thing at stake. After all they'd suffered, how could she tarnish Philip, the marquess, and the marchioness by bringing these awful rumors to their door?

Except they were no longer just rumors; now, they were truths.

Philip had wed her out of a sense of family duty, and despite his outward indifference and unwillingness to discuss the matter, she knew he wanted to be considered worthy of the title cast upon him. Having an illegitimate wife, who evoked scandalized whispers wherever she went, would be far from what he bargained for.

And worst of all … what if Holbeck was correct about the marquess? What if this damnable knowledge was enough to undo the small progress Lord Langley had made and hasten his final decline? That wasn't a risk she could take.

"Two hundred pounds." She uttered the amount out loud as she turned over the implications of it in her mind. It was no small sum, but neither was it an astronomical one. She didn't have that kind of money on her person, obviously, but if that's what it took …

"I trust you can wait two days while I make the necessary arrangements." The words made her sick, yet she had no choice but to speak them. "I'll have the payment delivered to you at the location of your choosing."

"Good girl."

The way his eyes lit up reminded her of her own when she'd seen herself smile in the mirror, and she clamped her arms tightly across her chest to keep from shuddering at the realization.

"However," he said, "I would like you to deliver the money to me. Here, at the same time as today."

"Is that really necessary?" For the first time that day, the magnitude of what she'd done fully hit her, and it took every shred of her remaining tenacity to prevent her from bolting and not looking back. Betsy had been correct all along: This was no place for a woman like her, and she certainly had no business cavorting with unsavory men. All the sights she'd observed before—the trees, the canal, the other patrons who sauntered in the distance—suddenly took on an air of menace until she wished she'd been like Betsy and concealed a knife in her shoe.

"Your personal delivery of the money? Yes." The man's expression turned cold. "Although if this location is objectionable to you, I suppose you could deliver it directly to my residence on Little Earl Street."

Little Earl Street? She pondered the unfamiliar name, trying to place it, until a flicker of recognition struck. "But that is in—"

"Seven Dials," he finished for her, "yes. I imagine you would find that location even more objectionable than this one. But suit yourself."

Indeed, as much as this meeting in St. James Park made her skin crawl, it was nothing compared to venturing into a notorious slum, a place to which she had never traveled but had heard whisperings of its nefariousness just the same.

"I will join you here, by this very tree, in two days' time," she conceded quickly. She had no time left to argue or question. She simply needed to leave. "I trust this concludes our meeting, and I'll bid you good day. Sir."

That earned her another half-smile, one that might have been almost charming under different circumstances, at some point in the past. "As you say. Good day. Daughter."

That word again, spoken so naturally, pushed her to her breaking point. She turned and sprinted across the grass, immune to the low notes of laughter that radiated from behind her. She didn't stop running until she'd made it across the leaf-covered grass and to the street, and even then, she kept up a brisk pace, not planning to stop until she'd reached Langley House in Berkeley Square.

"My lady!" Betsy called, her voice breathless as she dashed to catch up. Catherine slowed just long enough for Betsy to reach her side before continuing with her hurried steps.

"My lady," Betsy repeated, placing a hand against her heaving chest, "are you all right? You didn't look to be in any danger, although you had a face on you like you stood in a lion's den. What happened?"

Catherine swung her head in the lady's maid's direction. "Betsy, have you ever seen that man before?"

Betsy's brow creased before she shook her head. "I don't believe so. Although I can hardly think when we're walking this fast!"

"Very well." Despite how her brain screamed at her to keep going, she halted, clasping Betsy's palms in her own and peering imploringly into her flushed face. "Please, you must think carefully. Have you seen him anywhere at all during your time with me? Even just in passing on the street."

"I really cannot recall." For the first time, a hint of fear crept into Betsy's pale eyes. "Who is he, my lady?"

A valid question indeed. The man's name still echoed through Catherine's head: Holbeck. As he claimed to be a fourth son, perhaps she'd crossed paths with some of his relations at some event or another. But as she mulled over the plentiful list of acquaintances she'd amassed throughout the Season, she couldn't place anyone with that name. She would check Debrett's as soon as she returned home. Meanwhile, that wouldn't answer the question of what led a peer's son to blackmail his illegitimate daughter. If she wrote to Lady Bathurst or even Lady Langley, they might have information to impart on the man in question. But of course, she could never put the necessary words on paper without damning herself entirely. Besides, Lady Langley couldn't know too many details of the situation, for she would have never accepted Philip's choice of bride had she comprehended anything even approaching the truth.

"It is not important right now," she said, quickening her stride, immersing them once more amongst the pedestrians who meandered about the street. "We can discuss it another time. Meanwhile, you must say nothing of this encounter to another soul. Please."

That non-explanation was apt to leave Betsy burning with questions, but fortunately, she only nodded and then said nothing else, focusing her attention on keeping Catherine's pace.

Catherine gazed at her lady's maid a second longer in silent thanks before turning her attention to the street ahead, concentrating on how each footstep brought her closer to the safety of Langley House.

Nothing would feel better than retiring to her bedroom and awaiting Philip. Or better yet, maybe he had already re-turned home, and she could go to him directly and nestle herself in his warm, sturdy embrace. Even though nothing had been quite the same since their journey to London. Even though he concealed *something* from her, the signifi-cance of which she still hadn't ascertained. Even though she, too, now held a secret.

A moment in his arms would be enough to erase all that, at least temporarily. It would be enough to give her the strength to do what she needed to ensure nothing destroyed the unexpected happiness they'd found as husband and wife. If she could just get through the next couple of days, she could eliminate what threatened them, he could finish up with whatever sort of business matter he dealt with, and they would be free to return to the country and forget this unfortunate week had ever happened. And then, they would be happy once more.

Chapter 17

Philip ascended the stairs of Langley House two at a time, reining in his pace only when he reached the upstairs corridor that contained his bedroom. He'd arrived home later than anticipated that evening, expecting that Catherine would already be in the drawing room preparing to go in to dinner. Instead, Swift, the butler, had informed him that Lady Kendrick had retired to her bedroom with a megrim and was unexpected to come down. Therefore, despite his anxiousness to see her, Philip trod carefully across the uncovered floorboards as he approached their room. If she suffered a throbbing head, she surely wouldn't appreciate him clattering his boots down the corridor the way he'd done as a young boy. Well, before the illness had taken hold.

Their bedroom door was the third one on the right, and he pushed it open slowly, just in case she had gone to sleep. However, as the first crack of light from the room became visible, he could detect her sitting atop her vanity bench in the far corner, languidly running a brush through her unbound hair. She sat with her back turned to him, but her face reflected back to him in the vanity mirror, showing that she'd gone nearly as ashen as the drab gray dress she wore. Furthermore, her lips were pinched together, and her eyes had gone shiny, almost as if she'd been crying.

That was all it took for him to neglect his efforts at silence and shove open the door, crossing the room to her without another second's delay. "What's wrong, love? Is the pain very bad?"

"Philip!" She started to rise from her seat, but he placed his hands upon her shoulders, encouraging her to rest while he kneaded at the tight muscles. He leaned in to kiss the top of her head, the silkiness of her hair and the citrusy scent of her perfume reminding him just how much he'd missed her. And how much it ripped at his heart to see her in distress.

At least she relaxed backward into his touch, and a small smile crossed her lips. "It's nothing. Merely a head-ache."

"Is there anything you require? Have you taken head-ache powder?"

"I have, and I'm certain I'll be well soon. Thank you." She kept her tone light. However, that pained, unusual shin-iness didn't leave her eyes. Damn it, what if his actions had something to do with her distress? He should have insisted she stay back at Clifton Manor while he attended to matters in London. Or better yet, stayed back with her and found someone else to handle the whole thing. Hopefully, he could atone for his missteps now.

"Allow me." He motioned to the silver brush she still clasped in her fist, and wordlessly, she handed it over. He ran it across her scalp and over the curtain of hair, the locks shimmering like spun gold. She closed her eyes, and little by little, waves of tension seemed to exit her body.

"I have some good news," he said, keeping his voice soft. He didn't want to disrupt her revery, but at the same time, this was too important not to share. "I was later than anticipated returning home today, but that is only because I wanted to ensure the business matters were fully concluded. They are, for the time being, and we can depart London as soon as tomorrow. We can return to Clifton Manor if it pleases you. That is, if you don't mind residing under the same roof as my parents. Alternately, we could opt for Ravenfield in Norfolk, which is decidedly more rustic but would have the distinct advantage of affording us time alone."

He could almost close his eyes too and dream of having her to himself again, where nothing from the outside world would interrupt them. However, Catherine's eyelids flew open, and her troubled gaze returned to the mirror. "That sounds lovelier than anything. Only … I wish to stay in London a few more days."

"Do you?" He lowered the brush to the vanity, trying to keep perplexity from creasing his face. It would be inconvenient indeed if she developed a preference for London just as he'd grown to appreciate the merits of living away from the place. But based on her behavior of the past few days and the subtle rigidity with which she'd reverted to carrying herself, he had a hard time believing that was the case.

"I would like to go shopping. For a new ball gown or two. And hats. And shoes. And … and perhaps new drapery for my bedroom at Clifton Manor, if you have no objection."

Odd, she'd never expressed the slightest penchant for shopping before. Nor was she the sort who troubled herself with displaying the latest fashions. Nor did mention of the lengthy shopping excursion bring even a hint of joy to her countenance. But if that's what she said she desired, who was he to argue? "Whatever you wish, love."

"I shall require money."

He stared at her, for he felt certain he'd noticed her hands shaking as she delivered the request in a dull monotone. However, she quickly slipped them beneath her knees, the weight of her legs keeping them still. This situation was growing more peculiar by the minute. He racked his brain, trying to determine the reason for her discomfiture. Could it be related to the massive debts her father had accrued, which sent her and her brother to the brink of ruin? Fortunately, the marquess had no proclivities toward gambling that threatened the family fortune.

"You needn't worry," he assured her. "You will receive credit wherever you go, and I can settle the accounts later."

"Regardless"—she swallowed thickly, as if something unpleasant had caught in her throat—"I would like to have the money with me."

Over the past few weeks, he thought he'd begun to know his wife, but here she was, just as much an enigma as ever. What the hell was going on? A nauseated feeling washed over him as he considered that Catherine, despite her gentle innocence, deceived him in some way. Yet how could he dare complain when he kept secrets too?

"Take whatever you like," he muttered. "One hundred pounds. One thousand. Ten thousand. Name your price, and you shall have it."

"Thank you." Her lips twitched, presumably in an attempt to smile, but the expression turned to more of a pained grimace.

His bewilderment refused to be contained a second longer. "You can thank me, Catherine, by telling me what in God's name is the matter!"

"Nothing." She said the word adamantly, but her eyes glimmered even more brightly as if fresh tears threatened to fall. "Nothing. I'm just very, very … tired."

He reached out a hand to her, and she shifted to accept it, allowing him to help her to her feet. "You should rest," he said, leading her toward the bed, for amidst the tumult, that insignificant gesture was all he knew to offer right now. She drooped her weight against him, and he became aware of how heavy his own limbs had grown. The task of moving had turned so immense that as soon as he eased her onto the bed, he flopped himself down beside her.

He rolled to his side, pulling her toward him so her back rested against his chest. And while he momentarily tensed, uncertain of her reaction, she nestled herself into him more tightly, shaping her body to his as if they were one. She filled his senses—with her softness, her warmth, her scent—and for a fleeting moment, it was enough to make him forget everything else and simply lie with her in peace. However, her quickened breaths swiftly drew him back to reality.

He swept back the hair that covered her ear and brought his mouth next to it, keeping his voice just above a whisper. "You can tell me anything, you know."

He lingered there, silently willing her to trust him with whatever ran through her mind. Yet he'd made a discovery about Catherine, a fact that had become apparent since nearly the time of their first meeting. She didn't divulge her thoughts easily, and if she'd inwardly resolved to keep something concealed, no external force would convince her to do otherwise.

Which maybe he could accept, if only for the knowledge that her withdrawal into herself could have resulted from his own lack of openness. Once again, the truth of the reason for the trip to London swirled through his head, and he imagined it pouring from his mouth until every last detail was laid out in the open. Catherine was kindhearted, generous, and tolerant. Perhaps she wouldn't be angry. Perhaps she would even come to understand.

There would be no easier time to utter the words than here, now, when he leaned against her ear and nothing interrupted them. Except that his promise hadn't gone away, and those deathbed words would never leave him. *You must swear that no one else will ever know of this. Swear it, Philip, I beseech you.*

Blast it all. Why had he never possessed the foresight to think of his own future? To even consider that someday, he could turn into something more than just a careless rake who had only himself to trouble with. A wife had never been part of his trajectory, and certainly not a wife he cared for. Idiot that he was.

He sighed, releasing a stream of tension with his exhale, as inwardly, he pushed down the words he couldn't say. Still, he needed to at least make her understand one thing. "I just want you to be happy, love. With me, if I may be so lucky. But without me, if that's what it takes."

She flipped her body toward him, cupping his face in her slender fingers. "Please believe me when I say I want your happiness too. Rather, *our* happiness, together. And I would do anything to achieve it."

He kept himself perfectly still, absorbing the warmth from her touch. Many things remained unspoken between them; that much was clear. After the years he'd spent concentrating solely on the physical, he was the last person equipped to navigate the intricacies of an emotional bond. His heart thumped rapidly, raw and full and aching. And by the way she gripped his jaw and gazed at him, with her eyes wide and intent, he had to believe that some depth of feeling existed within her as well.

***

This time, Catherine arrived at St. James Park alone. The shame of what she did prevented her from disclosing the meeting even to Betsy, and she'd slipped out the front door of Langley House, adorned in her gray dress and veil, without uttering a word to anyone.

Worst of all had been her early morning conversation with Philip, who had offered to join her on her shopping trip if for no other purpose than to hold her parcels for her. Telling him she'd rather shop unaccompanied had sent an ache radiating through her body, despite how he'd brushed off her refusal with a smile and opted to go riding in Hyde Park instead.

Throughout her life, she'd always striven to act with honesty, and now she was a deceiver. But she did this for them. For him. So she could remain the wife he and his family needed her to be.

The clouds above threatened rain, which gave the park the advantage of having fewer patrons than the day before. The man was still there, though, in the same worn black attire, waiting behind the tree trunk they'd agreed upon. She'd looked up his family name and discovered him to be the youngest brother of the Viscount Allandale. Not that this knowledge signified much when she'd never so much as heard tell of the viscount. But that hardly mattered either. Not when she was about to cut off all association with the youngest Holbeck and would hopefully have no cause to encounter his relations either.

She hurried up to him, continuing to clutch the weighty reticule concealed beneath her thick woolen pelisse in a death grip. It was just as well to rid herself of this unwanted burden and get the unpleasantness over with.

Holbeck flashed her an affectionate yet dangerous smile, and he began to bow to her. However, she hadn't the patience for any of that. "Here." She cast the unwanted reticule into his hands before he'd even raised his head. "I've done just as you asked, and you will now have the means to repay your debts. As such, I can see no further benefit of an association between us. I bid you good day."

She spun away from him, not caring if he laughed at her this time as she fled from the park, but his hand shot out, grasping her firmly by the arm. She startled at the unexpected contact, his fingers caustic against her despite the layers of fabric that separated his skin from hers.

"Where are your manners, Catherine?" He spoke pleasantly enough, but his dark eyes had turned hard, inviting no argument or protest. "It's exceptionally bad form to treat your only surviving parent in such a way, rushing off with scarcely a greeting."

The bitter taste of bile stung her throat while her mouth grew so dry that she could barely manage to swallow it away. Her steadfastness hung by a fragile thread, and she needed to leave before the last of the frayed remnants snapped.

"I didn't see the point." She poured everything she had left into holding his gaze and keeping her voice from shaking, but even with her best attempts, her words came out as little more than a whisper. "We needn't pretend that you came to me out of affection. We had an arrangement, and now that I've fulfilled my share in it, surely you can see the necessity of us parting ways. Please, you must."

She bit her lip, choking back the sob that threatened to emerge. She'd begun this brief meeting considering herself in control, a woman taking care of an unfortunate situation so she could put it behind her. But he still gripped her arm, and her illusion of composure started to crumble, giving way to flickers of panic.

"I'm indeed pleased with your compliance, daughter." He gave her arm a gentle pat before swiftly retightening his grasp. "Only, I've been thinking. I do not believe two hundred pounds will suffice in covering my debts after all. Which leads me to another consideration. I may be better off leaving England and journeying to the Continent, leaving my debts behind. There is little here that binds me. I imagine that scenario would please you as well, given how disagreeable you seem to find our acquaintanceship. Of course, I would require quite an increase in funds to successfully execute this plan, but that shouldn't cause an issue for the future Marchioness of Langley. In fact, it would be a small price to pay, would it not?"

She cast her eyes downward, certain that her expressionless mask had turned to a look of pure horror, obvious even beneath her veil. He may as well have kicked her to the ground for the way his demand knocked the air out of her, leaving the world spinning about her in a nauseating haze. For she had just proven everything he believed of her to be true. She was an innocent, naive fool.

Why hadn't she possessed the foresight to realize that he wouldn't stop with one basic demand? Why would he, when she blatantly displayed how easily she could be manipulated? He could rest secure in the knowledge that his continued silence, or better yet, his disappearance, was worth any price to her.

"I do not expect you to deliver the funds so quickly on the next occasion," he said, inclining his head as if he offered her a generous concession. "While I would like to receive payment as quickly as possible, I understand that you may need to arrange for an augmentation in your allowance, or perhaps you have jewels to be sold. I can wait several days, even, if need be. By that time, I trust you will have secured a sufficient amount. Shall we say three thousand pounds?"

Catherine's head refused to turn upward, and her throat felt far too parched for speech. Yet she had to say something, if for no other reason than to free herself from his scathing grip.

"There is no need to delay," she mumbled, unable to control how the words wavered. "I will meet you again to-morrow."

For a long moment, she could feel his scrutinizing gaze upon her until, at last, he gave a brusque nod, seemingly satisfied. "Very well. Should you encounter any difficulties with our arrangement, you need only send a note to my lodgings on Little Earl Street. And likewise, though I do not often mingle in society these days, I still roam about the fashionable parts of London, even if I may not always be in view. Rest assured that whenever you are ready to see me, I'll never be far away."

Spoken under different circumstances, by a different man, these last words would have been ones of affection.

Instead, they resonated through her head as the worst kind of threat. He watched her. He knew far more about her doings than she likely even realized. He gave her no escape. Horror threatened to consume her, except suddenly, his hand lifted from her arm, and she staggered backward, at least free from his physical clutches.

He bowed to her in that overexaggerated manner of his as if they were two old friends parting ways after spending a pleasant afternoon in each other's company. "Good day, Lady Kendrick."

She had nothing to give him in return—no words, no gestures—but nor could she make the hasty retreat she so craved. Her legs had grown far too heavy for that, and her thoughts weighed her down too, swirling about her head in an anguished flurry.

Somehow, she mustered the strength to pivot away from him, pushing back the dread that threatened to take over and concentrating only on placing one foot in front of the other. Whether he stayed to watch her retreat, or laughed at her, or made his own departure, she had no idea. She focused only on walking.

She made it as far as the edge of the trees before the truth of what had transpired flooded her mind once more. As much as she wished she could turn her thoughts off and force her legs to carry her back to Langley House, where she would begin preparing for her journey with Philip back to the country, she couldn't do that now. Not with everything she'd believed lying in shambles at her feet. Instead, she crossed over to the north side of the park, wandering aimlessly across the near-vacant expanse of grass and trees as she attempted to make sense of her new reality.

She could give Holbeck the money if that's what it came down to. Philip wouldn't deny her request for more; he'd made that much clear. He hadn't even questioned her, though her ability to prevaricate effectively was dubious at best. He believed in her. He wanted to make her happy. *Name your price, and you shall have it.* A high-pitched sob escaped her at the reminder of her deception. The only thing that had made it tolerable was her conviction that one untruth would buy them a lifetime of joy. That childish belief had now vanished.

Yes, she could hand over the three thousand pounds, but then what? The sum was hardly enough for a man formerly of means to establish himself in a foreign land. He pushed her little by little, seeing how much money he could extricate, but there would always be a next time, of that she felt certain. Perhaps he didn't truly mean to leave England after all. Indeed, it would be far more profitable for him to stay in the place where his silence held value. Where he had a means of receiving payment whenever he felt the whim for more.

The cycle would continue for as long as they both lived, as meanwhile, her relationship with Philip turned into lie after lie until the connection they'd built eroded away, and nothing remained but her deceit. That was a fate even worse than the revelation of her shameful truth.

A few heavy raindrops splashed upon her pelisse, and she clutched her arms tightly around herself as if that would offer her protection from everything. From the weather. From the tears that threatened to flow down her cheeks and mix with the increasing stream of rain. From the truth.

A child's gleeful shriek piercing the air was the only thing that stopped her total descent into misery. She turned her head in the direction of the noise, watching as a man swept a tiny dark-haired girl into his arms, eliciting further giggles from her as he rose his greatcoat above her head to shelter her from the rain. He walked briskly, keeping his face turned toward the little girl so they could chatter to one another as he strode in the direction of Pall Mall.

Through her haze of shock and despondency, glints of recognition flashed in her brain. There was something about the man's deep green greatcoat. And his polished Hessians. And the top hat that rested on a head of thick, dark hair that lightly curled at the back of his neck. For that matter, there was something about the girl too. The shape of her eyes. The particular brown shade of her hair.

And though Catherine wouldn't have thought it possible to contain any more, a fresh jolt of uneasiness surged through her. Surely, it wasn't him. No, it couldn't be. Impossible …

Her previous shock made her skills of deduction slow; nonetheless, the truth of what she saw could only stare her in the face for so long before she recognized it. And in case that wasn't enough to make her realize the significance of the sight she beheld, the man paused and raised his head for just an instant before crossing the street, providing her with a fleeting glimpse of his features before he continued on his way.

She took a few hurried steps in his direction before halting. There was little use in catching up to him when she could never reveal herself. Could she? What would she say? Did she still possess the ability to speak? Once more, the world spun around her at a dizzying pace until nothing made sense.

But suddenly, she no longer needed to ponder what to do. A young woman, mostly concealed by a thick brown cloak, rounded a corner across the street and raised her hand in a wave before rushing toward the man and girl. The woman reached them quickly, and the three of them hurried off together to seek shelter from the rain, effectively ending any thoughts Catherine had of a confrontation. There was no need. All had become clear to her now.

She staggered to the nearest tree, leaning her weight against the trunk before her knees had a chance to buckle and cast her to the ground. Holbeck had shaken her to the core, debasing her so thoroughly she would have thought it impossible to sink any lower. Oh, but she'd been wrong. For the second time that day, reality swept down and crushed her, stealing everything she believed, leaving her tangled and broken.

She wished she could believe this was just an ominous daydream, the product of her despairing, panic-stricken mind. However, although they were far in the distance now, the figures of the man, woman, and child remained within her view for a moment longer before they slipped away onto a side street. And though her final sight of them was but brief, it was long enough to certify the painful truth she'd noticed but couldn't seem to fathom.

The man was Philip, carrying a child in his arms who looked just like him.

Chapter 18

Catherine thought of finding a horse and riding through the rain all the way back to Highfield Park. She thought of getting aboard the mail coach and journeying to the far reaches of Devonshire, where Lavinia and Lady Bathurst would take her in. She even considered roaming around the streets of London indefinitely, waiting for night to fall and allowing it to do with her what it would. But since none of those options seemed particularly feasible, she made her way back to Langley House.

No sooner had she stepped through the front door and removed her soaked pelisse than Betsy emerged from the corridor, her face awash with worry.

"My lady!" Betsy strode over to her as quickly as propriety allowed, eying Swift, who, having welcomed his mistress home, was still making a slow retreat from the entrance hall. She lowered her voice to a fervent whisper. "Oh, I've been beside myself. Everyone said you'd gone shopping, but you didn't take the carriage, and you told me nothing of your plans. Not that you're obliged to say a word, but I kept thinking of that man in the park, and I didn't know if something had gone wrong. I did as you asked and kept your secret, but if harm befell you because of that, I would never forgive myself. Please tell me you're all right, my lady. Did something happen?"

How could she even answer that question? Tell Betsy she was forced to choose between conceding to endless blackmail or bringing shame upon those she cared for, and that her life with Philip had become a lie?

As the truth was an impossibility right now, she merely shook her head. "I'm well." It seemed she remembered how to speak after all, although her tone came out quiet and pinched. "I apologize for making you fret."

Her words did nothing to remove the worried crease between Betsy's brows. "You're soaked through, my lady, and shivering. Let me help you out of those wet things and then arrange for a bath."

"No," she insisted at once, for though the entrance hall was airy and Betsy's voice gentle, the space began to close in on her while the whisper singed at her ears. She needed to go to her room without delay. Alone.

"No," she repeated, already moving toward the stairs, "thank you. I'll see to it myself and will ring when I'm ready for assistance. If you wish to help, please see that I'm not disturbed. By anyone."

"But my lady—" Betsy started to protest. However, Catherine was already halfway up the stairs, her legs sprinting in a sudden burst of energy born of her immense need to conceal herself from everyone and everything. She ran down the corridor, pulling at the hairpins that stabbed into her skull, letting her damp locks fly free. She just needed to be by herself, to sit before the fire in silence for an hour or two and ponder what next steps she should take.

She burst through the door of her room, letting out the breath she'd been holding and putting her hands to her knees as she sucked in desperate mouthfuls of air. And then, she froze.

Philip stood by the fire, seemingly in the process of getting redressed, for wet garments lay in a pile by his feet, and he wore only a pair of tan trousers. She hadn't accounted for that possibility. Given her discovery, she'd thought that this "business matter" would keep him away from home for hours yet, giving her uninterrupted time to think.

"Catherine, love!" He cast aside the shirt he'd been about to pull on and rushed over to her, glancing from the wet mats of her hair to the sodden material of her skirts. "Why didn't you take the coach? You would have saved yourself a great deal of discomfort. Not to mention, how did you carry home all your purchases?"

It was funny, really, how his voice made him sound just like the Philip she'd always known. He looked like the same Philip too, with his dark hair tousled upon his head and his gray eyes intent. In fact, having him next to her in a state of undress, displaying the taut outlines of abdominal muscles against his lean form and filling her nose with his masculine scent, caused the usual flutter low in her belly.

Outwardly, nothing had changed. But inwardly—it had all disintegrated into a pile of rubble. She'd let the guilt of her deception consume her as, meanwhile, he'd deceived her right back. Philip didn't have a business matter. He had a child.

Perhaps she should have suspected as much. After all, children were hardly an uncommon result of the activities of a flagrant rake. That in itself wasn't the problem. She had come to terms with his past. She could have come to terms with a child too, under the right circumstances, for if anyone was equipped to feel empathy for the plight of a by-blow, it was her.

What she couldn't accept was the duplicity of it all. The days she'd spent thinking they grew closer, that their relationship had become something real, while in reality, he kept this secret, never intending to fully allow her in.

She quickly straightened herself to her full height, pushing her back against the wall for support. And distance. "I didn't make any purchases after all." Her low voice echoed through the room in its usual tone, even though she would never be the same person again.

"Unfortunate, when you wished to stay in London for the purposes of shopping." He continued to stare at her, and her cheeks threatened to burn beneath his scrutiny. Fortunately, he gave his head an abrupt shake. "But no matter. Come by the fire and take off your wet things."

She gave a passing glance to his outstretched hand before crossing her arms across her chest and strolling to the fireside without him. The warmth seeped through her wet clothing, giving her a brief moment of comfort.

"Allow me?" Unnerved by her rebuttal, Philip followed close behind her, motioning to the row of buttons at her back.

Perhaps this was to become a trend, him assisting her with buttons when she least wanted the help. But the alternative—remaining in her soaked dress—would only add to her despondency. She shifted slightly, allowing him full access to her back, and he set to work with his usual nimbleness.

Blast it, why did those little flicks of his fingers, barely perceptible through the fabric, have to shake her so deeply? His touch seared her skin, bringing memories of pleasure, leaving her craving more. He reached the bottom of the row of buttons and brought his hands upward, beginning to push away the fabric at her shoulders.

"No." She spun away from him, clutching the dress tightly against herself. "That is, thank you. I can manage from here."

"Catherine …" He spoke her name barely above a whisper, that lone word containing so many notes. Bewilderment. Exasperation. Maybe even a hint of dejection. This was one of those rare moments when he didn't have all the answers. She could almost take pity on him. Except …

She hadn't only seen him with his child. She'd also seen him with a woman. The child's mother? Her hands started to tremble as she pushed down the wet, gray lump of a dress, for possibilities began floating through her mind that she hadn't yet allowed to flourish. Did he conceal the child's existence from her because he didn't want her to know about the woman? Did he see the woman often? Did he care for her? Did they still—

"Catherine," he said again, stronger this time. "Whatever the hell is going on, I've had enough. Why will you not speak to me? Why—"

She stepped forward, placing a lone finger to his lips. She couldn't endure his questions right now. Not when he was the one who deserved to be interrogated. She thought back to their evening beneath Lord Wellesley's desk and the way her hand had connected with his cheek in an indignant slap, and she briefly wondered if doing so again would bring her any measure of relief or satisfaction. However, the thought left her hollow. Instead, she brushed her finger along his upper lip, letting it trail to the rough surface of his jaw. She'd done this at the Wellesleys' too, tracing her fingers over him, discovering the contours of his face. Every angle was familiar to her now, and not just of his face but of his body as well. She ran her finger along the throbbing pulse point of his neck and toward his chest, the hard warmth of him luring her in, inviting her to take more.

She should hate him. She should shun him. But the feeling of heat and need that pooled between her legs whenever they were alone together hadn't learned to abate. She forced the wrenching memory of him walking side by side with the woman back to the forefront, and her chest constricted, her lungs feeling like they had filled with acid. However, that still wasn't enough to douse her yearning. Rather, jealousy fed it like kindling upon a fire. She wanted him to forget the existence of all other women. She wanted to be enough.

Before her mind had a chance to consent, her lips crushed against his. This was madness—insanity—that she should pull away from immediately, but he returned the pressure to her lips, running his tongue along them in a familiar, intoxicating caress, and she was helpless to do anything but remain in the kiss.

His tongue slid between her parted lips, connecting with hers, and she swirled it against him until a low groan emerged from his throat. He even tasted the same as always, despite the many truths that should have crossed his lips but he'd decided to keep hidden.

He pulled her against him, one hand kneading the fabric that clung to her bottom while the other flew to the ribbon of her shift. The sudden movement was enough to break the spell, and she wrenched herself free of his grip, holding the shift tightly in place, although the wet garment did nothing to conceal her.

"No." She glared at him, trying to contain the rapid rising and falling of her chest. Her skin was on fire, aching to be free of the shift and feel his touch on every surface. However, the day's events had already robbed her of every aspect of control, and she refused to cede it again now. She would do this on her terms and her terms only.

"No," she repeated, taking another step backward. "You may not touch me. Not unless I give my express permission."

Philip's mouth hung agape a moment before he pinched it closed, his eyes narrowing. "What is it you want, Catherine?"

She wanted to turn back time so this day had never happened, for ignorance had to be preferable to the ache that swelled inside her. She wanted to believe in the way he cared for her as a wife. She wanted to see the familiar look of desire upon his face as if he couldn't live without her. She wanted to immerse herself in pleasure until the pain ceased to exist. She wanted …

"I want you," she answered truthfully.

"Then why—"

She jerked backward as he reached for her again. "That changes nothing about what I just said."

They eyed each other in silence, neither of them daring to look away or to scarcely breathe. If she'd driven him to a state of frustration, so much the better. Suddenly, though, he ran a hand through his hair, pushing a stray lock away from his forehead in a gesture of nonchalance. "Very well. Do what you will, then. I won't move a muscle without your command."

"Good." Perhaps she sounded childish and spiteful. It didn't matter, as long as she held his attention and compliance. In her own best show of indifference, she ran her fingers over the ribbon of her shift, undoing the knot with one gentle pull. With another tug, she lowered the garment down her body, wriggling her hips until the damp, flimsy fabric slipped to the carpet and all that remained upon her was a pair of silk stockings.

She had never stood before him like this, naked in broad daylight while he remained clothed. She wouldn't have thought she possessed that level of boldness. However, his sharp intake of breath vanquished any feelings of inhibition that threatened to rise within her. She'd captivated him, just as she intended.

She sauntered past him, allowing her body to brush against the arousal tenting his trousers as she went. He made a low sound, almost like a growl, and she didn't need to look behind her to know he watched her every step of the way. She stopped at the side of the bed, her pulse growing increasingly rapid, and placed her hand upon the bedpost. She tried to make it a casual gesture. In truth, she required the support.

"You may join me." She spoke quietly, without turning back to him. Perhaps it would be better if he *didn't* hear her. Philip, though, was far too astute for that and appeared at her side in an instant. True to his word, he didn't touch her. He was so close though, his heat radiating onto her until her skin tingled. And since they'd come this far … "You may undress," she added, not daring to look at him.

She heard the quiet rustling of his buttons, detected the movement of his trousers as they dropped to the floor in a heap. And then, she whipped her head in his direction, unable to divert her eyes any longer. Nor could she suppress the sharp gasp that betrayed how greatly he affected her and how control of the situation slipped from her fingers.

Maybe, distracted by his increasing desire, he hadn't noticed. His pupils had grown so large that his eyes looked nearly black, glimmering with the look of all-consuming yearning that she'd come to recognize. The way his mouth twitched, though, with the tiniest hint of a wicked grin, suggested he *had*, in fact, heard her.

She clenched her muscles against the fire that burned through them, fighting to maintain composure, at least for a little longer. "You may lie down."

He obeyed her again without hesitation, reclining his lean, contoured form across the counterpane like a gift that was hers for the taking. A gift rather like the forbidden fruit in the Garden of Eden: one she should know better than to accept but too tempting to deny. His skin, practically glowing beneath the light flickering from the grate, begged to be caressed. She'd forbidden him to touch her but had made no such stipulation about touching him in return.

She knelt on the bed beside him and placed her hand on him tentatively, at the spot on his chest where she'd last left off. She shifted it to the left until it lingered above the rapid thudding of his heart. It would seem his body betrayed him as well, exposing his air of equanimity as nothing but a facade. Good.

She continued her journey downward, across the hard ridges of his stomach, over the sprinkling of hair that started below his navel. And then, giving him a warning glance to ensure his hands stayed firmly planted at his sides, she glided her fingers over his jutting arousal.

He drew in a harsh breath, his hands balling into fists against the counterpane.

Encouraged, she continued her exploration, encircling her fingers around him in a light grasp and sliding them back and forth along the rigid length of him. He *felt* the same as always too, the tantalizing combination of silk against steel. And he continued to gaze at her through heavy eyelids with the same look of intense need, as if she held the key to his existence.

Her blood had turned to fire, her body throbbing with unfulfilled longing, and she tightened her grip on him in response, intensifying the speed of her strokes.

He jerked beneath the power of her touch, his eyes widening into two dark pools of desire. "Christ, Catherine. If you do not cease, I'm going to—"

She could stand it no longer. Tearing her hand away, she swung her leg over him so his thighs were captured between hers, and her aching, heated sex brushed the tip of his arousal. That whisper of a touch was enough to consume her final shred of restraint. In one swift motion, she sank down onto him, her moan mixing with his as, at last, she gave in to the desire ripping through her. She raised herself back up, and this time when she came down, he thrust his hips against her, causing their bodies to connect at just the right angle.

They developed a frenzied pace, the tightness of Philip's features suggesting that he struggled to maintain his grip on sanity. This was exactly what she wanted. To feel their bodies consumed in each other. To experience pleasure so deep that it took everything else away, at least for a time. Then again, even time ceased to exist when she was with him like this. All that remained was the pleasure, along with her burgeoning need.

"You may ... touch me," she panted, unable to stop herself from reaching for his arm. She'd taken control and held him at a distance for long enough. None of that mattered now. Her yearning for his skilled touch overtook all reason.

He groaned as his hands connected with her skin, as if he, too, had finally been granted permission to consume a tempting but forbidden fruit. He knew exactly where to place his fingers, gliding them up her thigh, teasing the folds of her sex before finally hitting the sensitive peak that craved his touch.

She cried out, plunging down on him in a powerful motion that caused her to shatter. As the violent waves of pleasure consumed her, Philip began spasming within her, taken by his own release. From within her haze of bliss, she could detect him call a throaty version of her name and plant his hands firmly against her back, guiding her down to lie against his chest. She let her depleted body drop, nuzzling her face into his neck as the aftershocks of release pulsed through them both. She could stay like this forever, joined with him, her limbs boneless, her thoughts floating in a sated trance.

Yet with each passing moment, a little more of the euphoric fog melted away, bringing the real world back into far too sharp focus. Suddenly, the pleasant fluttering low in her belly turned to a feeling more like dread, and her weightless legs became leaden. Worst of all, his arms no longer held her in a comforting embrace. They confined her, forcing her to stay and remember all she had misbelieved and all she had lost.

In a burst of force, she rolled free of him, clawing her way to the edge of the bed. She couldn't lie here anymore. She never should have done so in the first place, for with the pleasure now dissipated, the pain that wracked her became all the more acute.

"Catherine!" Philip scrambled into a sitting position and peered over her, his face a mixture of confusion and alarm. "Are you well? What's the matter?"

Her eyes connected with his just long enough to detect a trace of something else developing in his expression: hurt. The knife in her chest twisted, and for just an instant, she pictured throwing herself back into his arms. But no, she couldn't. She had to get away.

She jumped from the bed and rushed to the fireside to retrieve her discarded shift. The warmth from the flames had dried it, mostly, and she thrust it over her head, desperate for concealment. She eyed the blob of rumpled gray muslin still on the floor, wondering if the dress was salvageable, at least to the point of making her presentable enough to run from the room.

"Devil take it!" Philip's sharp voice, made especially noticeable because of the uncharacteristic way it wavered, cut through her thoughts. He'd leaped from the bed and gathered his trousers, and he now loomed beside her in front of the fire, snatching up the shirt he'd previously been interrupted from putting on. "I've come to accept, even to enjoy, at times, the mystery you present to me. This, however, is beyond bearing. I may be a fool, but I'm not blind altogether. Why are you acting this way? Have I done something to offend you? Whatever it is, you need to speak to me! Tell the truth, Catherine, so I can attempt to remedy matters. But damn it, whatever you do, do *not* run from me."

How dare he make demands of her? He had no right to besiege her with questions when *he* was the one who had much to answer for. Very well, then. Though her head pounded and every inch of her skin prickled, awash with perturbed energy, she would stay and do exactly as he asked. *Then* she would see if he still felt so demanding.

She hadn't yet learned to yell in anger as her father—or at least, the former Earl of Ashton—used to do. Instead, she spoke in an even monotone, her gaze fixing on him, boring into him as if she could see right to the part where he kept his innermost secrets, so it would be futile for him to lie.

"Why did you not tell me you have a child?"

Chapter 19

Ever since the moment when that blasted letter had arrived from London and infiltrated the sanctuary he'd discovered with his wife at Clifton Manor, Philip's circumstances had been on a steady decline. But standing before Catherine's scrutinizing glower, absorbing the fury she radiated after asking the question he least expected to hear, delivered him to a new level of hell.

He opened his mouth and then swiftly closed it. How was he supposed to go about answering a question that brought forth a torrent of regret and forever altered the course of his life? He could request that she explain herself further, for indeed, inquiries as to the source of her question reverberated through his head. However, that would accomplish little. Through whatever means, Catherine knew what she knew, and there was no purpose to stalling or pretending otherwise.

As if sensing what poured through his mind, Catherine gave her head a barely perceptible shake, a look of warning flashing in her eyes. "If you are trying to invent some falsehood to placate me, you needn't bother. As it happens, I was in St. James Park today. A fact you clearly didn't anticipate, or I imagine you would have behaved with more discretion. In any case, you did not, and I *saw* you." She spat the last words at him, her voice on the verge of breaking.

He could have laughed at the irony of it, were the world not crumbling around him. For the past year and a half, while attending to family "business matters," he'd crept about London like a bandit, always looking over his shoulder for sources of detection. At the same time, he'd accepted it as a possibility, and though not ideal, recognition wouldn't have been deleterious. Not when anyone who knew him would have come to the same conclusion as Catherine and, given his reputation, likely thought little of it. Except, through some stroke of luck, no one *had* seen him, at least to the best of his knowledge. Not until today. Not until he'd been discovered by one of the few people who couldn't brush the knowledge away as something of little import. His wife.

He smoothed the shirt he'd hastily thrown over his head, trying to maintain his grip on the man he'd once been, the one who could make it appear as though he was unafflicted by any manner of difficulties. "You seem to have a talent for catching me in inopportune moments."

Whatever he should have said in that moment, these words were the exact opposite. Her eyes blazed, maintaining their hold with his for another moment before she abruptly bent down to grab the dress she'd cast to the floor. She shook it out, attempting to pull the wet, wrinkled fabric over her head as she strode across the room.

"Wait," he muttered faintly, although that didn't garner him so much as a second glance. She was far too focused on pulling her dress closed so she could march out of the room.

Damn it all, how could he make her understand that he'd issued a promise? That he'd sworn never to tell … Yet here she was, filled with hurt and anger that he'd been responsible for putting there, stalking away from him, reaching for the door handle—

"The child is not mine."

Catherine froze, her hand hanging in midair, until very slowly she turned back to face in his direction. "What?"

Now he was the one frozen in place, unable to form additional words. He'd just uttered the very thing he'd made a deathbed vow never to reveal. The one secret that, despite his many failings—his inferiority, his carelessness, his depravity—he'd treated as a matter of vital importance, concealing it at all costs. For it was the one time in his life anyone had entrusted something into his care, and though Charles might have done so out of delirium and desperation, Philip had refused to let him down.

He'd tried his best. He'd tried so bloody hard. However, losing Catherine was too great a price.

She neglected her wet dress once more, letting the loosely buttoned garment drop to the floor as she started back across the room, her face pale and drawn tight. She seated herself on the edge of the bed in a stiff motion, smoothing the counterpane beside her that was rumpled from their lovemaking. "You had best come and sit. I believe a lengthy explanation is in order."

So it was, despite how the weight of his broken promise threatened to crush him. He went to her, accepting the proffered seat on the bed, careful not to let any part of himself connect with her tense body. She parted her lips slightly, a

barrage of questions flickering across her face, but ultimately, she said nothing. Instead, she merely set her eyes on
his again, waiting.

This was his last chance to shove the remainder of the
secret away, untold. However, he had already come this far
with it. Catherine deserved nothing less than the truth.

"The child—Eleanor …" He paused, imagining the little girl's dark curls and delighted giggles. He brushed the
memory away with a brisk shake of his head and cleared his
throat. There was no point in delaying matters further. "The
child belongs to Charles."

"Charles …" Catherine let out a tiny gasp, her eyes
growing wide. "You mean your … your brother?"

"Yes."

There it was, the truth laid out plainly before her. The
enormity of betraying his promise to his dead brother still
rested heavily on his shoulders. But counteracting that was
a lightness that came from finally setting the knowledge free,
where it could no longer drive a wedge between them.

"But …" Catherine trailed off, her struggle to compose
her thoughts written plainly across her face. She took a deep,
steadying breath. "Why would you not have just told me this
to begin with? Did you think me too delicate to hear tell of
an illegitimate child? Because I assure you, I am not."

He reached for her hand, and surprisingly, she didn't
push it away. He stroked the soft lengths of her fingers, letting the feel of her ground him. "I know far better than to

underestimate you. The truth is that—at Charles's request—no one knows."

"Surely the marquess and marchioness must—"

"No one," he repeated. "Even *I* did not know until Charles's fever began to take hold, and he summoned me to his bedside. He had never asked me for anything before, but in this, he was most adamant. He had fathered a child, close to two years prior, who needed to be provided for, though her existence could never be revealed."

Catherine's hand twitched beneath his, her fingers burrowing into the counterpane. "I understand the need for discretion in such matters. However, why such absolute secrecy? Especially now. I hope you know me well enough to realize I'm not a thoughtless gossip. Likewise, given all they have lost, do you not think your parents deserve the knowledge that a small piece of their eldest son remains? Even if through unconventional means."

"Of course not!" An image of his brother's face, grown dark with revulsion, flashed through his mind. "All that would accomplish is shattering the illusion, the very thing Charles didn't want. It's why I agreed to claim Eleanor as mine, if it came down to it, rather than reveal her as the by-blow of Charles and some Vauxhall dancer who took his fancy. You're my *wife*, Catherine, and I refused to tell you that lie. But you must see why no one else can learn the truth, especially my parents. They already lost their exalted heir, their perfect son. Why, at this stage, lead them to believe he was anything less than that? Better to let the matter

rest with the son who has already proven himself a reprobate. Even though, I should perhaps add, I have always
taken precautions in an area where Charles seemingly did
not."

"Stop this!" Catherine's hand tensed, and suddenly she
was gripping him, her nails digging into his wrist. "I'm tired
of hearing about your inferiority to your brothers. Being
struck by illness did not render you less than them, and
though you may have tried to prove this belief you hold true
by performing any number of salacious deeds, that still does
not make it so. You may pretend all you want that you're
nothing but a scoundrel and have society whispering the
same, but I know better. Furthermore, though I sadly lacked
the opportunity to know either of your brothers, of one fact,
I am quite certain. They may have been valiant, proper gentlemen, but they still had flaws, just the same as you. Just the
same as anyone."

Philip stared at his wife, trying to grasp the meaning
behind her uncharacteristic outburst. A nagging voice within
him suggested that spurts of truth existed behind her words
if he cared to examine them further. However, he was in no
position to explore that possibility right now.

Catherine's gaze continued to pierce him as she awaited
his response, but after another moment of silence passed
between them, she merely sighed, her grip on his arm loos-
ening. "The woman who was with you today …"

"Eleanor's caretaker," he answered quickly, not wanting to allow the opportunity for misinterpretation as her

words faltered. "A widowed, childless cousin of her mother, who was carried off by fever several months prior to Charles."

"How sad." Catherine's face took on a faraway expression. "The poor little girl."

"Yes," he agreed, startled by the appearance of tears welling in her eyes. Given that the past few years had consisted of one tragedy after another, he supposed he'd never fully allowed himself to consider the gravity of it all. "But despite any misgivings I may have about her, she has kept Eleanor in good health and spirits, and for that, I am grateful."

"What sort of misgivings?" While he had intended to provide reassurances, she'd fixated on the first part of his response, her lips turning downward into a frown.

He felt a scowl of his own form as he pictured the periodic thorn in his side that had a tendency to present itself at inopportune moments. Such as this past week. He pressed a hand to his forehead, kneading the tension away. "Charles had the wherewithal to establish Eleanor with the cousin—Hannah—before his own illness set in. He asked me to ensure their continued wellbeing but assured me he had already arranged for them to receive more than sufficient funds. Nevertheless, in my first meeting with Hannah, she told a different story. Apparently, she lacked the means to provide Eleanor with all the necessities. I augmented her allowance at once, without question. But three months later, she wrote me a letter claiming the funds she received had once more become inadequate, and then the same thing two months after that, and so on and so forth."

The blood had drained from Catherine's face, and he paused, about to inquire after her wellbeing. However, she nudged her head toward him, encouraging him to continue.

He took a drawn-out breath, trying to release some of the exasperation that came from finally hearing himself speak of the aggravating situation aloud. "This time when she wrote, it was to say that their lodgings were no longer suitable and they would require something larger and better situated. Hence the need for my current trip to London. Now that I've seen Hannah set up in a respectable townhouse on Henrietta Street and given an additional increase in her allowance besides, she should be appeased. At least for the time being."

"But that's terrible!" Somehow, Catherine's complexion had turned even paler, and her voice wavered as she spoke.

He would be the last one to argue with her there. Yet she failed to see the purpose behind his actions. "Hannah was widowed young, and I'm not sure she truly has a desire for children of her own just yet. However, she's the only relation I know of who can care for Eleanor, and she does a sufficient job of it, as long as she receives the appropriate enticements. I cannot risk Eleanor's situation by refusing Hannah's demands, especially when parting with a little extra money here or there has minimal effect on the family coffers."

"That is not the point!" Catherine choked out, the tears shining in her eyes beginning to spill over. "Eleanor is your relation too, your one and only niece. You cannot leave her in the care of a woman who tolerates her only because she is well compensated for the task. Eleanor may be illegitimate, but that doesn't make her unworthy of love. She deserves better. Far, far better. Just as you deserve better than to live beneath the threat of an avaricious woman's demands!"

Philip reached up to brush the droplets away from her cheeks, his stomach heaving from the upset he just couldn't seem to stop causing her. For whatever reason, his story had awoken Catherine's vehemence, and he stroked her hair in a helpless attempt to be soothing.

She trembled, unaffected by his placating touch, giving her head an insistent shake. "No. You cannot continue on like this. If none of her mother's relations can give her a loving home, Eleanor belongs with us. You may tell others whatever lie you like about her parentage if it means she can be under our roof. I'll take responsibility for her care and love her like my very own child, if only—"

"It is not that simple," he exclaimed. "You do not realize the magnitude of what you ask."

Unlike him, she hadn't yet had the opportunity to spend countless nights pondering the situation, wondering about the best course of action. She hadn't yet realized the difficulty in balancing desires that were nearly impossible to make coexist. Despite his devil-may-care attitude and his trail of unsavory deeds, he valued his brother's final request, his niece's care, and his wife's happiness above all else. Yet he couldn't help but think that in the span of an afternoon, he'd managed to fail all three.

Catherine swiped at her eyes, impatiently brushing away a few stray tears, before planting her hands against his shoulders. She didn't tremble any longer. In fact, her features held fresh determination. "Could I at least meet Eleanor? Before we depart London, I mean. It can be a short, discreet visit at her home if you're concerned about detection. Only, I would like very much to meet her in some fashion. Please."

Perhaps it was a dangerous path to walk down, one that amplified the risk of his carefully guarded secret having consequences of unprecedented proportions. However, what he'd told her at the beginning of their marriage remained just as true today. When she looked at him, her eyes dark and imploring, and spoke to him in her even, gentle voice, he lacked the ability to refuse her anything.

"If you wish." He spoke before giving it another moment's thought and then waited for the pang of regret that would follow. Interestingly, though, it didn't come. Instead, another thought filled his head, one that, despite everything, nearly made him smile. Eleanor resting in Catherine's arms, giggling as Catherine showered her with affection.

She pressed her forehead to his, her eyelids fluttering closed. "Thank you," she whispered, and after an afternoon of trepidation and doubts, he finally felt he had made a correct decision. "Thank you for agreeing. Thank you for your honesty. I'm certain there must be a way to ameliorate the situation, for everyone. We'll find a way to set things right."

***

Catherine stared up at the bed curtains that surrounded her, their distinct damask pattern fading to nondescript gray as the last of the flames died in the grate. After a trying day, she and Philip had retired early, Philip falling into a deep sleep nearly the instant their heads hit the pillow and they settled into each other's arms. Given the utter exhaustion that had swept over her, she thought for sure she would do the same. Instead, she lay wide awake nearly two hours later, her mind still reeling with the day's events.

She'd been dragged through agony twice that day and come out of it with knowledge she never could have fathomed. It all pointed to one fact she'd previously had occasion to ponder but could now accept as the truth: She'd been wrong to doubt Philip. She'd let rumors and an ill-timed encounter cloud her judgment, but when she looked past that, only a man who was truly decent at his core remained. A man who now needed her help.

She had always marveled at his skill in keeping himself so composed, but sure enough, he carried burdens beneath the facade, just as she'd suspected. That he harbored his brother's deathbed secret and took responsibility for a child as a result, went far beyond any circumstances she'd conceived, and indeed, it had clearly cost him much to speak the truth. Ultimately, though, he had chosen to confide in her in a way he had done with no other. He trusted her. And if there had ever been any doubt in her mind, it had given way to certainty. She loved him for it.

Which is why she knew what she needed to do next.

Very slowly, she shifted out of his arms, watching his face for any sign that he stirred. However, he remained motionless except for the even rise and fall of his chest. Her body protested the departure from his reassuring warmth, but she couldn't give in to the desire to return to his embrace. Not while her own burden still weighed heavy on her.

She retrieved the silk shawl she'd left draped over her vanity bench, wrapping it around her shoulders as she tiptoed across the room to the escritoire by the window. Gently, she pushed back the curtain, allowing the glow of moonlight to shine in just enough to illuminate the little brass inkpot and the paper resting beside it. The light was dim, but it would be enough for her to accomplish the task at hand. She eased herself into the chair, taking up a quill but then twirling it in her fingers, her heart beginning to thump with more urgency.

Yet she had to keep going. Philip had given her honesty, despite the difficulties it presented. Now, she owed him the same. She'd known from the moment Holbeck made his increased demands that she could never let the secret of her parentage linger between them without it consuming her. The events that had since transpired only served to solidify that belief. She needed to tell him the truth, for better or worse.

Only … before that, it was crucial that she meet Eleanor. Under no circumstances could she stand by idly while an illegitimate child was used for financial gain. That cut far too close—and too deep. She just had to accompany Philip in visiting the little girl once, and then, somehow, she would convince him that his niece belonged with them. If this so-called caregiver was truly as high-reaching as Philip said, an additional payment would surely entice her to give up the child. Then, Eleanor could reside where she belonged, in a loving home. Even if it meant Philip had to lie about her origins. Even if it caused rumors to swirl, making Catherine the pitied wife of a flagrant rake.

That had to happen first. Then, she could divulge her own truth. The reason she felt such a connection with Eleanor. The meaning behind her request for money, her desire to stay in London, and her presence in St. James Park. As with the situation with Eleanor, she didn't know the best path forward once her secret sprang out in the open. Surely, though, they could find a way to move past it without being totally consumed by scandal. To avoid having the marquess's final days filled with shame. And if Philip decided he couldn't handle the disgrace of her parentage, well … at least she would have secured Eleanor's future before he cast her aside.

The scathing mixture of deceitfulness, shame, and apprehension roiled in her stomach until she was unsure whether she wanted to scream out her secrets and be rid of them without delay or clamp them tighter inside where they would never see the light of day. And since neither seemed a viable option, she lowered the quill in her unsteady hand, dipping it into the inkpot. If nothing else, there was one small gesture she could make to unload a little of the weight of what she concealed and begin her path toward the truth. She bent her head low to the escritoire, squinting so she could just make out the marks her quill left against the page.

Mr. Holbeck,

I regret to inform you that I will not be attending our meeting today. After careful deliberation, I have arrived at the conclusion that I am unable to provide you with the funds you seek, now or at any time thereafter. Please do not take the trouble to make yourself known to Lord Kendrick or Lord Langley. Any revelations regarding my parentage of which you feel they should be made aware, I assure you, I will have already divulged. As for your intention to disclose this information to the rest of society, you may do as you see fit. Whether anyone chooses to believe your claims, given that you do not currently enjoy a position of good standing within the ton, remains to be seen. Either way, I have decided that a scandal is far preferable to living beneath your demands. As such, I can see no further benefit to our continued association, and you will not hear from me again.

C

"Catherine?" Philip's voice, thick with sleep, echoed through the darkness just as she finished folding the page.

"I'm here," she uttered back as she dropped the letter into the drawer of the escritoire before silently closing it. "Just a moment."

She pulled the curtain closed again, ensconcing the room in total darkness. In the morning, she would give one of the stableboys a coin and request that he find someone to deliver the letter to Little Earl Street. But for now ...

"I didn't mean to wake you," she murmured, feeling her way back to the side of the bed. Her hands connected with the edge of the mattress, and she slipped between the sheets, wriggling her body into his protective embrace once more. "I was having difficulty sleeping, but I'm feeling more tired now. I'll try to rest once more."

He said nothing, merely stroked her lower back in a state halfway between wakefulness and sleep. It was all she could do to keep from sighing from the contentment of it and pressing against him even more tightly, as if she could form a bond with him that nothing could break. But since she didn't want to rouse him—in fact, she couldn't risk what might come out of her mouth if she did—she stayed where she was, silent and still. Perhaps soon, the even rhythm of his breath would lull her to sleep, especially now that she'd taken the first step toward freeing herself from this mess. She would escape Holbeck's clutches. She would see Eleanor brought to her proper home. And then, for better or worse, she would return Philip's honesty, and the incumbrance of secrets would no longer stand between them.

The truth would set her free. As long as it didn't destroy her first.

Chapter 20

For someone who had betrayed a long-upheld promise to his brother, Philip approached Henrietta Street with a surprising lightness in his step. Visits to Eleanor—especially in the early days, when the little girl's dark curls and wide brown eyes reminded him so much of the brother he'd just lost—had always put a smile on his face. But with them had also come a sense of trepidation. On the one hand, owing to Hannah and her relentless, unpredictable demands. And as a result came his fear that, by leaving her with that woman, he didn't truly do right by his niece after all.

Today, though, was different. As impossible as the idea was, he couldn't help but imagine what would happen if he brought Eleanor home with him, just as Catherine suggested. Difficulties and scandals aside, how freeing, how *right*, it would feel to have the child grow up before his eyes without him wondering what sum he would next owe to an unscrupulous caregiver for her continued wellbeing. Furthermore, Catherine had spoken so sincerely that he didn't doubt her ability to love Eleanor, despite where she came from. For beneath the exterior he had once considered frigid, Catherine possessed an ability for caring and compassion like he'd never known. And with her by his side, sharing in the burden of his secret, he could almost believe that there was a better way forward.

"Here we are." He stopped before a glossy black door, glancing up at the windows above it. In her previous lodgings, Eleanor had often waited with her face pressed to the glass if she knew he was coming. Today, however, the curtains remained drawn, with no dark, curly head poking out between them. He turned his attention back to Catherine, where she stood with her hand resting atop his arm. "Are you ready to go in?"

She gave a small smile, shifting the painted wooden doll, which she'd insisted they stop to purchase along their way, in her grasp. "Of course."

She straightened herself to her full height, her eyes shining so eagerly that he couldn't help but lean in to her before reaching for the door knocker, dropping a soft kiss against her forehead. "Thank you. For your acceptance. For—"

However, before he could utter another word, the door burst open, revealing a pale-faced Hannah. She stepped aside to allow them entry, her movements jerky as she dropped into a curtsy. "Good day, my lord. My lady."

"Good day, Mrs. Green." He watched her carefully as he stepped into the entryway with Catherine at his side, the faintest hum of unease beginning to vibrate through him. Hannah, in her guilefulness, usually had a ready smile and an air of confidence, but at the moment, she gazed at the floor, her features drawn tight. He tried to shake the sensation away, forcing himself to remember the formalities. "Allow me to present my wife, Lady Kendrick. And Catherine, this is Mrs. Hannah Green."

Catherine murmured a reply, and he became vaguely aware of Hannah doing the same. As for the exact words either of them said, he was too focused on Hannah's shifting gaze, darting wildly from wall to wall without daring to meet his eye, to notice. But more importantly ... why had he not yet heard the patter of tiny feet? Whenever he came to visit, Eleanor always liked making a game of running as fast as she could before leaping into his arms. Currently, though, the house stood eerily silent.

"Hannah, where is Eleanor?" Without meaning to, he began shifting his own eyes, on the lookout for the little girl to pop out from behind a doorway or come barreling down the stairs.

The woman's white face suddenly flushed crimson, and she stared down at her hands, wringing them together. Her voice, normally capable of issuing strongly worded demands, came out as a squeak. "Well, my lord, I don't rightly know."

"You *what?*" he thundered, his body abruptly seized with tension. "What do you mean you do not know?"

Hannah's face flushed an even deeper red, and her chin began trembling. "She was eager to see you and Lady Kendrick and wished to wait for you outside. I planned to go out with her, only I had to go upstairs to fetch my cloak first. When I came back, she was gone."

A curse broke from his throat, and he shoved the door open, tumbling back onto the street. He peered back and forth, looking for any sign of a small girl darting alongside building fronts or curled up in an imagined game of hide and seek. But except for a few passersby strolling hurriedly along, the street remained empty.

"She cannot have gone far," Hannah said from the doorway behind him. While she spoke more strongly than before, the wavering note in her voice betrayed her uncertainty. "She may have wished to explore her new surroundings and lost her way. I'm sure someone will see her and return her home. Or maybe she wandered to the back. Or maybe—"

"Go back and look for her in the house," he snapped, his composure treading a thin line. "Perhaps she reentered without your knowledge and is making a game of hiding."

He wished he could convince himself that were true. However, his former sense of unease had become a booming echo that pounded through his head and rattled his insides. Betraying Charles's secret was one matter. But failing to protect the one thing his brother had entrusted to his care, well … that was too abysmal to fathom.

At the periphery of his line of sight, a swath of dark blue fabric whirled back and forth. Catherine. He turned to where she paced alongside him, her steps uneven and her complexion so ghostly white that she appeared on the verge of swooning.

He fixed his hands against her shoulders, holding her steady. "We'll find her." He tried his best to speak with assuredness he didn't currently possess. "As Hannah said, she could simply be making a game out of hiding. Or perhaps she wandered too far in the wrong direction. Why Hannah wasn't more mindful of her, given that their surroundings remain unfamiliar, I do not know. Nonetheless, I'm sure we'll find her."

Catherine made a strangled sound, something between a yelp and a sob. "This is my fault."

Her body jerked, making the doll slip from her hands, and he tightened his grip to keep her from crumpling to the ground. He opened his mouth, about to make another attempt at reassurances, but she shook her head violently.

"Holbeck … my letter … my defiance …" Their faces were only inches apart, but her eyes had taken on a faraway expression as if she no longer saw him in front of her. "He did this because of me."

Her jumbled words mixed with the pounding in his head until everything ceased to make sense. He pushed his palms into her shoulders again, unsure whether he was now steadying her or himself. "What are you saying? I do not understand." His frustration was on the verge of boiling over. "Catherine!"

She startled at the abrupt way he called her name, her eyes snapping back to his. He recognized the look that appeared in the dark brown depths. It was the same expression that appeared when she was about to panic and flee, although, on this occasion, her terror was amplified tenfold. She took a shaky breath, visibly struggling to control the way her limbs trembled.

"He approached me. My father. My *real* father," she clarified in response to the confusion he felt creasing his face, "because it turns out I'm not an earl's daughter after all. I'm a by-blow, the product of my mother's affair with a degenerate gambler. And he's been watching me! Since our arrival in London, he must have been watching us both."

She shuddered, her voice tinged with hysteria. "I gave him money to make him leave us in peace, but then he came looking for more. I wrote him a letter denying his request. It was posted just this morning. This is his retribution. *I* caused this."

Catherine's words floated at the edge of his awareness, their meaning not fully sinking in. He stood numbly, trying to form a coherent thought. "It cannot be …"

"It is," she exclaimed, beginning to struggle within his grip. "I need to find him. I'll go back to St. James Park. Or to his residence. Yes, perhaps he's there. He said he has rooms on Little Earl Street."

She mumbled the last words to herself, lost in a trail of frantic thoughts again, as meanwhile, his own grasp on composure slackened more by the second. "Are you certain that is what occurred?"

"My lord?"

He whirled around in response to Hannah's call from the doorway, and he rushed over, a faint hope emerging that he would see Eleanor clinging to the back of her skirts. However, except for Hannah, the entryway stayed empty, and Hannah's face remained drawn.

"I looked everywhere. Under beds. Behind doorways. Within trunks and cupboards. Out the back windows." She turned her eyes to the floor, no longer able to look at him. "She's nowhere to be found."

"Damn it!" He spun out of the house just as quickly as he had entered it, trying to keep the chaos from consuming him altogether. None of it mattered right now. He would work out the details of whatever the hell was going on later. Presently, he just needed to focus. "Catherine, could you please tell me where—"

However, as he surveyed the street once more, the request died on his lips. Catherine, too, was gone.

Chapter 21

Catherine's lungs burned, and the muscles in her legs threatened to seize, but still, she kept running. She had paused for a split second at the end of Henrietta Street, presented with the option of which way to go, when a burst of pure instinct told her north. Toward Seven Dials. She could only hope she had chosen correctly.

In a total lack of foresight, she'd neglected her sturdy walking boots in favor of a pair of delicate blue slippers, which now threatened to disintegrate around her feet. Not that she would let that impede her. Not when each time her slippers hit the granite setts below her, they pounded out a rhythm: *your fault, your fault, your fault.*

She'd thought that by sending Holbeck the note, she'd done the right thing and taken the first step in freeing herself from a web of dishonesty. She'd never doubted that he would be angry with her decision. That perhaps he would even continue to approach her. But how could she have anticipated that he'd take his wrath out on an innocent child? For although it was common enough for young children to wander off or to become separated from their guardians, she felt certain this wasn't one of those instances. From the moment Hannah had revealed Eleanor's disappearance, a looming, relentless tug at her core had insisted this was Lawrence Holbeck's doing. Because she'd spited him. Because he watched her. Which is why she now had to locate him at all costs.

She continued her frenzied path as the streets around her became a congested hub of activity, swathed in a malodorous haze that left a bitter tang in her throat and roiled her stomach. She didn't imagine the eyes that watched her now, for she could see them plain as day. The sunken eyes of women in rags who hunched beside buildings. The glassy eyes of men who stumbled out of gin shops, seeking additional sources of entertainment. Only a fool would run blindly into a notorious slum alone, dressed in her fine silk dress and dainty slippers, with no means of defending herself. Yet she couldn't afford to retreat.

She had reached an open stretch of road, a confluence from which other side streets veered off in all directions. In this unfamiliar maze, how was she to determine which way to go? She had no choice but to pause, her head spinning as she whipped it around, trying to get her bearings.

"You look like you've lost your way, little lamb." A hulking, unshaven man staggered in her direction, his lopsided grin revealing a row of cracked, rotting teeth. "Daresay I can help you find it again."

Blast it; she should have known better than to stop for even a second. He extended a burly arm toward her, and she jumped, nearly colliding with a street vendor's cart before orienting herself enough to dart around it, out of the man's reach. She bolted toward the closest side street, blind to where she was going but knowing she had to get away. For while she had very little left at her disposal, she at least had speed.

She weaved through the throng of people bustling along this new street, keeping her momentum until the fatigued ache in her legs became more insistent. At least she had placed sufficient distance between herself and the original source of threat. However, it would only be a matter of time before a new threat emerged. And what good could she do without knowing whether she was headed in the right direction?

She allowed herself to slow again, just enough to take in the buildings she passed, examining them for signs that would alert her to where she stood. Yet nothing was familiar. An array of shopfronts stretched out before her, melding into one another until they all looked the same. Meanwhile, bodies pushed past her, and passersby continued to gawk, providing her with a constant reminder that in this boisterous throng, she could be snapped up at the slightest misstep.

Amidst the cacophony, a door flying open from a crumbling brick building toward the end of the street should have done little to warrant her attention. Yet her eyes fixed on the tall, lean figure who emerged, watching as he peered hurriedly up and down the street, clearly on the lookout for a specific something or someone of his own. His black tailcoat and beaver hat were remarkable only in that their quality surpassed that of the clothing of the other men who scurried past him along the street. But there was something else ...

She continued at her haphazard pace in the man's direction, as amidst the steady flurry of panic that radiated through her body, chilling jolts of recognition set in. Perhaps the sight was merely an illusion—or more accurately, a nightmare—that she'd conjured up in her overwrought brain. Yet the figure didn't vanish. Rather, he stayed just where he was, glancing around fervently, until she could have no doubt as to his existence. Despite her vow to keep moving, the realization of what she saw caused her to stop dead in her tracks. She had found him. Somehow, through all her frantic, directionless running, her legs had carried her exactly where she needed to go.

Suddenly, the fatigue in her limbs, the nausea, and the confusion all vanished. Nothing remained but a persistent fire, driving her, unthinking, toward her purpose.

She charged across the street, feeling one of her slippers at last give way as she barreled into Lawrence Holbeck, slamming her fists against his shoulders. Despite her inferiority to him in both size and strength, the unexpectedness of the assault caused him to stagger backward, sending them both tumbling through the open door and into a dank entryway.

"What have you done?" She grabbed hold of his coat, shaking him with all the force she could muster. As if she only pushed hard enough, she could wrench the truth out of him. "How could you?"

"Cease, Catherine." He wrenched himself free of her grasp, shoving her away like an annoying speck of dirt on his clothing. "Your behavior is rather unsightly, wouldn't you say?"

"Where is she?" His rebuke caused her to scream even louder, as every unnerving emotion she'd kept pent up inside came spilling out. She lunged at him again, guided by pure fury. "Tell me this instant. I demand it."

He seized her by the wrists, smirking at her misguided efforts as he held her in place, at arm's length. "Ah. It seems you do wish to continue your association with me after all."

"You have given me no choice!" Her shouted words broke into a sob as the direness of the situation began setting in. She had charged toward Holbeck with no plan, armed with nothing but her blind outrage. An action that felt foolhardier by the second. What reason would he have to cooperate with her demands? He held the power now, as he well knew. She held nothing.

"You may have whatever you wish." Speaking the concession caused a lump in her throat that nearly choked her as her skin prickled beneath icy needles of dread. Yet it was the only thing left to do. She swallowed forcefully, managing to continue talking in a stilted whisper. "The sum you requested. More, if you like. Take from me what you will. Only, please, allow the child to be safely returned."

The man's sneer widened, his eyes glinting with a malicious light. "I imagined you would come to your senses. And not to worry. I daresay I could help you locate what you're missing, if given the proper incentive."

He hadn't so much as batted an eye when she brought up the matter of Eleanor. On the contrary, he knew of exactly which child she spoke.

Her whirling head and shaking limbs could endure no more. Her knees buckled, and with that, Holbeck abruptly released her wrists, sending her crumpling to the floor. His snide chuckle reached her ears, although it did little to amplify the stifling sense of defeat that had already spread through her. Hastiness had made her careless, landing her at his feet and at his mercy. If only she were a more worldly woman, perhaps she would have had the shrewdness to plan her steps more carefully and have a means of defense, like Betsy with the precautionary knife in her boot. Instead, she no longer had even a pair of slippers upon her feet. But as for Holbeck …

The tops of his scuffed boots were at her eye level. At just the right place for her to detect the glint of silver against his calf. Could it be … She hurriedly turned her face back to the floor, unable to take the chance that he would notice her staring. This was the only glimmer of hope she had, and a faint one at that. Her heart pounded rapidly until it seemed about to burst from her chest. She'd berated herself time and again for her timidity. She'd heard how others referred to her as a cowering little mouse. Surely, she lacked the capability to perform the deed that raced through her mind, especially after she'd failed so miserably the first time. Yet she had to try again. For Eleanor. For Philip. For herself.

She lunged at Holbeck, her hands diving for the poorly concealed spot of silver. She tugged as soon as her fingers connected with metal and then scrambled backward, putting distance between herself and the dangerous man before a sudden burst of strength shot her to her feet. She had come away with something, yet the smooth, cool weight within her grasp didn't quite feel real. Without taking her eyes off Holbeck, who stood unmoving and wide-eyed, still trying to process what had just occurred, she raised her shaking hand until it met with her line of sight. The silver glinted enticingly, from the curved handle within her grip to the precise blade that extended beyond. Holbeck had taken something from her. Now, she'd returned the favor.

"What theatrics for such a proper little miss! You had best put that down." He still smirked at her as if she were a misbehaving child whose pitiful attempts at retaliation amused him. However, she hadn't missed the slight waver in his voice that wasn't there before. That waver brought her the power she'd previously lacked.

She kept her hand where it was, managing to still the trembling as she shuffled her feet, leaving him with uncertainty as to her next move. Finally, she had him at a disadvantage. Now, she needed to use that to accomplish what she'd come here to do. She cleared her throat, refusing to let her words quiver this time. "These are your lodgings, yes?"

He said nothing, merely continued appraising her with his dissecting stare. Apprehensive though he may be, he distrusted her ability to emerge triumphant in this situation; that much was plain.

"Answer me!" She thrust her arm forward, shifting the blade precariously close to his throat. The faint line of blood that appeared caused her stomach to heave, yet she would never let him see that. She returned his stare with even greater intensity, daring him to contradict her.

He tilted his head back by no more than an inch, but the movement didn't go undetected in her state of hyper-alertness. He sighed, keeping up the appearance of a man incensed by his daughter's childish antics. "You're correct."

He could pretend all he wanted, but a subtle glint had appeared in his dark eyes, one she couldn't miss because she had seen it mirrored so many times in her own. Fear. Perhaps he thought she had gone half-crazed, and in her current state, she couldn't say he was wrong. But the validity of the belief didn't matter at present. Only its ability to get her what she needed.

"Give me the key to your door." Very carefully, she removed one hand from the knife, extending it toward his coat pocket.

Again, he responded with infuriating slowness, looking at her but saying nothing. She could nearly see the wheels turning in his head as he calculated his next move, just as she did. He pondered his own ability to surprise, to make a sudden move for the knife and regain the upper hand. He considered the degree to which she posed a legitimate threat, no doubt realizing that she needed him to remain alive—and cognizant—to divulge the information she so desperately sought. Control was a slippery prospect to hold on to, and already, it wriggled within her grasp, threatening to fall away at any moment.

"I suggest you do as she says."

That voice. It cracked through the air like a whip, sharp and foreboding. She didn't dare take her eyes off Holbeck for even a second. However, she didn't need to in order to realize who had burst through the doorway and now stood behind her, breathing heavily with a mixture of exhaustion and vehemence. She knew him because he had come to her rescue before. Because she'd spent the weeks since then getting to know, and love, every aspect of him. And now, despite how miserably she had failed him, he'd found a way to come to her rescue again.

"Kendrick." Holbeck's chin quivered, his mouth dropping slightly askew. "Fancy seeing you here."

Philip's boots rapped against the weathered floorboards as he stalked nearer, a hunter encroaching on his prey. "I wonder at your surprise by my presence here," he said, his voice dangerously low, "when you have absconded with what I value above all else."

"Really …" Holbeck trailed off, his eyes darting nervously between the two people in front of him as if he suddenly feared he'd made a miscalculation. It took only a moment for him to regain his composure and the smirk to return to his face. However, the set of his mouth no longer suggested confidence but desperation. "I apologize for any inconvenience. This matter was intended to rest solely between my daughter and me, and it would have, had she not been so troublesome. As she could not follow through with her end of the bargain, I must now, regretfully, inform you of the unfortunate truth surrounding the woman you married. She may masquerade as a well-mannered earl's daughter, but in reality, the girl is a bastard and an aggravating one at that."

Philip struck too quickly for her to fully see what happened. The violent flurry of activity flashed before her eyes, as suddenly, she found herself jostled backward while Philip and Holbeck went crashing to the floor.

"Give me the key!" Philip roared, one arm pinned against Holbeck's neck as the other tore at one of the man's frayed coat pockets.

Wordlessly, Holbeck fumbled inside his opposite pocket, his face turning purple beneath Philip's restrictive weight on his throat. Philip's hand darted over at the first sign of the brass key, and with it secured in his palm, he eased the pressure from his arm just enough so Holbeck could take in a deep, hungry breath. "Which is your door?"

"Up the first set of stairs," Holbeck wheezed, all his former assuredness drained from his face. Philip's fist must have connected with his eye as they toppled over, for already it swelled into an angry shade of purple. "Second door on the right. No harm has come to the girl. It was all a misunderst—"

"Shut up." Philip slammed his arm down again, his expression murderous. "Catherine, do you think you might trade me your knife for my key?"

Watching the frenzied exchange unfold had kept her frozen in place, although his words prompted her to stagger forward, unclamping her fingers from the knife handle and releasing it into his palm. In turn, she snapped up the key he offered, and with it, a fire ignited within her anew. This is what she'd come here for. At least as a first step.

"I'll go up." She forced her legs back into action, stumbling toward the dark, narrow stairway. "To see if … if …" A lump caught in her throat, causing the power of speech to fail her. The thought of Holbeck taking Eleanor and confining her here was too terrible to put into words. Yet the alternative—that he had brought her elsewhere, and this exchange had done nothing but waste valuable minutes—was even worse. She moved more quickly now, a fresh burst of alarm propelling her stockinged feet up the splintered staircase. One way or another, she had to find out.

"Yes, do." Philip's voice called after her with an eerie calmness. "I'll stay here with Mr. Holbeck. For if any of what he said turns out to be untrue, I'm afraid he will have a *very* serious problem on his hands."

She reached the upstairs corridor, a dark, mildewed space that smelled of rot and unwashed bodies, and sprinted the last few steps to the second doorway. With the key securely in her grasp, she thrust it into the lock, her pulse thrumming erratically in that moment of anticipation. Thankfully, mercifully, the key turned beneath her frantic jostling, producing a quiet click.

She burst through the door, trying to survey all corners of the dim room at once. And there, immersed in the subtle light that peeked through the lone grimy window, was a dark, curly head with a face pressed to the glass. The little girl spun around in response to the sudden commotion, her eyes wide. "I do not want to play hide and seek any longer. I wish to go home."

Catherine shot her hand out against the wall to steady herself before gradually letting her wobbly knees sink to the floor. She'd done it. She'd located Eleanor. And most importantly, the girl appeared unharmed. Tears of relief welled in her eyes, and her mouth stretched into a shaky smile.

"You shall, darling. I'm your aunt Catherine, and I've come here with your uncle Philip for that very reason. He's waiting downstairs. Shall I tell him I have found you?"

At Eleanor's nod, she turned her head toward the doorway. "Philip," she called in a singsong voice, careful to keep her tone gentle, "I've located Eleanor. She is ready to return home now."

She heard a grunt, followed by Philip's voice floating up the stairs, equally as placid. "As you wish, Eleanor, sweeting. Just stay with Aunt Catherine a moment longer, if you please. I'll be up directly."

She turned her attention back to Eleanor, extending a hand in her direction. "Would you like to come sit with me? While we wait for Philip?"

Eleanor looked her up and down, her expression hesitant. Of course it was. The woman before her with hair tumbling from its pins and a missing shoe was a stranger, and this day had already brought Eleanor much upset at a stranger's hands. However, after another moment's appraisal, she tottered forward, placing a chubby fist into Catherine's outstretched palm.

Catherine closed her fingers over the little hand, still replete with babylike softness. Eleanor's eyes were light gray, much like Philip's, and she currently used them to assess her newfound aunt once more. Catherine waited, unmoving, keeping her lips turned up in a smile. And then, with an approving nod of her head, Eleanor dropped herself into Catherine's lap, snuggling her body tightly against her.

Only then did the tears brimming in Catherine's eyes slip down her cheeks. She'd told Philip of her intention to love and care for this unfortunate, parentless child, yet she hadn't understood the extent of that desire until this moment. Already, a fierce, protective sensation swelled in her chest as she encircled Eleanor in her arms, and she knew, beyond a doubt, that she would care for her with a love that knew no bounds. Her throat grew tight as she considered all the tumult she had caused this day, and she tried her best to cast the memories aside before they caused her to fall apart altogether. She pulled Eleanor a little closer, reminding herself that the child was safe. She would spend the rest of her life making it up to Eleanor, atoning for what happened. That is, if Philip would still give her the chance.

Footsteps raced up the stairs, and just as with the familiar voice that had called out from the doorway below, she had no need of seeing their owner to know to whom they belonged. Her stomach fluttered, anticipating what was to come.

Philip rushed through the doorway, his shoulders immediately sagging as he surveyed the scene that greeted him. He looked back and forth, from her face to Eleanor's, before he, too, sank to his knees beside them. Slowly, he reached out to touch one of Eleanor's curls as if needing to ensure that he hadn't just imagined her presence. Catherine nodded, a silent reassurance that Eleanor was here, apparently unscathed. And with that, he brought a hand to her hair as well, pushing back a stray lock that had clung to her forehead with beads of perspiration. She closed her eyes, savoring that one brief touch. Turmoil lurked behind and in front of them, but at this single moment, it was just the three of them, and they had found safety.

He stilled his hand, letting out a deep exhale that sounded like he'd held in for a very long time. "Well, Catherine. And Miss Eleanor. I believe it's time we went home."

Chapter 22

Catherine cracked open her eyes to find rays of early morning sunlight pouring upon her through the lace-curtained window. Where was she? These weren't the usual heavy curtains and the darkened room that greeted her when she awoke, nor was the pink-flowered counterpane that covered her the one under which she typically slept. She turned, her eyes meeting with a curly dark head and tiny body that nestled against her in sleep. And then, it all came rushing back.

After Philip had seen her and Eleanor back to Langley House the previous day, the little girl had stuck to her like a shadow, especially with Philip having to rush off again to deal with matters regarding both Hannah and Holbeck. That had suited Catherine just fine. By focusing her attention on Eleanor—getting her familiar with the house, sending a servant to the shops to purchase children's books, clothing, and playthings, and simply talking to her to make sure she felt comforted and safe—she could take her mind off the chaos that swirled around them. However, she hadn't meant to fall asleep, which she must have done upon settling Eleanor into one of the guest rooms and lying down to hum her a lullaby. Not when she and Philip had so many unanswered questions—and unspoken truths—to discuss. And for that matter, had he even come home last night?

The feeling of disquiet that had been her constant companion yesterday began trickling back, and she inched herself out from under Eleanor's soft weight and tiptoed away from the bed. Early the previous evening, she'd parted herself from Eleanor just long enough to wash away the day's grime and change her clothing, but now that she'd slept in the clean white muslin dress she'd donned, that had become creased and unsightly too. Meanwhile, it would have to do. She needed to discover Philip's whereabouts without delay.

She eased open the door, careful not to let it creak on its hinges, planning to rush downstairs and ask Swift if he knew of Lord Kendrick's whereabouts. However, a shadow in the corridor stopped her. Philip sat against the wall next to the doorway, also in the rumpled clothing he'd thrown on yesterday before rushing out of the house. His head rested atop his knees, his eyes lightly closed.

She clamped her hand to her mouth to keep from crying out as a swirl of varying emotions hit her all at once. He glanced up at her immediately and then through the doorway. "Eleanor?"

"Still asleep," she whispered, gently pulling the door closed behind her.

He pushed himself to his feet, and she was overcome with the urge to launch herself into his arms and cling to him until she could be certain that no threat would come between them. But she couldn't. Too much had transpired, with too many things remaining unsaid. Perhaps she now caused him revulsion, and he no longer wanted …

No, she couldn't even think it. But at the same time, there was no point in prolonging the uncertainty. For better or worse, she needed to talk to him. She took a deep breath, trying to slow her rapidly rising pulse. "Perhaps we might speak to one another before she awakens."

He gazed at her, his expression unreadable. "Yes, I think a conversation is very much warranted."

She started away from Eleanor's bedroom before she could lose her nerve, treading down the corridor with Philip at her heels. Without thinking, she found herself at the door of their own bedroom, where she suddenly halted. Was this still an appropriate place for them to converse? Maybe she should have led him down to the drawing room, or some other location without connotations of intimacy, which they might no longer possess. However, though he hung back slightly, keeping his arms planted against his sides, Philip looked at her expectantly, waiting for her to enter. She scurried inside, not giving her thoughts another second to get the better of her, and made for the settee by the window. She supposed this was as good a place as any for her to issue the largest apology of her life, as well as to ask the burning questions of how he'd resolved yesterday's events.

Philip, though, spoke first. "I would like you to tell me everything that transpired with Holbeck." He lowered himself to sit beside her, his gray eyes intense. "I trust that, given present circumstances, you no longer feel the need to conceal this information from me."

"No." She swallowed back the heavy lump of regret that formed at the back of her throat. "No, of course not."

The matters she wanted to ask about would keep. Right now, she would do as he asked and give him the truth he deserved.

She told him about everything. The furtive letter. The meeting in St. James Park. Her attempt at buying her true father's silence and her refusal to do so again. And then, worst of all, the vengeance that came as a result.

"I'm sorry." Her voice had turned tight, and she choked back the lump that once more emerged. "I miscalculated my ability to manage my fa—that man. I gravely underestimated the depravity of which he was capable. I should have had the foresight to handle matters differently throughout all of this. I suppose I should be on my knees thanking fortune for leading me to Eleanor yesterday, despite all the missteps I made. And for you, for somehow knowing how to find me at just the right time, as you always seem to do."

"Yes, well." He shifted his hand into his pocket to retrieve an item, holding out his palm to display it to her. The remnants of her blue slipper. "Whether intentionally or not, you left me a clue."

She gawked at the ruined object as a flash of memory came of it flying onto Little Earl Street as she ran. She could almost smile at the serendipity of it. Almost.

He stuffed the ruined slipper back in his pocket, and with that, his shoulders stiffened. "I hope it will please you to know that Holbeck is no longer in England."

A shudder rippled through her at the unexpected news. "But how …"

Philip's expression darkened, his face becoming like steel. "He would have been transported for what he did. But given the time it would have taken and the resulting scandal … I merely sped up the process. I saw him placed on a ship bound for the West Indies, and he knows better than to attempt making a return. Due to his profligate behavior, his family disowned him years ago. I used to encounter him at the gaming hells from time to time when I first stepped out in London, and even then, he was on the fringes of society. From what I understand, he's been living in hiding of late, trying to elude debtor's prison. There's nothing left for him here. Not to mention the consequences I explained, very graphically, that he would endure were he to show his face again."

"I'm glad he is gone." She clasped her arms around herself as if to retain the small measure of comfort that came from the knowledge of never having to see the man again. Yet how would she ever bring herself to fully forget his face? She would see his dark eyes looking back at her every time she looked in the mirror. And worse, Philip would see them too.

"I didn't know about him previously, I swear it!" she burst out, unable to carry the weight of her unspoken words any longer. "Vague whisperings, perhaps, but one never knows how much stock to put in the ton's rumors. I didn't intentionally deceive you about my parentage. I would never want to cast that type of shame upon you or your family either, especially with your father's health so fragile. I didn't mean to ruin everything."

He blinked rapidly, a deep crease forming between his eyes. "What do you mean, ruin—"

"My lord?"

The butler's voice, accompanied by an insistent knocking at the bedroom door, cut Philip off mid-sentence.

"Go away, Swift," Philip snapped, still staring at her with his brow furrowed.

Outside the door, Swift loudly cleared his throat. "My lord, Lady Langley has just arrived. Shall I tell her you are indisposed?"

Philip shot off the settee, as meanwhile, Catherine's heart sank low in her stomach. "Your mother is here?" she uttered in a strained whisper, trying to process this unexpected piece of news.

"Tell her I'll be down to meet her in the drawing room in a moment," he called to the doorway before turning his attention back to Catherine. "Yes. I wrote to her yesterday saying that a matter of great urgency required her presence here. Meanwhile, I didn't anticipate her being so hasty. She must have traveled in the dark. It's for the best, though, that I explain the circumstances to her myself before rumors have an opportunity to reach her from another source. She should know about Eleanor, and the full truth of who sired her. And while I'm in the midst of divulging shocking information, I think it prudent to also tell the story of Holbeck and your association with him. If you have no objections, that is."

She found the strength to shake her head, because he was right. Of course he was. The marchioness needed to learn of her granddaughter without delay, whatever she decided to do with that information. It was just as well that she discovered the truth about her daughter-in-law's origins so all secrets could finally be vanquished. Nonetheless, Catherine hadn't prepared herself for that to happen quite so soon. Having Lady Langley hear of her disgrace would make it all the more real. Along with potentially bringing an abrupt end to so many things she held dear to her heart.

"I should go down." Philip made a futile attempt at smoothing his clothing as he made his way to the door. The deep wrinkles in the wool, along with the shadows under his eyes, made her wonder if he'd passed a good deal of the night sitting in the corridor. "If you would like to take a few moments to yourself, I'll check in on Eleanor on my way, in case she has awoken. In any case, I'd like to see for myself how she fares and determine if she would be amenable to an introduction to another stranger. That is, if the marchioness requests it."

The look of uncertainty that clouded his face caused a sudden knot to form within her. She had once thought him so overconfident, unable to be phased by anything. She knew better now. Despite the assured front he presented to the world, he did worry—and struggle—when it came to matters regarding those he cared for most.

"Yes," she murmured, turning her face toward the window so it was no longer visible to him, "do that." Drat it, if he didn't depart the room quickly, she would become a distraught ball of tears at his feet. "I'm sure Eleanor will be pleased to see you."

His footsteps paused for just a moment before he made his way into the corridor. "I suppose. But from what I hear, *you* are the one who has truly captured her affection."

Her eyes darted back to him, just in time to see the slight smile that crept across his face. And then, he was gone.

She pushed her hands across her forehead and through her disheveled hair, trying to clear her head. She should take out the few lingering pins from what remained of her coiffure and change her dress. Perhaps ring for Betsy and ask for assistance in making herself presentable again. Yet how could she make those minute details signify when something else prodded at her with far greater intensity?

She rose from the settee, about to head for her vanity table, when suddenly, her feet pivoted toward the doorway. There was something else she needed to do instead. Before she could give herself the opportunity for trepidation or second-guessing, she hurried from the room, knotted hair and all. But whereas Philip had gone toward Eleanor's room at the back of the house, she turned in the direction of the stairway, gliding down each step and then through the main floor corridor until she reached the threshold of the drawing room. Her heart thrummed forcefully in her chest, insisting to her that she should turn around and run back upstairs. She stepped into the drawing room anyway.

"Catherine!" Lady Langley pushed herself up from her chair by the fire the moment Catherine entered the room, her face etched deeply with lines of concern. "What in heaven's name has happened? Philip explained so little in his letter, merely that he had an urgent need to see me. Is he well? And are you?"

"I'm well," she said, although by the way Lady Langley looked her up and down, from the tangled hair that drooped down her back to the wrinkled folds of her skirts, she must look anything but. "As is Philip. He'll be down in a moment to speak with you. I simply wished to see you first. To tell you that I … I … Or rather, that Philip …"

As she struggled to find the appropriate words, Lady Langley's eyes widened knowingly. "Has Philip done something to displease you?" She tilted her chin with a frown. "Perhaps behaved in a manner unbefitting of a newly married man?"

"No! No, of course not," Catherine exclaimed with newfound conviction. She'd begun to think she had taken leave of her senses by approaching Philip's mother like this. She was in no place, especially now, to lecture a marchioness. However, Lady Langley's disparaging assumption served as a reminder to why she'd entered the drawing room in the first place, and it validated her reasons for doing so. The matter at hand was far too important from which to back away.

She squared her shoulders, forcing herself up to her full height. "I do not wish to overstep or to cause you pain. I know you have suffered much tragedy in recent years, and I cannot begin to imagine the heartache that comes from such a loss. Philip told me of his illness and how he is not the son who was expected to remain, yet ..." Her voice caught in her throat, and she swallowed heavily, prodding herself to continue. "I don't believe that makes him any less worthy of an heir."

Lady Langley's hand flew to her mouth before she abruptly cast it down, ready to make a reply. But Catherine had to continue first before she lost her resolution.

"He wishes to do right by you and the marquess." She took a step closer to Lady Langley and then another, the intensity of what she needed to communicate propelling her forward. "Despite any impressions he may have given to the contrary. Please do not hold my own failings against him, because he was oblivious to the truth and blameless in what transpired. Whatever happens, please say that you and Lord Langley will encourage and accept him as your son and heir. He will do you proud, if only you give him the opportunity."

Lady Langley's mouth hung slackly as she processed Catherine's words. The lady undoubtedly had a myriad of questions, her confusion over what had occurred growing greater than ever. However, Catherine could speak no more.

After all the fears she'd been forced to confront over the past few days, in ways more terrifying than she could have dreamed, she was done with fleeing from minor upsets.

She *did* possess the ability to manage them, if only she gave herself the chance. However, yesterday's confrontation had left her shaken and depleted, and now that she'd managed to convey the basic premise of her message, the small scrap of her resolve that remained was quickly slipping away.

And so, she gave an abrupt curtsey, and just one more time, she allowed herself to make a hasty retreat, all the way back to the safety of her bedroom.

Perhaps Lady Langley found her nonsensical and impertinent, and as it stood, she wouldn't have entirely disagreed with the marchioness on that front. Nonetheless, she couldn't let Philip disclose these shocking, detrimental revelations without at least attempting to explain his lack of guilt. Along with that secret part of him that she'd discovered, the one that really *did* care and seek acceptance, which he concealed so well that it seemed even his mother might lack knowledge of it.

She had said her piece for whatever good it might do. The rest was Philip's story to tell.

Chapter 23

When he first stood before his mother in the drawing room, Philip briefly debated softening the truth. He could omit certain parts and hope she never discovered the reality of things, or fabricate small details that would lessen the blow. His mind kept returning to that day earlier in the year when he'd stood in this very location and watched, with helpless emptiness, as his mother's tears had flowed onto the plush gold velvet of the sofa. As if she had nothing left, and life had broken her. Yet she'd proven her resilience. Somehow or another, she'd found the determination to keep going, proving her ability to overcome even the direst of troubles. He would discredit her by thinking she couldn't do so again. Besides, he was damn tired of lies.

They sat on the sofa together, his mother on one end with her hands so tightly clasped that the knuckles turned white, and him on the other, his trepidation suddenly numbed so that he could think only of what needed to come next. And then, he told her everything.

He spoke of Charles and Eleanor. Of the deathbed promise and the arrangement with Hannah. And of Catherine. The woman who had upturned his life in more ways than he could name. The woman whose origins had suddenly jumped out to haunt her and brought this whole maze of lies full circle.

His mother said nothing. Much to her credit, though her head must have been racing with questions, she didn't interrupt even once. Instead, she simply allowed him to speak, and he plowed ahead until he'd explained every last detail, and his voice had grown rough from the effort.

She was statuesque in her posture, giving not so much as a flinch while he delivered information with the power to make her world come crashing down around her. By the way she sat there, close-lipped and rigid, one would think she attended a lecture on mathematics or listened to the lines of a complex sonnet. Nothing betrayed her outward stoicism until he finished speaking, and her gray eyes became watery, glittering with the sheen of unshed tears.

It would seem they had both numbed themselves for the length of his explanation, but seeing his mother's eyes caused that ache of uncertainty to come back to him, along with the recurring vision of her sobbing into the sofa. He'd never intended to bring her back to that place. But what if these revelations were the thing that pushed her too far? He clenched his teeth, powerless to do anything but sit and wait for despondency to overwhelm them both.

His mother, though, still didn't falter. She kept her dignified pose, looking at him as if the tears that blurred her vision weren't there, until she at last found the ability to respond. "You say the girl is here?"

"Yes," he answered quickly, desperate to keep the dangerous silence from filling the room again. Yet between his haste and his weariness, the word came out as a rasp, and he cleared his throat, needing to try again. "Yes. Upstairs, settled into the back bedroom. Where she belongs. I should have recognized that earlier, but nonetheless, she's here now. After receiving a final bit of compensation, Hannah was more than willing to relinquish all claims to her."

The marchioness blinked rapidly, and just as quickly as the tears had sprung into her eyes, they were gone. She unclenched her hands, twisting the onyx ring that adorned her finger. "Do you think I might see her?"

His chest had tightened with the fear that he'd miscalculated his mother's ability to endure these revelations, but hearing her question sparked an inkling, for the first time, that perhaps he'd done right after all. "Of course. If that's what you want."

She peered down at her hands, continuing to twirl her ring back and forth as if the glittering stone held the answers to all the confusion that surrounded her. When she looked up, though, her eyes were clear, and her mouth was set in a determined line. "It is. If you'll only give me a few moments more to remain here and compose myself. Besides, there's something I need to say to you first."

"By all means."

"Philip ..." She swayed in her seat, uncertainty seizing her once more. However, just as before, a look of resolve crossed her face, and she shuffled nearer to him on the sofa. "There are few things more terrifying to a mother than the thought of losing one's child. When your fever struck, I believe I took that as a reason to distance myself. So that when the inevitable happened—as the physicians assured me it would—perhaps the blow would hurt less. I will not claim I did right. Quite the opposite, actually. Yet fear causes people to behave in irrational ways, as I think you know all too well."

He nudged his head in a semblance of a nod, too surprised to give a reaction beyond that.

"I've come to realize something over the years," she continued, her stiff shoulders giving just the tiniest hint of quivering. "One cannot always anticipate these types of events. Sometimes, fate intervenes in the most unexpected ways. I confess, the task of seeing beyond what I lost has often felt colossal, beyond my abilities. However, I would be mistaken in not recognizing—and allowing myself to embrace—what remains."

She shuffled closer again, and suddenly, for the first time he could recall since the day the fever got so bad that he thought it would be his last, her hand was upon his, giving it a gentle squeeze.

"You went above and beyond to fulfill Charles's final request. Not to mention how you did the same for your father. I hope you do not resent us for our part in entangling you in marriage. By the way I've seen you look at Catherine, right from the start, I rather think the arrangement is to your liking. And she loves you dearly in return, of that I'm certain. You need not worry about her too much, I daresay, for she holds far too high a position to warrant the ton's eternal scorn. She will grow into a fine marchioness. And you, a fine marquess alongside her."

He could feel himself gaping at her. How could he help it when an assortment of phrases he'd never dreamed he would hear had emerged from her mouth in succession? For just an instant, he returned the pressure of his mother's hand, squeezing the weathered fingers in his own. Then, he pulled himself away, before his astonishment could lead to something as untoward as having his own eyes grow misty. "Are you ready to meet Eleanor?"

"Eleanor." His mother tried out the name for the first time, the syllables causing a faint smile to cross her lips. "Yes, I believe I am."

He staggered to his feet, his limbs prickling after he'd held them so stiffly for all that time. "Let me go up first to make sure she's ready, and you can follow in a few minutes. I already spoke to her about having a visitor, and she seemed agreeable, but after all she's been through, I want to take extra care not to startle her."

"Of course." His mother set her hands back neatly in her lap. "I'll wait here and will be up in a moment. Actually, Philip?"

"Yes?"

She glanced at him serenely, having readjusted her posture to be as regal as ever. "While I'm waiting, could you ask Catherine to please come and join me? I need to speak with her a moment."

So did he, more than anything. However, now that his overwhelming dread had given way to a sense that, just maybe, everything would be well after all, he could let his mother speak to her first. His turn would come soon enough.

***

"You wished to see me?" Catherine poked her head around the doorway of the drawing room, taking great care not to let her voice falter as she addressed Lady Langley. No small feat when her heart raced uncontrollably, pounding out a warning that she was about to receive a setting down. Philip had been so infuriatingly calm when he stood on the threshold of their bedroom and informed her that the marchioness awaited her in the drawing room, his voice and expression giving no clues as to the nature of this meeting. Then, he had departed just as quickly as he came, saying he needed to prepare Eleanor for a visit with his mother. Surely, that had to be a promising sign that Lady Langley had reacted with at least a degree of acceptance to Philip's shocking revelation about the child. But as for where the marchioness stood with Catherine ... well, Catherine couldn't help but imagine the worst. Especially after her impertinent outburst.

Surprisingly, though, the expression on Lady Langley's thin face didn't betray any signs of antipathy or indignation. Rather, she unclasped her hands, patting the vacant space on the sofa cushion next to her. "Yes. Would you please sit a moment?"

Catherine forced herself forward, one foot after the other, until she arrived at the sofa and lowered herself to the proffered seat. Philip must have inherited his aplomb from his mother, for short of this small gesture, Lady Langley still displayed no signs of how she felt about the woman sitting next to her. Catherine attempted to clear away the dryness in her throat so she'd be prepared herself to speak again. Perhaps she should just apologize upfront. For the way she'd spoken out of turn, even though she couldn't bring herself to truly regret her efforts to come to Philip's defense. And more importantly, for the way the truth about her parentage would make them all a source of gossip and derision.

But no. She'd already had the opportunity to voice her thoughts without relenting. Now, it was Lady Langley's turn to take the floor. And whatever the marchioness said—however she chose to react to the daughter-in-law who had filled their house with turmoil and scandal—she would find a way, somehow, to accept it.

"I believe I already told you that your mother and I were friends many years ago."

Lady Langley's voice was so gentle and even, and so different from the harsh reprimand Catherine had been expecting that she nearly sagged from the wave of relief that crashed into her. She nodded, willing the lady to continue.

"As such, her relationship with Lawrence Holbeck was never a secret to me. I never understood it, really. Even all those years ago, the man was a bit of a reprobate, but then again, Georgina always had a rebellious streak …"

Lady Langley's cheeks pinkened just a touch, the first sign that something rattled her composure. "Forgive me, I'm veering off course. My point is, I do not know what

Holbeck told you, but he deceived you terribly if he made you think we would view revelations about your parentage as astonishing. As I said, I'm speaking as your mother's friend, as someone with intimate knowledge of her affairs. Meanwhile, if I'm being honest, the fact that she and the earl were estranged for a good decade or more was well known amongst society. When it became obvious that she was with child despite the estrangement, the whisperings came and went and were ultimately accepted. To have them come to light again now would hardly be revolutionary. Nor should you blame yourself for circumstances you had no hand in creating and have no power to change. These types of … situations … are hardly uncommon within the ton, and I would like to see anyone dare try to shun you for bygone disclosures that hold little significance at this point in time. The earl accepted you as his daughter while he was living, just as Lord Langley and I accept you as our daughter now. If that still does not suffice for a few ridiculous gossips, who take no issue with being on the bad side of the future Marchioness of Langley, then the more fool them."

Catherine could feel herself blinking as she fought to comprehend everything the marchioness had just disclosed. Had Lady Langley—the distant, somber Lady Langley— truly just revealed that she accepted her? She peered into the clear gray eyes that reminded her so much of Philip's. That subtle hint of sadness remained, as it likely always would. But now, other notes had crept in. Warmth. Eagerness. Maybe even hope.

Catherine leaned in, and before she could think on it any further, she threw her arms around the marchioness. "Thank you." She'd never had a parent to comfort or hug her. Yet here was Lady Langley, who'd been a friend to her mother despite her imperfections and was now willing to welcome Catherine despite hers. She knew no other way to express her gratitude.

She withdrew without lingering from the contact that proved unfamiliar to them both. Not, though, before Lady Langley reached up, giving Catherine's back a subdued pat.

"Indeed." The marchioness straightened her pale lilac skirts, attempting to resume her dignified stance. However, the pink in her cheeks had deepened, and her mouth twitched upward despite her apparent efforts to keep her face impassive.

The sight elicited Catherine's smile as well, one that she couldn't hold back. Hearing that Lady Langley didn't hold her in contempt or view her as the ruination of the family— as she had so vividly imagined—was the best news she could hope for. Well, almost. She and Philip had had so little opportunity to talk that she still didn't know where they stood with one another. Had he possibly said something to his mother? She debated asking the marchioness, but despite her anxiousness to know, she reined herself in. That was a conversation she needed to have with Philip alone. Besides, Lady Langley was already rising to her feet, squaring her shoulders with fresh determination.

"Thank you for speaking with me. But now, if you'll please excuse me." She nodded a farewell and crossed the drawing room, her soft voice floating back just as she reached the doorway. "It's time for me to meet my granddaughter."

Chapter 24

Despite being told that Lady Kendrick hadn't yet come downstairs, Philip didn't at first see her when he reentered their bedroom. The bench before her vanity sat empty, as did the bed and the armchair by the fireplace. But then, he turned to the settee by the window, where Catherine sat with her forehead resting against the glass, watching the bustle of the street below. A dense mist had overtaken the earlier morning's sunshine, but even though that made the light around her dim, he could still see she was deep in thought.

He took a couple steps toward her, keeping the tread of his boots light. "What are you contemplating, love?"

She spun around, her dark eyes widening. "Philip! I didn't hear you come in. I … I suppose, in all honesty, I was thinking of how much I miss the quiet of the country. But it doesn't signify. Please, tell me about Eleanor and your mother. Have they met? Did the visit go well?"

"They have, and yes, I would say so." He grinned, recalling the scene he'd just left behind in the back bedroom. "I never imagined my mother as the type to sit on the floor and administer pretend tea to dolls, but here we are."

Catherine made a breathy sound approaching a laugh. "I'm so glad to hear it." She smiled, although any joy she might have felt didn't fully show in her eyes. On the contrary, her brow remained tense, giving her the same look of trepidation he'd noticed ever since retrieving her and

Eleanor in Seven Dials. Or to some extent, ever since their arrival in London, when her scum of a sire had cornered her, and she'd felt prohibited from seeking help. The thought gnawed at his insides, and he did his best to focus only on the task at hand before memories of recent events could lead him to a fresh burst of ire.

"I've been asked to tell you of your invitation to the tea party and bid you to join right away." Remembering Eleanor and the way she'd delivered the command in a high-pitched yet assertive babble helped restore his equilibrium. "Meanwhile, I hope Eleanor will forgive me if I take up a few moments of your time first. We started a conversation earlier that we didn't get to conclude. I would like to finish it now."

She nodded her assent, and he joined her on the settee, resuming the same position he'd taken earlier before they'd gotten interrupted. As she still radiated hints of hesitancy and aloofness, he took care not to touch her, given her tendency to turn and bolt. He thought they'd moved past that stage, but at the same time, after all the revelations they'd dealt with over the past few days, they needed to get to know each other all over again, in a way. The last words she'd spoken prior to Swift's knock still echoed through his head, and he needed her to explain them. "Catherine, why do you believe you have ruined everything?"

She made that sound approaching laughter again, but this time it lacked humor. "Is it not obvious? You wanted to make a match worthy of a marquess, and instead, you ended up wed to the illegitimate daughter of a reprobate. I was so afraid of what that knowledge would do, especially after everything else you and your parents have endured. As it turns out, your mother was beyond gracious in her acceptance of me. But still … I was dishonest with you, Philip, and my mistakes could have had disastrous consequences. Are you very angry?"

"Of course I'm angry," he exclaimed, but upon seeing the hurt that shot across her face, he immediately softened his tone. "But not, perhaps, in the way you think. I'm angry that you didn't feel you could come to me. I would have helped you, you know. I would go to the ends of the earth for you."

He inched closer to her, aching to reach out and touch her, but he kept his hands pressed against his knees. He couldn't risk anything interfering with this conversation before he had the opportunity to speak all the words that needed to be said. "Meanwhile, I cannot condemn you for dishonesty when I, too, withheld the truth. For that, I'm angry with myself. I wish to God we had been upfront with one another right from the start. We could have saved ourselves a great deal of torment."

"I know." She gave a tiny, rueful sigh. "Believe me, I know."

"But as for this belief you ruined everything … Do you truly think I care who your parents are? I trust I need not remind you of my own reputation and the things people say.

Let the ton gossip as they see fit. It changes nothing about the way I feel for you."

Throughout the significant conversations he'd already held that day, something his mother had said kept coming back to him. *She loves you dearly … Of that, I'm certain.* Which forced him to confront something he'd suspected but never fully allowed himself to embrace.

It had presented itself as a strange, insistent pull in his chest that occurred when they sat pressed together under Lord Wellesley's desk. And again, when he fell asleep for the first time with Catherine in his arms. And yet again, when he watched her with Eleanor and saw the little girl's face light up with natural adoration. It was foreign and unnerving. Certainly not befitting of an infamous rake. Yet he'd never felt so certain about the rightness of anything before, and he couldn't go another second without confessing it, terrifying though it may be.

"It changes nothing about the way I love you."

She took in a sharp breath, staring at him as if trying to establish that she'd heard him correctly. And suddenly, that air of reserve in which she'd enshrouded herself melted away, and she was pressed against him, her arms clasped about his neck. "I love you too! So much. That's why I couldn't bear the thought of hurting you or anyone you hold dear."

He rested his palm against her chin, finally getting to savor the feel of her soft skin beneath his fingertips. It was one thing for his mother to proclaim that Catherine loved him, but hearing Catherine speak the words herself brought a rush of warmth within him—a feeling of completeness— like he'd never known.

He wished he could ask her to repeat the phrase over and over. Then, he would carry her to the bed, where they would tumble together in an endless stream of pleasure, all while he explained each and every reason that he loved her in return. However, the last part of her declaration left them with one final point they needed to discuss, for it appeared she might still feel flickers of anxiousness on account of it.

"This week in London has brought us to hell and back." He placed his free hand lightly over her thigh. "There are so many things to regret about the way events transpired. Yet I cannot regret the outcome. Eleanor is with us now, as she should have been all along. I have you to thank for that. For giving me the opportunity to unburden myself of a secret that I didn't know how to keep carrying and for making me see things differently. I focused so heavily on the vow I made to Charles that I neglected to consider whether, in upholding that vow, I did right. Eleanor had only been with Hannah a short time before Charles became ill, so it's very possible that he lacked the opportunity to see the woman's avaricious nature. I should have had the sense to intervene sooner. For although the current situation is far from what Charles requested, I hope that, at least in some sense, he would consider it an amelioration."

"His child is being not only cared for but esteemed and loved by her closest remaining family. What more could a worthy parent ask for than that?"

Catherine spoke so adamantly that it was difficult not to believe the truth behind her words. "Indeed. But Catherine ..." He paused, hating to have to bring up another point of conflict. "I will not lie on the subject of Eleanor's parentage. Again, I only have to hope that if Charles could reevaluate matters, he would see the merit in acting with honesty so that his daughter need not grow up in a tangle of secrets and lies, never fully knowing to whom she belongs. However, that won't stop some people from recounting my past behavior and jumping to erroneous conclusions. There could be talk of an unpleasant nature to which you may be subjected, as much as I wish otherwise. For I would never want to hurt you either."

She leaned in, letting her head rest on his shoulder a moment before looking back up. "You have agreed to cast any rumors about me aside as if they were nothing. What makes you think I would do differently for you? I love you. And I told you right from the time I learned of her existence that I would love Eleanor too. That love is unconditional. It cannot be altered by frivolous gossip. Let people say what they like about any of us. Beneath it all, we'll know the truth. We need only place our faith in one another, and I think— no, I *know*—we can be very happy."

He pulled her closer to him, nestling his face against her neck and dropping a kiss against the silky skin. She smelled so good. Of delicate orange blossom perfume and soft femininity. And of home.

He'd spent so many days, weeks, *years* in the pursuit of pleasure, trying to make himself forget his identity as an invalid turned heir. He'd grown increasingly extravagant with his misdeeds, cavorted and caroused, and enjoyed himself very much on a superficial level, to be sure. Yet nothing had ever taken away the sting of the past, or of loss, or of secrets. A gaping hole, buried deep inside, always remained, and no amount of revelry or carnal pleasure could erase it.

What he had now, though, was different. All his former pursuits—the gaming hells, the parties that continued for days, the endless stream of eager women—were gone. And it mattered not a whit. From the moment Lady Catherine Adderley had stumbled into his arms, something within him changed. With her quiet presence—which, when peeled away, revealed fathomless depths of determination and passion and love—she grounded him. She caused him to confront his deeply sheltered insecurities and still feel adequate despite them. She helped him discern the right path forward. And she made him feel complete.

"Come with me," he murmured, pulling them both to their feet and backing toward the bed with her tightly ensconced in his arms.

She dropped her weight against his chest, staggering along with him, when suddenly she bolted upright, her eyes darting toward the door. "The tea party! I should go. I fear the hostess will be displeased with my lateness."

He took in one more breath near her hair before reluctantly releasing his grip, suppressing a groan as the alluring heat of her body slipped away.

"I'll try not to be long." She smoothed her skirts, her breathy voice suggesting that she, too, had been caught up in their embrace and now struggled with its loss. "If Eleanor and your mother are enjoying each other's company, perhaps they wouldn't mind if I slipped away early. If nothing else, I'm sure the promise of real tea and biscuits in the kitchen will provide a distraction, at least for a time."

While certain parts of him strongly protested her departure, deep down, he knew she was right to go. This was their life now, one in which they were accountable not just to each other but to a child as well. The first of many, if Catherine's wish for a large family came true. Funnily, the more he thought about it, the more he wanted the same thing. No doubt it would make seeing to their own undertakings increasingly more challenging. But the sense of rightness, completion, and love would make it more than worthwhile.

Besides, he had once told her they had no need to rush their intimacy. Her brief absence now would only make what they did when she returned that much better.

"I'll return soon." She leaned in to brush a quick kiss against his lips, and then, before they could let the gesture distract them into something more, she was gone.

He paced up and down the room a few times, trying to get his pulse to slow as he debated what to do next. After spending the night in the corridor, on alert for any sounds of distress coming from the room where Catherine and Eleanor slept, he could greatly benefit from falling onto the bed and closing his eyes for a few minutes. Or perhaps he should change his clothes, given that, like him, they were a bit worse for wear for how they'd spent the night. It was fortunate he'd requested for Robertson to remain behind at Clifton Manor for the week, for if the valet had known that Lord Kendrick conducted several of the most monumental conversations of his life wearing such clothing, he would have had a conniption. Then again, the activities Philip had in mind for when Catherine returned required very little in the way of clothing.

Ultimately, he opted to shirk his disheveled garments in favor of a striped banyan, and he sprawled across the bed, atop the untouched counterpane. Not sleeping, but closing his eyes and resting in contented, anticipatory silence. Secure in the knowledge that he had a wife—an impassioned, uplifting, loving, soul-completing wife—to come back to him. Not just this morning but for the rest of their lives.

And he would always be waiting.

Epilogue

January 1820

Catherine stood before her vanity, leaning forward enough so that each detail of her ensemble was reflected in the gilded mirror. The pearl bandeau stretched neatly across her intricately arranged curls, while her dainty pearl and diamond earrings glittered in the candlelight. The tiny puffed sleeves, trimmed with delicate silver tulle, revealed just a hint of her shoulders, while the low neckline of her vibrant blue bodice rested appealingly against the swell of her breasts. However she might feel about overcrowded balls, at least she could look the part of a well-dressed, effervescent hostess.

"My lady, you look magnificent," Betsy said as she reappeared in front of the mirror with the pearl bracelet Catherine had requested as a final touch. Betsy draped it around her wrist, deftly fastening the clasp and giving it a tiny pat. "I think this is your most lovely gown yet, if you'll allow me to say so. Are you pleased?"

"I am. Thank you for your assistance. You've helped me to style it just right." Catherine glanced down at her pearl-encrusted overskirt to ensure it hung properly before turning her attention to the silk that draped over her stomach, smoothing it tightly to reveal the bump that had begun to grow there. Giving a little smile, she released the fabric, causing the evidence of her condition to vanish. Yet who knew what some sharp-eyed society matron might notice over the course of the evening.

She turned away from the mirror, planning to retrieve the matching blue slippers she'd waited until the last minute to put on because of how they pinched her feet. Instead, her eyes fell upon an unexpected object on her nightstand, and she gave a tiny jump. "Betsy, where did this come from?"

Her skin turned icy as she inched nearer the nightstand for a closer look. It was only a letter, a smooth, folded page marked with an even scrawl. But after that day several months ago, when a lone, fateful letter had awaited her in the drawing room, threatening life as she knew it, she couldn't help the spurt of apprehension that popped up now.

"I'm so sorry, my lady," exclaimed Betsy, taking one look at Catherine's face before rushing forward to snatch up the letter and pass it back to her. "This came in the post earlier. I brought it up to you as soon as it arrived, but you were asleep, and I didn't wish to disturb you."

Catherine's heart rate began a steady descent back to normal as she accepted the proffered letter. While overall, she'd felt well since learning of her pregnancy, the one pesky side effect that plagued her was bouts of extreme fatigue, causing her to nap with a frequency of which she'd never imagined herself capable. She'd obviously slept through Betsy's entrance earlier and had then been so groggy when her lady's maid roused her to begin getting ready for the ball that the letter had escaped her detection until this point. At least now, she could see that she'd overreacted, for the handwriting on the page belonged to none other than Lavinia.

Her slippers currently forgotten, she sauntered toward the bed, pulling at the letter's wax seal. Correspondence from Lavinia had been surprisingly scarce of late. And while the Bathursts must have been in London by now, given how they'd accepted the invitation to the Langley House ball, Catherine had seen no sign of her nor received her calling card. She unfolded the page and began to read, eager for news of her friend.

My dearest Catherine,

I hope this letter finds you well. As I do not want to risk missing today's post and not having this reach you in time, I will keep my words brief and merely write, with regret, that I am still in Devonshire and unable to attend your ball, which I was so looking forward to. I'm sure it will be a smashing success. Alas, something has happened, and I do not anticipate visiting London at all this Season—

"Exquisite." She started, for a low voice filled her ear as a wisp of breath brushed against the side of her neck. "You are absolutely, perfectly exquisite."

"Philip." She tilted her head, giving him ample room to press a kiss against her throat. She'd been so caught up in her letter that she didn't hear him come in.

Her perplexity must have spread across her face, for his forehead creased as he looked at her. "Is something wrong?"

"No, nothing." She quickly scanned the letter for additional news, but the last few lines contained only good wishes for Catherine's health and a promise to write again soon. "It's merely a letter I just received from Lavinia, stating that she cannot join us this evening after all."

"Unfortunate, although there will certainly be no shortage of guests in attendance. I looked down the stairs on my way back from the nursery, and they are already starting to arrive in surprising numbers. It seems even scandal cannot drive the ton from the Langley homestead, if for no other reason than curiosity."

"Whatever it takes, I suppose," she said, quelling a sigh. Of course, a ball under her roof, filled with people who came to whisper and gawk, was the last thing she wanted. Nonetheless, even she could see the necessity of it.

After that fateful week in London in the autumn, they'd made a hasty retreat back to Clifton Manor, where they'd all but secluded themselves from others, instead focusing on getting Eleanor settled and being near the marquess. Much to everyone's surprise, their presence—especially that of Eleanor, with her infectious laugh and endless supply of caresses—coincided with a slight improvement in Lord Langley's health. He was still weak, mostly confined to his room, and no one could doubt the severity of his condition. However, having a small piece of the son he thought forever lost to him—along with knowing that they anticipated a new baby to fill the nursery later in the year—put a smile on his face and returned a little of his former zeal.

And because the marquess didn't appear in imminent danger, Lady Langley had insisted on the rest of them partaking of a trip to London to show themselves for at least some of the new Season. Remaining holed up in the country, as rumors swirled about a mysterious child and the reason for Lawrence Holbeck's sudden disappearance, would be tantamount to admitting guilt and shame. That, of course, would not do. And so, not only had they traveled to London, but Lady Langley had planned an elaborate ball at Langley House, sending out invitations in the hundreds. What better way, she said, to celebrate Philip and Catherine's marriage and show her acceptance of this new member of the family, along with the fact that they had nothing to hide or cower from. Regardless of any whisperings that circulated throughout the ton. Judging by the number of invitations they'd seen accepted, along with the persistent buzz of chatter that already floated up from downstairs, her plan was a success.

"As much as I would prefer spending my evening exactly where we are," Philip said, tracing a finger over the pearl detailing at the neckline of her bodice, "I suppose that would rather defeat the purpose of the ball. Shall we go down and help in greeting the guests? I feel I should attempt doing my duty at least for a time. But, be warned, the need to rush back upstairs with you in my arms could strike at any moment."

"Noted." She pressed his hand tighter against her chest, absorbing his warmth and strength. "Yes, let's go down."

Grudgingly, she left his embrace, returning to her initial task of retrieving her slippers. "And all is well with

Eleanor?" she asked, wriggling her toes into the smooth but confining silk. While the little girl typically had a sunny disposition, she'd been quite perturbed when her nurse informed her that she wouldn't be permitted to stay up late enough to go down to the ballroom and dance a waltz.

"It appears so." He gave a reluctant smile. "She seemed appeased by my promise of leftover pastries when she awakes in the morning."

"A fair compromise." Her feet resting securely in her slippers, she crossed the room to where Philip had moved to await her by the doorway. And then, because she could think of no other tasks or questions to delay the inevitable, she placed her arm atop Philip's, allowing him to lead her out of the room. It was time.

The noise of conversation intensified as soon as they stepped into the dusky corridor. Guests must be arriving with surprising promptness and in a steady stream. No doubt, the marchioness stood near the front entryway welcoming each one, wondering why Philip and Catherine hadn't yet appeared. All the more reason for them to hurry downstairs, although Catherine's legs had gone heavy.

All the whisperings she'd overheard about herself last Season—talk of her timidity and ineptness, and yes, even her parentage—along with the fresh rumors she could only imagine were circulating now, threatened to overtake her thoughts, causing the familiar heat to begin spreading across her cheeks. She quickly forced the memories down, turning her attention to placing one foot in front of the other. She would *not* let herself cower at this point.

They reached the end of the corridor, arriving at the point where they would turn to approach the stairs, when Philip halted, drawing her near him against the shadowed wall.

"We can wait a moment if you'd like to, love." He placed one hand around her waist while the other traced absently over her midsection. "Prolonging our entrance into the lion's den will garner no complaints from me. We can remain here, just the two of us, for as long as you need."

How tempting it was to agree. To be alone with Philip a little longer, away from the noise and chaos and prying eyes.

At one time, she would have accepted the proposition without question. Yet so much had happened since she'd stepped into her first ballroom, more than a year ago, as a woman out in society. She had conquered Lady Wellesley's house party. She had fought her way through scandal and ended up married to a man she loved as a result. She had found the strength to confront the threat to their security and had found her way back to happiness once more. If she could do all those things, then she could do this too.

"No, I don't need to wait." She gave her dress one final tug, smoothing away invisible wrinkles. Then, setting her shoulders straight and holding her neck high, she stepped around the corner, away from the shadows and into the abundant candlelight that illuminated the stairs. "I'm ready."

Bonus Content

Sign up for Jane's monthly newsletter to get access to free bonus content, including a subscriber-exclusive prologue for *Rumors and a Rake*. You will also be the first to know about new releases, giveaways, special promotions, and more!

Join now at: www.janemaguireauthor.com/newsletter

About the Author

Jane Maguire is a Canadian author whose lifelong passions for history, writing, and love stories inevitably led her to begin penning historical romance novels. While her love of historical fiction spans all eras, she focuses her writing on high society in the glittering regency period. She enjoys crafting stories with lots of angst, which makes giving her characters their happily ever afters all the more satisfying.

When she isn't at her computer writing and researching, you can find her vacationing in the Rocky Mountains, playing classical music on the piano, or simply curling up with a cup of tea and a good book. She lives with her husband, two kids, a five-pound guard dog, and a foodie cat.

You can find Jane online at
www.janemaguireauthor.com.

Made in United States
North Haven, CT
30 April 2023

36071945R00189